I0579513

THE RECOGNITION REJECTION

Recognition Book 2

HENRY VOGEL

Copyright © 2017 by Henry Vogel

All rights reserved.

No part of this publication may be reproduced, stored in a retrieval system, or transmitted in any form or by any means, electronic, mechanical, photographic, or otherwise, without the prior written consent of the publisher.

Published in the United States of America by Rampant Loon Press, an imprint of Rampant Loon Media LLC, P.O. Box 111, Lake Elmo, Minnesota 55042. "Rampant Loon Press" and the Rampant Loon colophon are trademarks of Rampant Loon Media LLC.

www.rampantloonmedia.com

Cover design by

ISBN: 978-1-938834-96-7 (ebook)

ISBN: 978-1-938834-97-4 (print)

First publication: December 2017

PRAISE FOR THE RECOGNITION RUN

Book 1 of the Recognition Series

PUBLISHERS WEEKLY BOOKLIFE PRIZE CRITIC'S REPORT:

"Struck from the template of classic space opera, this tale of intergalactic adventure hits all of the right notes. It has a likable hero and heroine, nasty villains, a plot full of intrigue and unforeseeable surprises, and a colorfully rendered outer-space backdrop against which its well-paced events unfold."

AMAZON READER REVIEWS:

"The characters are well-crafted, the pacing is absolutely perfect, and any reader who's enjoyed Robert Heinlein or Andre Norton will absolutely love this book!"

"A great new series by Henry Vogel. In addition to his usual scifi thriller/adventure story, Vogel has added a generous splash of mystery, a computer slicer (hacker) character, and an atmosphere of political intrigue among royal families, reminiscent of C. J. Cherryh's *Foreigner* series [...] I can't wait to see how the mystery unfolds."

"Nobility, corruption, succession scandals, and old grudges fill this book, and take it beyond the great majority of space sf."

"This is my first book written by Henry Vogel—definitely won't be the last! This is more than Science Fiction—it has elements of the mystery/thriller, as well. His characters are well-drawn and you actually like them and care what happens to them. Danger and twists abound as Jeanine and Drake try to solve a mystery which could affect the galaxy (and has ramifications all the way to the royal family). Look this one over—get it—read it—and enjoy!"

MY PERFECT MOMENT

Olivia

Intricate music echoed around the palace ballroom. Dignified music. Royal music. Traditional music. Safe music. Boring music.

Pastel couples flowed and swirled around William and me. My sapphire blue gown separated me from the noblewomen, just as William's golden suit did with the noblemen. Yet, our clothes only separated us by color. Every stitch of every article of women's clothing in the ballroom was a subtle variation of my gown. The same was true of the suits worn by the men. Everywhere I looked, I saw our own clothes reflected back at me a hundred times over. Everywhere I looked, I saw the same safe, boring, traditional clothing.

William, bless his male heart, didn't notice. He had eyes only for me. My ladies-in-waiting spent hours on my look to ensure just that, of course, but every woman enjoys having her man's admiring eyes roam over her body.

Held close in his arms as we danced, I whispered, "Don't worry, William, you get to unwrap me once the ball is over."

"Do you torture me on purpose, Olivia? These trousers are quite constricting. My natural reaction to your suggestion will be both obvious and uncomfortable."

Despite myself, I giggled. That is one of William's most endearing traits. He can make me feel like a young girl mooning over her first crush. The intellectual part of me knew he honed this ability to more easily woo women—noble and commoner alike—into his bed. The emotional part of me blushed and lost itself in William's dark eyes. On our one-month anniversary, there was no doubt that my emotions overruled my intellect. Still blushing, I moved closer to William and pressed my hips against his. We dipped and twirled, subtly grinding against each other. Even through several layers of clothing, I felt William's reaction.

His eyes closed in obvious pleasure even as he protested, "God above, Olivia, I'll never be able to conceal *that* from our guests!"

"Good. Now every woman in the room will see what awaits me when the ball ends." Still, I took pity on my husband and pulled my hips back. "More importantly, you know what awaits you."

"I do so love you, my dear."

He showed it by kissing me gently on the lips. It was a romantic kiss, lingering and loving. We didn't realize the music had stopped until we broke apart. Our guests encircled us at a distance, watching and smiling fondly. William laughed, lifting me by the waist and twirling me about. I let my head fall back and laughed with joy. As William put me down, our subjects applauded and joined in my laughter.

This was what I needed. This moment. This adoring crowd. My husband smiling. All eyes on me. All attention on me. What should have been at my wedding, now *was* at my ball.

My perfect moment.

And the bitch ruined it.

The herald banged his staff on the floor twice.

"Lady Jeanine, Duchess of Neert, Duchess of Gaunner, and her husband, Captain Drake Haral."

Of course, I invited her. As the ruler of two duchies, I had to. But I never imagined she would accept the invitation.

Every eye turned away from me, abandoning me and leaving my perfect moment in ruins. Every eye watched as that woman glided down the stairs, with her common-born husband at her side. His suit was dark gray, complimenting his dark hair and gray eyes, with a bright white shirt providing just the right contrast. Compared to this sea of strutting peacocks, Captain Haral exuded quiet power. I'm probably the only person in the ballroom who even noticed the man, because of what his wife wore.

Quiet gasps sounded from the women when they saw the bitch's gown—if you could even call it a gown. There was so much wrong with it, I didn't even know where to start.

It was emerald green—both contrasting and complementing her long red hair—and it stood out among the boring pastels surrounding me in the same way my own sapphire gown did. Her neckline plunged in a sharp V, proudly displaying cleavage where the other gowns only hinted at it and hid it in loose folds. And the *hemline*—it didn't brush the floor, as a proper gown's hem should. It barely brushed her thighs!

The gown was wrong. Utterly and completely wrong.

But she made it work.

And I wished I was daring enough to have worn it.

Damn her, yet again!

I forced my eyes away from the couple descending the stairs, but I was the only one who did. Around me, jaded courtiers watched the bitch in admiring silence. In a flash, I realized what these unoriginal women would wear to my next ball, just as I realized most of them could never do justice to the look. *I* could —and I wanted to. But I couldn't let *her* dictate fashion on the capital!

Then again, how could I even stop her?

I looped my arm through William's and said, "We must greet our newly arrived guests."

"What?" William replied, his tone distracted.

I looked up at him and found his eyes riveted on the descending couple. Oh, who am I kidding? His eyes were riveted on the red-headed interloper. On her breasts. On her legs. On her swaying hips. Would his trousers be even more constricting now than when I was rubbing against him? I was too proud to look. But I did carefully grind a heel into his foot. William's eyes snapped to me and he gritted his teeth against the pain.

"I said, we must greet our guests, William."

"Of course, my dear."

He smiled, perhaps hoping I didn't notice how he had stared at the bitch. More likely, he was aware that I noticed and was worried he wouldn't get to unwrap me after the ball ended. Of course, he would get to unwrap me tonight. Denying William would only accentuate my rival's appeal. But my plans for a loving, sharing, fun romp in the sheets had been completely shattered. Instead, I would have to work hard to drive Jeanine from my husband's mind—and my own mind. I was going to have to advance my timetable and be more sexually adventurous with William than I ever wanted to be this early in our marriage. I was going to have to cede some of the marital upper hand to William and I'd have to do it such a way that he never realized *why* I was doing it.

Damn her! Damn her for ruining my wedding. Double damn her for ruining my first ball as royal hostess. And triple damn her for ruining my night with William.

We reached the bottom of the stairs and I plastered a false smile on my face.

"Lady Jeanine, what a lovely surprise! We didn't expect you."

"I couldn't let myself miss your first ball, Your Highness. When I realized we could attend with only a minor delay in our journey, I told Drake we just *had* to come."

William bent over Jeanine's hand, no doubt taking a closer look at her breasts, and said, "I hope our little celebration didn't take you away from anything important, Lady Jeanine, though

I'm sure I speak for all of my subjects when I say how pleased I am you chose to join us."

"It is something important, Prince William—our first official visit to Gaunner—but we couldn't let our shared, anniversary pass unacknowledged."

My smile broadened and became partially genuine. Jeanine thought she was wounding me with her 'shared anniversary' quip and her remark about my former duchy. But, in truth, she did just the opposite. She was *finally* visiting Gaunner. At last, all my secret plans and preparations could come to fruition. With that knowledge warming me, I danced and enjoyed myself with William, after all. Because, once the bitch landed on Gaunner, her days were numbered.

THE FIRST MOVE

Jeanine

It was late when Drake and I returned to our Xapreathean palace. Or it was early, since midnight was three hours ago. The cool night air felt good on my exposed skin, dissipating the heat built up from hours of dancing in a room closely packed with people. The quiet of the grounds felt good to my ears, soothing away hours of listening for any hint of conspiracy or treachery. The dark felt good on my eyes, relaxing after hours spent in the bright glare of noble attention.

As the car pulled away, I took Drake's hand. Holding my shoes in my other hand, I pulled him away from the walkway and onto the lawn.

"It's really peaceful out here. Can we walk a bit and just enjoy it?"

"Of course, we can, babe," Drake said. "Just remember that the surveillance cams cover every square meter of the grounds. If you try to take advantage of me, the guards will know about it."

"And come running to save you from my amorous clutches?"

"God, I hope not! I'll happily let you clutch my brains out—anytime and anywhere. Even if your guards *are* watching."

I laughed and wrapped my arm around Drake's waist. He did the same to me and we made our circuit of the grounds with our hips swaying against each other. Just before we reached the front door, I pulled Drake into a deep shadow next to the palace. Putting my arms around his neck, I pressed against him and gave him a slow, gentle kiss.

Drake grinned as our lips separated. "You know the guards can see us clear as day on the cams, right?"

"Have I ever told you that you talk too much?"

Before he could answer, I covered his mouth with mine and slid my tongue against his. Smart boy that he is, Drake ignored my question and concentrated on returning my kiss.

"I think," Drake said when we broke apart, "that we had better get to the bedroom. Quickly."

"As my captain commands."

No doubt the guards alerted the staff to our activities. The normally bustling entry hall—yes, it was busy even at this late hour—was empty but for the palace's butler. He bowed and took our jackets.

"Thank you, Brice," Drake said.

Brice inclined his head slightly. "My lady, shall I leave word you're not to be disturbed in the morning?"

Much as I wanted to answer otherwise, I said, "No, we need to be onboard the ship no later than ten. Have breakfast sent up at eight-thirty. Send Jana to us at nine."

"Very good, my lady."

We climbed the stairs and entered our suite. The second the door closed, Drake loosened his tie and unbuttoned his collar.

I grabbed his hands and pulled them away from his shirt. "What do you think you're doing, mister?"

"Getting undressed for bed?"

"Right, but *I* get to undress you."

"And then I get to undress you?"

"Among other things."

Tired as we were, we didn't get much sleep before breakfast arrived. Jana showed up precisely at nine, looking disgustingly well-rested. We met her in the suite's sitting room and damned if the slicer didn't curtsy.

"You wanted me, my lady?"

I crossed my arms and glared at Jana. "Since when did *you* start calling me 'my lady'?"

"Since you had me meet you in this palace. The staff is so formal—I mean, they call me 'Miss Ward'. Drake is 'Captain Haral'. And you're 'my lady'. I guess the formality just sort of wore off on me."

"Well, unless we're in a formal situation, I want you to stop it."

Jana's eyes sparkled. "As you wish, my lady."

I rolled my eyes. "Drake, please whip our slicer for insubordination."

Laughter bubbled in Drake's voice as he said, "As you command, my lady wife."

I glared at him. "Do you ever want to get laid again?"

"Right. Um, Jana, don't do that ever again or bad things will happen."

"Like what?" Jana asked.

"Well," Drake replied, considering the question, "at the very least, I'll be extremely cranky."

"I can't have *that* on my conscience," Jana said. She spun back to me, her long, blonde hair flying out briefly. "Are you finally going to tell me why you brought me with you to the capital? You were awfully secretive back on Neert."

"I know, and I'm sorry. Have you noticed that security is less attentive at home but is pretty tight here?" Jana nodded, so I continued, "I can't be certain Olivia doesn't have some spies working in the palace on Neert. We have a few on Gaunner, so it seems likely she has more on Neert. Here, though, we only have the palace and the grounds to secure. Sitting in the middle of...I guess 'enemy territory' is the right phrase...far more precautions are taken when hiring staff. Since I was Recognized, I've also had the entire palace swept for bugs every day."

"Okay... Now I'm starting to get worried," Jana said. "You aren't going to ask me to assassinate Princess Olivia or something, are you?"

"What? Good God, no, Jana. If I want the royal bitch dead, I'll kill her myself. I'm far better trained at that sort of thing than you are. But what I'm going to ask you to do *is* dangerous. People have disappeared forever for doing it."

Jana's furrowed brow cleared and she grinned. "You want me to find out everything there is to know about the Star Stone!"

"How did you guess?"

"I've already gotten a bit of a start. The stuff I found out while digging into the Recognition Ceremony was so intriguing that I've kept digging since the ceremony. I know all about the disappearances and the people who've been driven insane."

My eyebrows rose. "Just researching the Star Stone has sent people tumbling into insanity? Maybe it's too dangerous after all."

"No, no—they were driven insane during Recognition. It doesn't happen often, though, so there's nothing to worry about."

"I don't—"

"Jeanine, you've *got* to let me do this!"

"Why?"

"Because it's the *Star Stone*! The ultimate challenge. Finding out what it is and what it does makes breaking into the Royal DNA Database look like child's play."

I looked into the woman's eyes, shining with anticipation, and sighed. "Promise me you won't take any unnecessary chances. After all, when Drake and I hold that fancy wedding you said we should have, I'm going to need bridesmaids."

"Thank you, Jeanine! I'll be very careful and—" A look of surprised realization came over Jana's face. "Wait, did you just ask me to be a bridesmaid in your wedding?"

"Yes."

"Wow, I'm...Oh my gosh, I don't have anything to wear! What—"

I laughed, "Relax, Jana. We haven't even set a date for the public wedding yet. I take it you'll be a bridesmaid?"

"Of course! I've never been a bridesmaid before. And now I'll be extra careful researching the Star Stone!"

"Good. Now, tell me what you've learned about the Star Stone so far."

Before Jana was finished, it was time for us to go. I hugged her, told the staff to treat Jana's requests as they would mine, and then we boarded the ship. Ten minutes later, we broke through the atmosphere and were on our way to Gaunner for my first official visit as their duchess.

Drake and I caught up on our sleep for the first several hours of the trip. After that, we went over our itinerary for the visit to Gaunner.

"God, Drake, there are so many minor nobles I have to meet and reassure, I don't know how I'm going to keep their names straight."

"Oh, that's easy enough," Drake said. "At my first Space Patrol posting, there were a bunch of noble scions fulfilling their military obligation. That mostly amounted to taking the easiest jobs and ordering commoners to handle all of the actual work. It was simple enough picking out the high-born from their vacant expressions, but they came and went so quickly that none of us bothered learning their names."

"So, what did you do?"

"Bowed and said 'Yes, my lord' or 'As you instruct, my lady'."

"I don't think bowing and scraping and accepting orders from people I'm supposed to rule will help all that much."

"No, but the 'my lord' and 'my lady' bit will. Even if you get it slightly wrong, you'll be close enough that no one will take offense. They'll probably take your slip-up as an indication of good things to come for them. They definitely will *not* correct you."

"No wonder nobles end up so thoroughly messed up. How can anyone learn anything if everyone around you tells you you're wonderful when you're an ass and that you're right when you're most definitely wrong?"

"That's yet another reason I joined the revolution, babe. Though, to be fair, there are some quite reasonable noble families who don't surround themselves with sycophants—House Musgrave, for example."

"The planet Bragua, where we met Jana, is in their duchy, right?" At Drake's nod, I added, "I thought Sir Gilbert treated us quite fairly when Sir Phillip tried to stop us from leaving the system."

"Sir Gilbert has a good reputation, as does Lord Musgrave. The revolutionary council even had plans to approach Musgrave for support." Drake gave me a sidelong look. "Of course, that was before a more suitable—and far more beautiful—noble appeared on the scene."

"Drake, are you trying to distract me from studying this boring list of nobles and, say, lure me into bed?"

"What?" Drake looked surprised. "No."

I tossed the data pad onto the table. "Why not?"

Drake blinked his eyes a few times in surprise. "Because I'm an idiot?"

"I wouldn't go that far, dear. Though if you continue sitting there and staring at me, I might have to entertain that possibility."

Standing, Drake scooped me up and carried me into the bedroom.

We were dozing lightly when our ship transitioned from hyperspace into normal space. I slept through it, but an experienced pilot like Drake can't help but notice the ship's subtle changes during the transition. Even if he isn't the one flying the ship. He woke quickly, which pulled me into wakefulness, too.

"Sorry I woke you, babe."

I kissed him lightly on the cheek and sat up. "I need to get dressed, anyway. That list of nobles won't memorize itself."

We passed the next two hours in companionable silence. Then, the comm buzzed.

Lorena Tucci, the ship's captain and pilot, said, "My lady?"

"Yes, Captain Tucci?"

"We might have a situation, my lady."

"Explain."

"We entered the Vollec system about twenty minutes ago and everything was normal. The system is a common waypoint for traffic between Xapreathea and Gaunner, so it's not unusual to pick up a dozen or so drive signatures, which we did."

Drake, perhaps frustrated by our civilian captain's round-about approach to the potential problem, said, "Skip the buildup, please. What's the situation?"

"Two new drive signatures appeared on our screen a moment ago, sir. They're in-system from us and along our route."

"I assume they're too deep into the star's gravity well for it to simply be ships exiting hyperspace?"

"Correct, sir. They're also close enough to intercept us easily if we attempt to reverse direction and go back the way we came."

Drake gave me a grave look. Without a second thought, I said, "Captain Tucci, Drake is taking command of the ship until further notice."

Relief was evident in her voice when Tucci said, "As you command, my lady."

"I'm on my way to the bridge. Have the crew man the guns," Drake said, standing. "Also, prepare to hand the controls off to me."

"Aye aye, sir."

"Is there anything I can do, Drake?"

"Stay here and strap in. This is the best-protected section of the ship." He paused at the door and looked back at me. "We've been waiting for Olivia to make her first move against us. It looks like the waiting is over."

$$\overline{}$$

PIRATES

$$\overline{}$$

Drake

Captain Tucci was sliding out of the pilot's seat when I charged into the cockpit. Once I was behind the controls, she motioned her copilot to vacate his seat and took his place.

"What are your orders, sir?"

"We'll maintain our current course and thrust for the moment." I fished a small memory stick out of my pocket and handed it to the astrogator. "Plug that into your console."

The man gave me a puzzled expression but did it. "May I ask what this is, sir?"

"Unless it's an emergency situation and you've been given a direct order, you may always ask questions. That memory stick holds a series of astrogation formulas devised by a friend of mine." The ship's astrogator looked uncertain, so I added, "I worked a lot with Grant in the Neert Space Patrol. He's a certified genius and knows what he's doing."

The man still didn't look convinced, but he didn't question me any further. Next, I looked at the scanner tech.

"What can you tell me about our two friends out there?"

"We've held off giving the ships a full-spectrum scan, so I don't have much to tell you." She looked back at her screens as if checking notes. "They look like a couple of regular freighters, sir.

They are mid-sized, nothing you don't see all over the Star Kingdom. Independent traders use that sort of ship all the time."

"So do pirates—and for that very reason." I waved a hand in the general direction of the two freighters. "Ships like that are so common that no one gives them a second glance—until it's too late."

"So you think it's pirates?" Tucci asked.

"If we're lucky, they are—but I suspect they're mercenaries hired to target Jeanine." The bridge crew were all from Neert, so they didn't have to ask who would have hired mercenaries. "Captain, how many of the crew have combat experience?"

"A couple of the gunners are Space Patrol veterans, but that's it."

"That's about what I expected. Okay, I'm going to do my best to avoid a fight. And, if we have to fight, I'm going to do my best to make sure the odds are entirely on our side." I looked back at the scanner tech. "Go ahead and hit those two ships with a full-spectrum scan. There's no real advantage to pretending we aren't suspicious and maybe they'll go ahead and show their full capabilities while we still have time to do something about it."

"Aye, sir."

"Please give me a comm channel throughout the ship." The communications officer flipped a couple of switches and nodded at me. "Everyone, this is Drake Haral. By now, I suspect you all know we have two unidentified ships closing on us. I've temporarily taken command, while we deal with this situation. Gunners, we are performing a full-spectrum scan of the unknown vessels and will be feeding the information into your systems. I'm going to do my best to avoid a fight, but that may not be possible. I'll keep everyone informed as best I can. Please do not call the bridge with unnecessary questions or comments —that includes you, Jeanine. Bridge out."

"Sir?" the scanner tech asked. "I'm getting very odd readings from those two ships."

"Let me guess, you're picking up far too many drive signatures."

"How did you know, sir?"

"Back in my Space Patrol days, I saw more than my share of mid-sized freighters converted into carriers by pirates and mercenaries. It's a good trick, if you can afford starfighters. Most ships can't do a full-spectrum scan—they usually don't have equipment good enough to perform one—and that's the only way to pick them up until they launch. They make for a nasty surprise if you don't know they're there."

"From these readings, it looks like each ship carries four fighters," Captain Tucci said. "Even knowing they're there, I doubt we can defend against that many ships."

"I agree with you," I said. "I just hope they go ahead and launch, now that the element of surprise is gone."

Captain Tucci gave me an odd look. "I don't understand. Wouldn't it be better for us if they launched at the last minute? If we can build up enough velocity, they might only get one run at us before we're past them."

"If we go to maximum acceleration, they'd launch the fighters anyway. And, with that many ships, they'd send half of them directly at us and have the other half positioned to match velocities with us and pretty much pound us into oblivion."

Sounding abashed, Captain Tucci said, "Oh, I hadn't thought of that."

"It's nothing to be ashamed of, Captain. I had to learn it the hard way." I looked over at the astrogator. "Load the third formula from that memory stick. It's the one labeled 'micro-jump'. Plug the star system's data into it and let me know when it's ready."

"They're launching fighters," the scanner tech announced. "The freighters are decelerating, sir."

"You're planning a micro-jump with *my* ship?" Captain Tucci asked.

"The engines can take it. I've checked."

"I'm not worried about the *engines*, sir. I'm worried that the calculations will be off and you'll scatter this ship and everyone on it across half the system."

"You've seen the same scan results I've seen, Captain Tucci. Do you think we have any chance against those fighters?"

"No, of course not. But you haven't even hailed them. Maybe they'll accept our surrender. They can extort a huge ransom for Lady Jeanine, after all."

"I'm positive they want to kill Jeanine and any witnesses, not grab hostages. So, I'm willing to take my chances with a micro-jump."

"Using a formula concocted by someone who's not even here?"

"Grant is the guy who plotted our jump away from Gaunner —the one where we jumped into hyperspace a hundred kilometers above the planet. He wasn't with us then, either. So, yeah, I'll trust him with my life, with your life, with the crew's life, and especially with Jeanine's life. Better we take a chance with his formula than the certainty those mercs represent."

Captain Tucci sighed, "You're in command."

"That's the spirit, Captain!" I turned to the astrogator. "Have you plugged all the data into the formula?"

"Aye, sir, but the options aren't good."

"Explain."

"The *best* coordinates beyond the freighters only have a forty-one percent chance of success. They don't get any better, either —at least not before those fighters reach us."

"Damn... All right, calculate our best chance if we jump between the fighters and the freighters."

"Once I saw the initial results, I went ahead and did that, sir." The astrogator tapped a button and coordinates appeared on my console. "That gives us a sixty-eight percent chance of survival."

"Not what I hoped for, but better than facing those starfight-ers." I switched my attention to the scanner tech. "Let me know when those fighters pass the midway point between us and the freighters they launched from."

"Will do."

"To everybody on the ship, I'm sure you all heard that exchange and know we're going to attempt to micro-jump. It's dangerous, but less dangerous than facing those fighters. Gunners? I want all weapons aimed forward. If this works out, you're going to have point-blank shots at those two freighters. If we take them out, we strand the fighters. Any questions?"

There weren't, so everyone settled in to wait for the fateful moment. Two tense minutes passed in silence.

"Sir, the fighters have passed the halfway point."

With a quick prayer to the god of chance, we jumped into hyperspace.

Virtually every display on the bridge went blank as the ship slid into hyperspace. Velocity, nonexistent. Scans, null. Thrust, zero. On the view screens, a dull gray mist replaced the pinpricked darkness of normal space.

Our transition into hyperspace was successful, as expected. The true danger came when the ship returned to normal space, which it would do in three seconds.

Two seconds.

One second.

The mist vanished from the view screens. The controls flared to life. And the proximity alarm blared as the scanners picked the two freighters, both within a thousand kilometers of us.

"Gunners, fire at will!"

The soft whine of firing lasers sounded just ahead of my command, probably the work of the two Space Patrol vets. The other lasers weren't far behind. Most of those first shots missed, but a few burned away pieces of the two freighters.

Next came the thunk of launching missiles. Both launchers had a target lock on the respective freighters. The missiles flashed across the short distance almost as fast as the lasers, giving the enemy crews no time to deploy countermeasures.

Flaring circles on the scanner screen marked devastating hits to both ships. One disintegrated into a fiery ball that was quickly spent in the vacuum of space. The other ship broke into three pieces, but somehow did not explode.

"Missile incoming from—"

That was all the scanner tech had time to say before the ship rocked from an aft explosion. But 'aft' didn't tell me whether my wife was safe.

Disregarding my own orders, I called, "Jeanine?"

A long second ticked past, then she said, "I'm fine, Drake. Now, concentrate on your job."

"Yes, my lady." I shifted mental gears, away from being the worried husband and back to being the ship's commander. "Damage report. What did the missile hit?"

The ship's engineer came over the comm. "The starboard engine took the hit, sir. We're still assessing the damage, but the engine is offline. I've routed all power to the port engine, but even with that you've got no more than fifty-five percent of our normal thrust."

"Understood, Chief. Was the hyperdrive damaged?"

"I can't say yet, sir, but it's possible. I'll contact you as soon as I have something to report. Engineering out."

Turning my attention back to piloting, I said, "Have we got a scanner reading on those eight fighters?"

"Yes, sir," the scanner tech said. "They're coming about, though I don't know if they're going to help the remaining freighter or keep chasing us."

"There's nothing they can do for that freighter, so you can be sure they're coming for us." I gradually brought the port engine up to its full thrust. "It will take them a while to reverse course and even longer to exceed our velocity. Captain Tucci, please take the controls for now. I have to confer with Lady Jeanine concerning our next course of action."

"Aye, sir. And may I say it was a pleasure watching you fly the *Lady of Neert?*"

"She's a good ship, Captain, and has a fine crew."

Everyone on the bridge beamed at my heartfelt compliment. With a nod to each of them, I rose from the pilot chair.

"Jeanine, I'm coming back there."

"I heard, Drake," she replied. "Could you have the ship-wide comm turned off, first? I don't think the rest of the crew needs to hear us arguing."

The communications officer grinned at me as he did as his duchess requested. Wondering why Jeanine thought we were going to argue, I headed for our small suite.

Jeanine was leaning against a high-backed chair with her arms crossed. "We're continuing on to Gaunner, Drake."

Jeanine was right—we were going to argue.

"You can't be serious, Jeanine," I said. "If Olivia has the resources to set up an ambush in the middle of nowhere, imagine what she's got waiting for us on her home planet."

"I understand that, Drake. But I also understand that I have to visit Gaunner sometime—and the sooner the better. I've got to show the citizens that they are equal members of my duchy."

"And we will, but not until we're backed up by half of a battalion of troops."

"Oh, that'll be just great—I'll show the citizens of Gaunner just how much I trust them by landing at the head of an invasion force. I'm sure it'll be a piece of cake to win them over to our side after that."

"You're not going to do anyone on Neert or Gaunner any good if you're dead. I know my plan doesn't get us off to a good start with the people of Gaunner, but after you've ruled them for a while they'll realize that you have their best interests at heart."

"When exactly is that going to be, Drake—right before or right after I give my public support to the revolution?"

"That's not–"

The comm buzzed, interrupting our argument. Still glaring at me, Jeanine answered the comm.

"Yes?"

Captain Tucci's voice issued from the comm. "I'm sorry to disturb you, my lady, but the chief engineer has compiled a damage report. He asks that you contact him immediately."

"We'll do that, Captain. Thank you." Jeanine reached for the comm switch and then paused. "I have a question, Captain. Are any of the other ships in the system close enough to lend us a hand in this fight? I can make it worth their while—assuming we survive."

"No. The closest ship is at least five hours away at its maximum thrust. Honestly, my lady, none of them would come even if they could reach us in time. We're far more heavily armed than any of the other ships in the system, so they'd just be flirting with disaster if they tried to help us."

"Understood, Captain. Is the Royal Navy also too far away to reach us in time to help?"

"Unless a navy ship is already in hyperspace and approaching the Vollec system, it would take at least eighteen hours to reach us from the nearest naval base." Captain Tucci paused for a few seconds when someone on the bridge spoke to her. "I've just received a report on the status of the fighters' pursuit. May I relay it to Captain Haral?"

"Please do," I said.

"Based on their current thrust, the fighters will exceed our velocity in an hour and nineteen minutes. If they maintain that thrust, they will be within firing range forty-seven minutes after that."

"So, we've got about two hours to figure out what to do."

"Correct, sir. I'll await your orders after you've had a chance to talk to the engineer. Bridge out."

Jeanine immediately opened a connection to engineering. "Chief Engineer Mills? I'm told you have a damage report for me?"

"Aye, my lady. Only two systems were damaged, but they're both important ones. The starboard engine is a complete loss and will have to be replaced next time we're in port. We can limp along without it until then, though the other damage probably makes that a moot point. The hyperdrive was also heavily damaged."

Jeanine's shoulder's sagged. "So, we're stuck in the Vollec system?"

"Effectively, my lady. The hyperdrive *might* work for one jump, but I wouldn't count on it."

"I assume repairs are out of the question?" I asked.

"Correct, sir."

"Was any of the damage attributable to my micro-jump?"

"Not at all, sir. It was all from the missile hit."

"Life support is okay, though, Chief Mills?" Jeanine asked.

"All of the ship's systems are operating well within tolerance, my lady."

"I have one more question, Chief Mills. It's an odd one, but..."

The chief chuckled dryly. "I've heard plenty of strange questions, my lady. I doubt yours will be any more strange."

"The freighter that broke into three pieces—if its hyperdrive survived the explosion, can you install it in our ship?"

"I stand corrected, my lady," the chief engineer said. "That is the single strangest question I've ever been asked."

"But can you do it?"

"I'll need a detailed scan of the engineering section of that freighter before I can give an answer, my lady."

"Get it. That's your absolute top priority right now."

"Aye, my lady. Perhaps you could call the Captain and pave the way for my request?"

"She'll comm you momentarily. Oh, and chief, contact me the second you know whether that hyperdrive still exists and will work in the *Lady of Neert*." Jeanine punched up a connection to the bridge. "Captain Tucci, give Chief Mills everything he asks for. No questions. No delays. He takes priority over everything else."

"Of course, my lady," Captain Tucci replied.

Jeanine closed the connection and looked at me. "I'm going to need your help planning this."

"Exactly what do you have in mind, babe?"

"We need to send the chief engineer to the broken mercenary ship to get the hyperdrive. The pinnace has to avoid those starfighters and the *Lady of Neert* has to stay alive long enough for the engineer to return with the hyperdrive and install it."

"Oh, is that all?"

"I know it's a tall order, but you've pulled off some pretty impressive miracles in the past."

I nodded absently, already pondering the question. I was so deep in thought, I didn't even hear the chief engineer comm our suite or Jeanine's conversation with him. Her gentle touch on my arm pulled me back into the here and now.

"The chief engineer says he can make the other hyperdrive work, assuming it wasn't too damaged when the ship broke apart and assuming that we can get it and assuming that the *Lady of Neert* is still around to install it in and... Well, you get the idea."

I nodded. "That's a lot of assumptions—but we *might* be able to pull this off."

Jeanine's eyes brightened. "You've thought of something?"

Smiling grimly, I said, "It's a long shot—scratch that, it's a series of long shots—but I've got a plan."

BUT IT'S NOT PROPER

Jeanine

"Okay..." The look on Drake's face made my pulse race. I didn't know what his plan was, but obviously it put him in harm's way. "Start with the worst part—the part where you do something very dangerous."

"So, you figured that out?" he asked.

"You're trying too hard to keep your face expressionless. At the risk of revealing one of my secrets, that's a dead giveaway."

The ghost of a smile appeared on Drake's face. "I'll have to remember that."

"Good, you're planning for a future beyond whatever it is you want to do." I resisted the urge to cross my arms defensively or hold my hands in supplication. "Now, tell me what it is."

"My plan is to launch the ship's pinnace, run dark until the starfighters pass us, fly to what's left of the freighter, board it, get the hyperdrive, and come back. While I'm gone, Captain Tucci will do her best to evade the starfighters without getting too far away from what's left of the freighter."

"Why are you the one piloting the pinnace?"

"I thought that was kind of obvious, babe. I'm the only pilot around here with combat experience. On top of that, if anyone is still alive and trapped in the remains of that freighter, I also have experience performing boarding actions—both hostile and humanitarian."

I closed my eyes and concentrated on breathing. Only after my pulse slowed did I respond to Drake's plan. "Who are you taking with you?"

My question surprised Drake. "You're not going to try to talk me out of this?"

"I want to, but you're right. None of the other pilots on this ship have combat or boarding experience. So, who are you taking with you?"

Drake gave my question careful consideration before saying, "The chief engineer, obviously and a few of your guards."

It was a reasonable list and I couldn't think of anyone to add to it. That didn't mean I was quite ready to accept Drake's plan. "What about negotiating with the starfighter pilots? They're stranded out here. We can offer them a ride back to civilization and, if anyone is still alive on that freighter, we can offer to rescue them."

"I think that's a great idea. Hell, they might even go for it. But I think you should wait until the pinnace is away before you begin negotiating."

"Won't you ruin my negotiating position when the pinnace powers up and appears on their scanners?"

"Probably," Drake said, "but you can still try talking sense into them."

"You will give any survivors on the freighter a chance to surrender, right? Coming back as your prisoners has got to be better than dying on what's left of their ship."

"You'd think so. Let's hope they're reasonable."

I sighed. "You're not very good at reassuring your wife that everything is going to work out just fine."

"No, but I'm quite good at being open and honest with her. Call me crazy, but I think she prefers it that way."

I went to Drake, wrapped him in a tight hug, and breathed, "She does."

The next ten minutes were filled with frenzied action. Members of the crew rushed to prepare the pinnace for launch while Drake sat with the bridge crew and gave them a crash course in evasion tactics. That left me to talk to the chief engineer.

Chief Mills added a nice twist to the plan. "If you can give me an extra few minutes, I can mount a couple of life pod boosters on the pinnace. If we launch her in the direction of that broken freighter, the boosters will reduce the pinnace's velocity to zero. We'll reach the freighter that much faster since we won't have to waste time with reverse thrust."

"Won't the starfighter pilots see the boosters firing on their scanners?" I asked.

"Yeah, but they'll ignore it unless they're a bunch of idiots," Mills said. "Boosters don't read like regular engines. Those pilots will know what they are and will assume we're trying to throw them off our trail. By the time they learn their mistake, they'll have little chance of catching the pinnace before it reaches the remains of the freighter."

I nodded, appreciating the addition to the plan. "You're sure it will only take a few minutes?"

The engineer gave me a stern look. "Life pods don't have engines of their own, my lady. Those boosters are designed for quick mounting and dismounting. I wouldn't have suggested it if I wasn't sure it would work."

"I didn't mean to question your competence, Chief, but–"

"Your husband is going to be flying the pinnace. I understand, my lady."

"It's not just my husband I'm worried about. I don't want to lose my chief engineer or any of my guards, either."

Chief Mills smiled, "I'll do my best to make sure they all get back safely, my lady. Particularly, your chief engineer."

Leaving the man to his work, I went to Captain Pennington to select a boarding party. He never once met my eyes while I described the plan to him, but I was getting used to his ways. I knew he was absorbing every detail and already sifting through his guard roster.

When I finished speaking, he said, "Including me, four members of your guard contingent have boarding experience. May I have your permission to leave your side and join the boarding party, my lady?"

"Of course, Captain. If all goes according to plan, you won't have anything to do on the ship anyway."

Then again, if *nothing* went according to plan, he still probably wouldn't have anything to do on the ship. The starfighter pilots didn't want to board us, they wanted to blast us into little pieces from a distance.

"Thank you, my lady. I'll inform the three others joining us and have all of your guards suit up." He looked my way for the first time and added, "May I suggest you have everyone remaining on the ship put on spacesuits, too?"

"You may, Captain, and thank you for the suggestion. I'll issue the orders now."

"My team and I will report to the pinnace as soon as we're ready, my lady. Rest assured, we will do everything in our power to keep Captain Haral safe and whole."

I spent the next several minutes getting into my spacesuit and trying not to worry about all the things that could go wrong. The former was far easier than the latter. And then it was time to launch the pinnace.

I gave Drake a quick kiss on the lips. "Don't get yourself killed."

Drake grinned at me. "I shall endeavor to accede to your orders, my lady."

Despite myself, I grinned back. Then I looked at the boarding party and the chief engineer. "The same thing goes for all of you, too."

Then, they boarded the pinnace and the rest of us cleared the launch bay. Captain Tucci cut thrust and spun the ship so the launch bay was facing back the way we came. Drake fired the boosters and the pinnace vanished into the distance.

People who get their ideas about space travel from watching adventure vids have no concept of just how boring space pursuits and battles can be. In a vid, the starfighters would scream past the pinnace's location a few white-knuckled minutes after it launched and get within firing range of my ship just as the pinnace fired up its engines. In the real universe, the pinnace launched from the *Lady of Neert* at least an hour and a half before the fighters would get close enough to fire on us. Our pursuers wouldn't even reach the pinnace's current location for another forty minutes.

I spent a few minutes on the bridge, assuring myself the starfighters hadn't changed their course or thrust after the life pod boosters fired. It was too early to proclaim the fighters were doing exactly as Chief Mills predicted, but the early signs were hopeful.

Satisfied there was nothing else I could do on the bridge, I stood. "I'm going to make sandwiches for the crew. If you have any special requests or allergies, tell me now."

If I had announced Drake and I were going to have sex in the pilot's seat, I think it would have shocked the crew less than my offer did. Half-a-dozen stunned faces looked at me as I waited for sandwich orders.

Captain Tucci found her voice first. "My lady, that's not proper! We have crew members to handle that."

"No one has mess duty at a time like this because every crew member has an assigned emergency station. They're all busy running system checks. Which is exactly what they should be doing right now, Captain." I smiled brightly, trying to put the captain at ease. "I'm the only person on the ship without an assigned station, so it makes sense that I should make the sandwiches."

"But you *do* have an assigned station, my lady! You should be in your quarters where you will be as safe as possible."

I raised one eyebrow. "Are you honestly suggesting I should spend the next hour and a half cooling my heels in my room when I could be doing something useful like fixing lunch?"

"No, my lady, I'm telling you that your safety is our paramount concern!"

"Fine, Captain, I'll be careful to use dull knives when I'm making the sandwiches. I'd hate to cut myself and send the crew into paroxysms of despair."

I'd hoped for a laugh from someone on the bridge. I didn't even get a vague smile.

"But... It's not—"

"Proper. You've already said that, Captain." I sighed and looked around the bridge. "Look, I know you've got a mental picture of how a duchess should behave, but I'm *not* what you'd call a typical duchess. I cleaned the apartments my grandfather and I lived in—and those apartments were usually smaller than my suite on board this ship. I shopped for food. I cooked for my grandfather—who loved sandwiches, by the way. So, yes, I think I can handle making a couple of dozen sandwiches for people who are about to risk their lives to protect mine."

I followed that little speech with a glare that froze Captain Tucci with her mouth open. I don't know how long the standoff might have lasted if the scanner tech hadn't spoken up.

"I'd just about kill for a good BLT, my lady."

"Sarah!" Captain Tucci said.

Sarah shrugged at her Captain, "Well, she asked."

I laughed, "Sarah is a very practical woman. Are the rest of you equally as practical or do you just want to watch her eat a sandwich?"

That broke through their resistance and I took orders from everyone on the bridge. Before heading to the galley, I said to the communications officer, "Please check in with the rest of the crew and gather orders from them. Relay those to me once you have them."

"Yes, my lady," he said, turning back to his console. "I'll have their requests for you in a few minutes."

The simple task of preparing lunch for two dozen crew members kept my mind occupied just enough that I didn't worry about Drake. I won't say I didn't think about him, because he's always lurking in the forefront of my mind. But I didn't worry about him.

When I showed up on the bridge with a trolley full of sandwiches, it was too much for Captain Tucci. She found two crew members who didn't have much to do and ordered them to take over sandwich delivery duties. If she wasn't so conscious of the difference between our stations in life, I'm pretty sure she'd have given me a stern lecture about my lack of duchessly decorum. So, I handed off the sandwich trolley, grabbed my own sandwich, and settled into a spare seat on the bridge.

Around bites of my roast beef sandwich, I asked, "I assume there's been no change in the situation?"

Captain Tucci hurried through the bite she was chewing, practically swallowing it whole, so she could respond all the more quickly. "I would've called you had anything changed, my lady."

"I know that, Captain. That's why I said 'I assume'. How long do we have before the starfighters reach the pinnace's location?"

Unlike her captain, Sarah did not hurry through her bite of bacon, lettuce, and tomato sandwich. She followed the bite with a quick swig of water and then said, "Ten minutes at the most, my lady. The starfighters show no sign of decelerating or changing course, so it's a safe assumption they'll fly right past it. And thanks for the sandwich—it's really good."

Captain Tucci looked like she wanted to lecture her young crew member but, once again, she had a mouthful of ham and cheese. I made sure the captain saw my broad smile.

"You're more than welcome, Sarah. Would you like another one?"

Sarah's eyes cut toward Captain Tucci before she said, "No, thank you, my lady. We've already taken up far too much of your valuable time."

I considered correcting the woman's mistaken idea that my time was any more valuable than hers—at least while we were on board the *Lady of Neert*—but decided I had bucked enough traditions for one day. Instead, I leaned back in my seat, concentrated on enjoying my sandwich, and waited for something to happen.

Ten minutes later, the pinnace's engine flared to life on the scanner screen.

"Two fighters are breaking off their pursuit of us and swinging about to chase the pinnace." Sarah studied her screens intently for a moment and then said, "The fighters might catch the pinnace before it reaches the remains of the freighter. It's going to be very close."

"How close?" I asked.

"I can only make an educated guess right now, my lady, but I'd say within one minute, either way."

"Captain Tucci, is there anything we can do to help the pinnace?"

"No, my lady, I'm afraid not." Captain Tucci looked over her shoulder at me, "Perhaps it's time to contact those fighters and open negotiations?"

I gave the question careful consideration before saying, "Not yet. That's more of a last chance response, anyway."

"As you say, my lady." Captain Tucci turned her attention back to the piloting console. "With your permission, I'll begin plotting our evasion course. We've got a very tricky slingshot maneuver around the outer planet coming up relatively soon."

"This is your bridge, Captain," I said. "You never need to ask my permission to do your job. In fact, I'm going to leave you to it. Do you mind if I visit the various duty stations and have a brief word with the crew?"

"You don't need my permission, my lady!" Captain Tucci protested. "After all—"

"I'm the duchess," I interrupted the Captain and finished her line. "I know, but you are the captain of this ship."

Captain Tucci nodded, accepting my explanation. Perhaps there was hope for her, yet. "I'm sure the crew would enjoy getting to know you, my lady."

"Thank you, Captain. I'll enjoy getting to know them, as well."

With a smile and a wave, I began my rounds.

MISSILES LAUNCHED

Drake

The starfighters flashed past us, just a couple of thousand kilometers away—the space-equivalent of right on top of us. Of course, without our passive scanners, we'd never have even known they were there at all.

I checked my course and thrust calculations for the eleventh time. Our margin was slim, but I was confident we would reach the aft piece of that freighter before any of the starfighters could reach us. Chief Mills and I based our calculations on all the data we had for Meteor-class starfighters. Assuming the merc company hadn't made some major modifications—not a particularly safe assumption, but it was the only one we could make—those ships might get within firing range, but only if they maintained maximum thrust the whole way. That would deplete their ships' standard fuel load and start drawing from their reserve tank. We were gambling the mercs would save enough fuel to let them rendezvous with potential rescue ships rather than burn it all chasing us.

It was time to find out if we were right.

I fired up the pinnace's engines and, as quickly as was practical, brought them up to full thrust. At the same time, Chief Mills brought up the full scanner suite.

"Two fighters are breaking off from the main group, Captain Haral," Mills said.

"Not a huge surprise," I replied. "It's what I'd have done in their place. Can your scanners get us any more details than the *Lady's* long-range scan picked up?"

Mills snorted, "Not likely, given the inferior equipment installed on this ship. Remind me to upgrade the scanners on all our ships' boats when we get back to Neert."

I gave the chief a sidelong glance. "When was the last time a pinnace needed a better scanner suite than what's already installed?"

"Um..." Mills stared off into space—literally, in this case—and considered my question. "This is the first time, sir."

"In other words, you want to spend a hell of a lot of money to install top-of-the-line equipment that may never be needed again?"

"I wouldn't put it that way, sir. And I'd have thought a pilot like you would back me one hundred percent."

"Pilots who don't have to pay for their equipment always want the best, whether they need it or not. I'm a ship owner, Chief, and spent years balancing what I wanted against what I needed."

"I see your point, sir, but *you* won't have to pay for this stuff —the duchy will."

"And my wife is...?"

"Lady Jeanine." The chief's eyes widened as he finished following my train of thought. "Okay, I guess you sort of *will* end up paying for the upgrades. But I still think it's a good idea."

"When we get back to Neert, work up a proposal—including costs and potential justifications *besides* scanning ambushing starfighters—and submit it to me. I'll consider it."

"Right you are, sir."

The chief pulled out his pad and entered a note on it. While he was doing that, I looked over my shoulder at Captain Pennington and his three guards.

"Do any of you gentlemen have any questions?"

"Do you have any idea what we'll find inside the aft section of the ship, sir?" Pennington asked.

"Guesses, at best, Captain." I had given that question a lot of consideration since we left the *Lady* and took a few seconds to order my thoughts. "Our best-case scenario is that everyone in that piece of the ship is dead. We won't face any opposition, letting us get in and out without a running battle and without risking any of our lives."

"I get the idea you don't think that's likely, sir?"

"No, I don't. The remaining ship pieces are too big. It's likely the emergency seals closed quickly enough to prevent a complete loss of the ship's atmosphere. Since our target includes engineering, it's entirely possible that some life support systems are still operational. I'm afraid we're going to find survivors—possibly as many as thirty of them."

"That's...more than I expected, sir."

"It's not as bad as it sounds. Most of them will only have makeshift arms—big-ass wrenches, hammers, stuff like that. Things could get bad if we end up in close combat, but I think we'll have the advantage at range."

"They know the terrain, sir. If they've got any sense and plan properly, we *will* end up fighting them hand-to-hand."

"Perhaps the second-best case scenario will play out and they'll just be desperate for a ride off of the ship. If so, we may be able to negotiate with them."

"They're mercenaries, sir. I expect they'll just try to take the pinnace from us."

"That's part of the worst-case scenario, Captain—and why you and your men are here."

Since our departure from the *Lady*, Chief Mills had been busy working with the deck plans for the class of freighter used by the mercenary company. He changed them to match how he would have modified the freighter to act as an ultralight carrier. He shared his updates with Captain Pennington and his men and the five of them began planning the actions we would take once we reached what was left of the aft part of the ship. Since I didn't have much piloting to do at the moment and had a lot of experience in this sort of thing—especially boarding heavily damaged ships, something the Space Patrol did on a routine basis—I joined in the discussions.

As is usually the case in these situations, we didn't really make a plan so much as put together a branching collection of contingencies. Still, within an hour of getting our first look at the Chief's updated plans we had a plan we could all live with. In situations like this, that's usually the best you can hope for.

During our long approach to the wrecked freighter, the two starfighters maintained full thrust. They gained on us inexorably, which made my passengers increasingly nervous. With ten minutes left in our journey, I realized I needed to say something about the situation.

Jerking a thumb over my shoulder in the direction of the pursuing starfighters, I said, "It's nice of those guys to burn all that fuel catching up with us. I didn't think they were going to do us such a big favor."

Corporal Sams—'Sammy' to his fellow guardsmen—said, "Getting close enough to shoot at us is doing us a favor, sir?"

"They are going to shoot at us eventually, Corporal. The difference is, this way they only get one shot. They won't have enough fuel left to do anything else and I know a little bit about evasive maneuvers. If they don't fire braking thrusters in the next minute or two, it's going to take them hours to turn around and come back after they've taken their shot."

"What happens if they start braking now?"

"That's not too bad, either. We'll be docked and the chief will probably be halfway through disconnecting the hyperdrive by the time they show up. Unless they want to risk killing their friends, they won't fire on what's left of the freighter—that means they also won't fire on our pinnace. They'll have to hang around and wait for us to leave and they should be almost out of fuel. The pinnace carries a few hand-launched rockets—they're designed for use when we're on the ground, but any Space Patrol vet can tell you they work in space, too."

"But—"

"That's enough, Corporal," Pennington said. "Captain Haral is our pilot and he likes the current situation. That's good enough for me and it should be good enough for you."

"Yes, sir. My apologies, Captain."

I gave the man a thumbs up and returned my attention to piloting. A minute later, our situation got more interesting. One of the starfighters fired braking thrusters while the other maintained full thrust.

"Well, that was unexpected," I said, "and about as clever as they can be in this situation."

"What does it mean for us, Captain?" Pennington asked.

"It means we're going to get shot at *and* we get to find out how well those hand-launched rockets work. On the plus side, I'll only have to evade one starfighter instead of two."

Having said that, I changed course toward the forward piece of the freighter.

"Uh, sir?" Chief Mills asked. "You do remember the hyperdrive isn't in that piece of the freighter?"

"Yes, Chief, I'm fully aware of that. But that guy closest to us doesn't know where we're going. He's going to waste even more fuel changing to a new intercept course. And when he launches missiles, I think I can fool them into locking on to the forward freighter piece. We don't need anything from it, so it's no loss to us if the starfighter shoots it."

"But what about our fuel situation, sir?" Corporal Sams asked.

"We've got plenty of fuel, Corporal. Don't worry about that."

Seconds later, the closest starfighter's maneuvering engines lit up as he shifted to an intercept vector for our new course.

"Nice going, Captain," Chief Mills said. "Can't you just keep changing courses and make him run out of fuel before he even gets close enough to us to fire?"

"No, Chief. If I change course again, the pilot will just pick something in between the two courses and stay on that heading until I make a final decision."

When the scanner showed we would reach the forward piece of the freighter in one minute, Chief Mills asked, "Shouldn't you begin braking, Captain?"

"Almost. And, guys, this is going to be rough."

"Won't the inertial dampeners–" Corporal Sams began.

"Pinnaces don't have inertial dampeners," Chief Mills said. "Those are only installed on hyper-capable ships."

Then it was time for my maneuvers. I spun the ship so the braking thrusters would press us into our cushioned seats rather than our harness straps and increased the main engine thrust. Despite several gravities pushing against him, Chief Mills kept his eye on the scanner screen.

"The starfighter has target lock on us, Captain," Mills gasped.

"Acknowledged."

"Missiles launched. Looks like four."

I kept my eyes on my own screens, working to pass as close to the forward freighter section as possible. My goal was to loop around the freighter, throwing off the missiles, and letting the starfighter pass us before he could get a second target lock.

"Missile strikes in ten seconds."

The mangled front section of the freighter appeared in our viewports.

"Nine seconds."

I fired our maneuvering thrusters and the pinnace rushed toward the freighter.

"Eight seconds. Seven seconds. Six seconds."

We slid past the trailing edge of the freighter, no more than fifty meters from it.

"Five seconds. Four seconds."

My fingers danced across the console and the maneuvering thrusters slowly moved us up and around what was left of the freighter.

"Three seconds. Two seconds."

The freighter now filled the entire forward viewport. I had done everything I could do. Now, our lives were in the hands of fate.

"One second."

The pinnace completed its half loop of the freighter. As open space appeared in the viewport, I brought the main engines to maximum thrust. Light blossomed below us.

"Two missiles hit the freighter," Chief Mills said. "Another missile was destroyed by debris from the explosion. The other... The fourth missile lost target lock. Nice flying, Captain."

"What about the starfighter?" I asked.

"He just passed us and is headed out into deep space. He did spin around to face this way and launched four more missiles at us. He's working on a hope and a prayer because he doesn't have any kind of target lock on us."

"He's going so fast in the other direction, those missiles will burn all of their fuel just offsetting that velocity." I eased back on the throttle and the pressure on my chest eased, as well. "We've got a clear path to the aft section of the freighter."

"I hope the boarding goes as easy as that did!" Sams said.

Chief Mills looked over his shoulder at the guardsman. "Son, that was only easy because Captain Haral made it look easy. There aren't a lot of pilots who can do what he did."

"You're going to make me blush, Chief," I said. "I just hope Captain Tucci is as fortunate evading the six starfighters chasing the *Lady of Neert*."

EVASIVE MANEUVERS

Jeanine

Feeding the crew kept my mind occupied more than I expected. It wasn't the simple task of making sandwiches, but the simple courtesy of speaking to the crew members I was serving, that did the trick.

I learned this was the last voyage for the assistant engineer, Alex Hewitt. He and his wife were expecting their first child—a girl—and the man meant to be one of those fathers who came home to his family every day. Alex told me this with some trepidation, as if he was afraid I would disapprove. Instead, I offered truly heartfelt congratulations and threatened him with a displeased glare if he didn't bring his wife and soon-to-be newborn daughter to the palace so I could meet the wife and coo over the baby.

After word of my talk with Alex spread, the rest of the crew opened up to me more readily. I saw pictures of spouses and sweethearts back on Neert, of children ranging in age from newborn to young adult. When I returned to the bridge, Captain Tucci even surprised me with pictures of her grandchildren.

I deflected requests for financial advice—having little experience beyond simple household finances—but promised to line-up experts to advise the crew.

I recounted the story of how Drake and I met—leaving out Grandfather's request that Drake get me 'properly laid'—but otherwise telling the truth.

I even let Sarah, the scanner tech, cry on my shoulder after she told me how her most recent boyfriend dumped her, without explanation and by leaving a message on her pad, mere hours before she reported to the *Lady of Neert* for this trip.

Patting the young woman—she was only a couple of years younger than me, but the difference seemed greater—on the back, I asked, "Do you want me to have my secret police pick him up, lock him away in a dungeon, and torture the reason out of him?"

Sarah stopped crying and pulled back in alarm. "No, my lady! I just want answers, not torture!"

"That's good, Sarah, since I don't have a secret police force, a dungeon, or any intention of torturing anybody. It was supposed to be a joke."

"Oh. Well, that's okay, then."

"I'm just guessing, Sarah, but you're probably better off without this guy. Your ex took the coward's way out. A man worth having will always be up front with you. So, wipe your eyes and straighten your back. A smart and pretty girl like you will have guys falling all over themselves to replace that jerk."

"You think so? That's what my mother said when I called her, but...well...you know how mothers can be."

I didn't, really. Not in the way Sarah meant, anyway. But I did know my mother, at least. And even if I'd only met her a little more than a months ago, I thought I could imagine how she would have reacted in a similar situation.

"You know, just because she's your mother and wants you to be happy doesn't mean she isn't also right."

"Yeah, I know," Sarah said, her cheeks coloring slightly. "But a daughter's rebellious habits can be hard to break."

Eventually, when I'd spoken to every member of my crew, I settled into my suite to wait for things to happen. Captain Tucci kept an open line to the bridge so I could hear what was going on up there.

She gave me a stern look when I made that request. "May I speak freely, my lady?"

"Please do, now and at all times in the future, Captain Tucci. I have no illusions that I know everything simply because my biological father was a duke."

By this point, the bridge crew felt comfortable enough with me to smile at my remark. I considered that a big step in the right direction.

"I have no objection to your request, my lady, provided you only speak to us if you have something vital to say. During our upcoming maneuvers, none of the crew will have the time or attention to spare for idle questions."

I knew that, but appreciated the captain's forthright comment. "My life will be in your hands and the hands of your crew. I'd have to be pretty foolish to distract you at a time like that."

"You'd be surprised how many people don't understand that, my lady."

I thought back to the parties I'd attended on Xapreathea and the astounding levels of self-absorption evident in most of the nobles. Princess Olivia, alas, was one of the few who didn't suffer from that affliction. She still thought she was oh-so-superior to her peers, but I was honest enough to admit Olivia actually *was* superior to them. So was I, for that matter, but I didn't go around trying to kill my political opponents. Then again, I am preparing for a revolution, so perhaps my own self-satisfaction had more than a tinge of smugness to it.

I suddenly realized Captain Tucci was waiting for me to say something. "No doubt, Captain. So, let me assure you that *I* am not one of those twits."

"In that case," the Captain smiled, "I will happily agree to your request, my lady. Do you want to try negotiating with the fighter pilots?"

"No. I don't see the point, now that they've split up. I don't have time to negotiate with two groups. Besides, I like the plan Drake thought up."

I waited thirty long and quiet minutes for something to happen. Then things happened all at once. I watched my own screens as the *Lady* drew closer to the system's outermost planet. Captain Tucci constantly adjusted our course, always angling closer to the planet.

"The starfighters are following our course, Captain," Sarah said, her voice calm, professional, and a far cry from that of the woman who cried on my shoulder.

"Acknowledged," Tucci said. "Gunners, do you copy that?"

A dozen voices chorused, "Aye, ma'am."

"Good. You are weapons-free until I say otherwise, gunners. Do not—I repeat—do not wait for my order to fire. If you have a shot, take it."

"Aye, ma'am," the voices said again.

"Assistant Engineer Hewitt? What is the status of your engines?"

"They are operating at peak efficiency, ma'am, though I must also add that they are Chief Mills' engines."

"He's not on the ship, Hewitt. That makes them your engines until he returns."

"Aye, ma'am." I could almost hear the man grinning at the Captain's comment. "My engines are ready for anything you ask of them."

"That's good to know, Hewitt."

A few seconds passed in silence before Tucci said, "We're moving behind the planet now. Sarah, give me a running count of the number of starfighters still showing on your scanners."

"Yes, ma'am," Sarah said. "We've got six at the moment... Now five...Four...Now two...One...The scan is clear, ma'am!"

The maneuvering engines roared as Captain Tucci fired the

ship's braking thrusters, but I felt nothing. The inertial dampener protected us from what would, otherwise, have been a severe number of gravities.

"Entering the atmosphere now," Tucci said.

Everyone felt the ship shake and shudder as the relatively thin atmosphere caught the *Lady* and helped slow her down.

"Sarah, alert the gunners ten seconds ahead of the starfighters' projected arrival above us."

"Aye, ma'am." Seconds that felt like hours dragged by before the scanner tech said, "Gunners, ten seconds to arrival on my mark...Mark!"

The ship shuddered more as Tucci angled it back toward space and shut off the braking thrusters. The much deeper roar of the main engines grew as the Captain increased the throttle.

The pursuing starfighters suddenly appeared on my screen and raced across it. I felt more than heard the missile launchers firing, accompanied by the whine of laser batteries firing at the tiny targets.

A missile track intercepted one of the fighters and Sarah sang out, "A hit! One down...And another! Two fighters destroyed."

Then the dots slid off the far side of my screen and the fighters were beyond our scanner range.

"Six missiles never got a good target lock, Captain," Sarah said. "I recommend the gunners send self-destruct orders to them."

"Gunners, do as she suggests," Tucci said. "We fired ten missiles. We've got two hits and six misses. What about the other two?"

"Still in pursuit, Captain, though I doubt they'll catch their targets. The gunners should be prepared to destroy them when we finish our loop of the planet."

A minute later, actual scans matched Sarah's prediction. Still, considering the conditions the gunners were working under, two hits was a pretty impressive score for the gunners.

"My lady? The emergency is over. Do you have any questions?"

I asked the only important question I had. "Can the four remaining fighters threaten the pinnace?"

"No, my lady. That was central to Captain Haral's plan. Those fighters are heading off at a right angle to the pinnace and going much too fast. If they conserve fuel by gently firing their braking thrusters, they *might* be back in this area in about two days."

"Good job, everyone. I'm proud of you," I said. "Now, let's rendezvous with the pinnace and get a hyperdrive."

LET'S MAKE LIKE PIRATES

Drake

By the time we reached the aft piece of the freighter, the missiles launched by the starfighter as it passed us were slowly moving toward us. With a velocity of just under a thousand kilometers per hour, no fuel for the main engine, and little fuel left for maneuvering, I wasn't worried about the missiles at all. They might eventually reach the remains of the freighter, but they weren't a danger to the pinnace unless it was still docked there when the missiles hit. But if we were still on the freighter several hours from now, we would probably already be dead from something else.

We could actually see the aft section spinning in our forward viewport. Part of what had to have been the fighter bay yawned, open to space. I was tempted to dock in the bay. Even as mangled as it was, the partial fighter bay would be the most secure docking location available. It was also farther from engineering, making it a poor option for us. If no one was alive in the freighter, that wasn't a problem, but the pinnace's scanners weren't up to the job of discovering whether there were survivors or not. I hoped the short range would remedy the problem.

"Chief, any luck picking up survivors on the scanner?"

"No, sir. I've got some readings that are probably survivors, but I can't tell you whether it's one person or a dozen."

From behind me, Sams asked, "Why didn't we have the *Lady* do a complete scan before we left the ship, sir?"

"That wasn't an option, Corporal. A scan that intensive would have lit up the scanners on those starfighters like a King's Birthday light show. There's no chance they'd have ignored the life pod boosters we used to launch this pinnace."

"Oh. I hadn't thought of that, sir."

"Pilots and scanner techs are about the only ones who *do* think about that stuff, Sams."

"Sir?" Mills said. "I think I've found a good docking location. You're going to have to match that rotation and then get the pinnace within fifteen meters of the hull. Then I can use the pinnace's grapples to pull us down to the hull and lock us in place. Oh, and unless you're incredibly lucky or the best pilot in the kingdom, we're going to have to cross part of the deck to reach the airlock."

"I am both of those, Chief, but I *want* to leave space between the pinnace and the airlock."

The Chief snorted. "Typical pilot. No matter how far off-target your landing is, it's always 'I meant to do that'."

"Or," Captain Pennington said, "our pilot knows the vacuum of space will protect the pinnace from potential boarders and we won't have to leave someone here to guard the ship."

I grinned at the Chief. "What he said."

After that, everyone fell silent while I maneuvered the pinnace into a spinning, twisting orbit around the aft piece of the freighter. It wasn't easy and I was extremely happy the remaining starfighter was still too far away to shoot at us. As slowly as the pinnace was moving, the pilot couldn't have missed it if he tried.

After ten minutes of stressful, shoulder-hunching flying, I said, "Reel us in, Chief."

The Chief Engineer wasted no time activating the grapple. A

few seconds later, we heard a clang as the pinnace fastened itself to the hull. I rolled my head around, stretching my tight neck muscles, and flexed my shoulders, happy to finally release the flight controls.

Taking my spacesuit helmet down from its secure mount, I said, "Gentlemen, let's make like pirates and plunder this hulk."

Corporal Sams, at least, got into the spirit of the moment. "Aaarrrr!"

Through Pennington's faceplate, I saw him wince. "Please, sir, don't encourage the Corporal."

Shrugging an apology, I sealed my suit. The Chief and I checked the other's suit seals, while the four guardsmen did the same among themselves. Satisfied, I led the way to the airlock. We cycled through and onto the hull beyond the pinnace.

I walked carefully across the deck and tried the airlock's controls. As expected, nothing happened. Circuitry burns out quickly when a ship undergoes the kind of trauma this one had. Captain Pennington signaled two of his men who replaced me at the hatch. They worked the manual control and slowly cranked the hatch open. Once the opening was large enough for each of us to fit through, we entered the airlock in single file.

During our approach to the aft piece of the freighter, we'd held a lively discussion about what to do in this situation. Closing the outer hatch before opening the inner one was the humane thing to do. On the other hand, flushing the atmosphere and killing any survivors without spacesuits was the tactically smart thing to do.

Much as I wanted to be humane, I wanted to get the hyper-drive and get away from the Vollec system before our enemies could send more forces after us. So, we anchored ourselves inside the airlock and the two guardsmen manually cranked the inner hatch open, too.

We couldn't hear the air hissing through the widening opening, but we could see the results. With the artificial gravity gone, small items floating in the corridors were blown out of the ship by the escaping air. As the hatch cranked farther open, the flotsam grew in size. We hugged the sides of the airlock so none of it hit us.

And then the first person ricocheted down the corridor. He clutched at any handhold he passed, all in vain. The man's eyes widened as he flew through the inner hatch and he reached for Corporal Sams. Out of reflex, Sams began extending his hand. Pennington caught Sams' arm before the Corporal caught the extended hand. We all watched the man tumble out into space, his face a rictus of terror.

In quick succession, a woman and two more men followed the first man out into the void. They all reached for us, their eyes pleading for salvation that would never—*could* never—come.

"I know this is difficult, men," Pennington said, "but remember that these people laid in wait for us. They would have destroyed our ship, our friends, and our duchess without a second thought."

"Your captain is right," I said. "The disgust you feel at our necessary actions are what separates us from the likes of them."

The others responded in a subdued and ragged chorus. "Yes, sir."

To everyone's relief, the next human blown out of the ship was already dead. Shortly after the corpse vanished into the endless night, the wind slackened. A minute later, it stopped all together.

Captain Pennington signaled for Sams to take point. One of the two privates fell in behind Sams. The Chief and I were next. Pennington and the remaining private brought up the rear.

"Chief, you're the one with the deck diagrams," I said. "Which way do we go?"

The chief checked his suit's display and said, "Straight ahead for thirty meters."

With nothing but our headlamps lighting the way, we passed through the inner hatch and into what was left of the ship.

Six beams of light stabbed into the utter darkness inside the freighter. Bobbing and swinging with every move we made, they could have easily disoriented us. During my Space Patrol training, our instructors spent weeks teaching us how to handle situations like this, both for military and humanitarian operations. All patrollers had to pass stringent boarding tests before graduation.

If they weren't desperately needed at the regular posts, I'd have taken the two Space Patrol veterans among the *Lady's* crew. Since I wanted the best people available fighting to protect Jeanine, I never even mentioned the possibility of taking those two men. I knew she'd have insisted I take them, and for exactly the same reason I wanted them to stay at their posts. While Captain Pennington's three men hadn't gone through patroller training, they had experience in the real thing.

That meant Chief Mills was the only one with us who had never done this before. So, I wasn't surprised when he was the one who broke the silence.

"Damn, this is spooky! You think there are any other survivors out there, sir?"

I bit back the curt order I'd have issued to a rookie patroller, or even to one of Pennington's men, if they'd spoken. The Chief was nervous, as any reasonable man would be in this situation, and he didn't see much sense in keeping silent. The vacuum around us silenced everything—which only added to the Chief's 'spooky' feeling—and meant sound wouldn't give away a waiting ambush.

"Yes, Chief, it's extremely spooky and I'm sorry we had to drag you into something like this," I said. "But just because we can't hear anything that doesn't mean we should say anything beyond what is absolutely necessary. The quiet lets us give all of our attention to sight and touch, such as vibrations coming through the decks or the bulkhead."

Belatedly, the Chief mimicked the rest of us and put a hand

against the bulkhead next to him. "I'm sorry, sir, I'll be silent except to give directions."

"No harm was done, Chief."

Half a minute passed, then he said, "Take the next corridor on the left."

When we reached that corridor, Corporal Sams pulled a portable scanner from over his shoulder. 'Portable' is a relative term, since it massed fifty kilograms, but Sams handled it with relative ease. Gazing into the screen, Sams extended the sensor around the corner. He twisted the controls so it swung to the right, first.

After studying the scans in that direction for twenty seconds, he said, "Five branching corridors to the right where survivors could be hiding. Nothing else to report in that direction. Checking left."

Sams fiddled with the controls and the sensor swung to the left. It was halfway through its rotation when a flurry of blast bolts lit up the corridor. One hit the sensor and the energy from the blaster shot fried the circuitry inside the scanner. Sparks flew as Sams shoved the unit away from himself. It floated into the cross-corridor, where another flurry of shots reduced it to a twisted wreck.

"I've detected enemy activity to the left, sir," Sams said in one of the driest tones I'd ever heard.

"I guess that answers the question about survivors, Chief," I said. "Does your modified deck plan show a less direct way to reach the engine room than down that corridor?"

"Yes, sir, but we'll still have to cross this corridor."

"That's better than charging into the teeth of that ambush, Chief."

"Sir?" Captain Pennington said. "We could try negotiating with them. I can't believe these survivors would rather die than surrender and get a ride out of here with us."

"Wouldn't they just plan on killing us and taking our pinnace, sir?" one of the privates asked.

"To what end, private?" I asked. "They'd still be stuck in the Vollec system with no friendly hyper-capable ship to go to. I think your Captain's suggestion has merit. All of you, scan through the local comm channels and try to find a member of the crew I can talk to."

We split up the channels and began flipping through them looking for activity. It took less time than I expected because the survivors were using one of the standard emergency comm channels.

"Got them, sir," the private up front with Sams said. "Channel eight sixteen."

I dialed in the channel and my headset filled with chatter.

"Did anybody see what we shot?"

"No. Whatever it was sparked a lot, though. I bet they really needed it."

"It was just our portable scanner," I said. "And, thanks to all that shooting, we have a really good idea where you are."

The chatter stopped as soon as I spoke, but I still heard breathing.

"Someone stayed on the line," I said. "That's good, because I can't negotiate if I can't talk to any of you."

"Negotiate what?" a voice asked.

"Your survival."

"We already survived just fine."

"My mistake. Since you have everything under control, we'll just take our ship and leave."

"Now, hold on," a new voice said. "Fredricks don't speak for everyone."

I smiled at this admission of division in their ranks. "That's good to hear. Who am I speaking with and what was your position in the crew?"

"I'm Engineering Apprentice Holloway. Who are you?"

"Captain Drake Haral. My wife is the Duchess of Neert and Gaunner. I mention that last bit so you'll know that my word carries a considerable amount of weight."

"Yeah, we recognize your name," the first voice, Fredricks, said. "And it doesn't matter what my apprentice says. I'm the ranking officer here and I'd rather die than negotiate with you."

"There ain't no ship left, Fredricks," Holloway said. "Your rank don't mean nothing anymore. You been outvoted, so just shut up."

Chief Mills caught my attention and signaled for me to switch to our team channel. I motioned for Captain Pennington to monitor the survivors while I spoke with Mills.

Before changing channels, I said, "I have to confer with one of my team. I'll be back on this channel soon. Please try to figure out your own situation before I return."

I switched channels. "Yes, Chief?"

"Did you hear how Fredricks referred to Holloway? He called him *his* apprentice. Only one person would say that."

"This ship's chief engineer," I said.

"Right, sir. I just wanted to make sure you knew the situation before you got on with the negotiating. Fredricks could sabotage that hyperdrive beyond repair in under a minute—so don't let on what we're here for until we're in a position to keep him from doing that."

"Got it, Chief—and thanks for pointing that out. I missed it entirely."

Switching back to the survivors' channel, I heard the same argument as before.

"I'll see you all brought up on charges of mutiny!" Fredricks snarled.

That struck me as a pretty lame threat, considering the situation. Holloway agreed.

"Who are you going to report the charges to? If the Captain ain't dead, he's in the same boat we are and won't give a good goddamn about your stupid mutiny."

"Gentlemen," I interrupted, "I can offer salvation, but it's a limited time offer. You have one minute to give me a final decision or I'll toss a grenade down there and be done with it."

"You hear that, Fredricks? You're gonna get us all killed if you don't give in."

"I heard, all right. So tell me, Holloway, why didn't he just chuck a grenade at us to begin with? Either he's bluffing or he needs something down here and is afraid he'll damage it."

Damn, that threat backfired quickly. Chief Engineers are usually pretty sharp, but Fredricks sounded sharper than most.

Holloway's voice rose a notch. "Hey, where you think you're going, Fredricks?"

"The only thing back here is my engines. I'm going to fix it so that man can't use them at all."

Time for one more less-than-humane act.

"Fredricks is right," I said quickly. "And if you don't stop him, these negotiations are over."

Silence stretched for two long seconds, then I heard three muffled blaster shots. Fredricks cried out and then fell silent.

"Okay," Holloway said, "we stopped him. Now, what's the deal?"

A minute later, the blasters floated down the corridor. Then the six remaining survivors stretched out in the corridor. I left Captain Pennington and his men watching our new prisoners while Chief Mills and I went to the engine room.

An hour and forty-six minutes later, Chief Mills had the hyperdrive disconnected. With some misgivings, we got the prisoners to carry the drive. I threatened immediate death if they did anything to damage it. The threat was superfluous, since they did exactly what Chief Mills told them to do. Everything went incredibly well, though. We got back to the airlock and cranked the inner hatch the rest of the way open. Then Sams and one of the privates went to do the same with the outer hatch.

"Um, sir?" Sams said. "We've got a problem."

I joined him at the hatch and immediately saw the problem.

The second starfighter, the one that fired braking thrusters, was floating no more than a hundred meters away and pointing right at our location.

COMING TO TERMS

Jeanine

Relieved that the worst of this ambush was over, I asked, "Captain Tucci, how long will it take us to reach the pinnace?"

"That depends on whether we want to conserve fuel, my lady," she said.

I hadn't thought of that. "What's our fuel situation? Is it very low?"

"Not at all, my lady. We could run at full thrust for the rest of this trip and still have plenty in reserve. But fuel is expensive and—"

"Screw the expenses, Captain. I want my people safely back on board as soon as possible."

Especially Drake, though I wouldn't admit as much aloud. I had no doubt the crew knew he was my highest priority, but part of ruling successfully is acting as if all of your subjects are of equal importance. Besides, we couldn't get Drake without getting the rest of the men.

"As you command, my lady. Commencing full burn now."

The muted roar of the engines deepened. I also thought the deck vibrated a bit, though that was probably just my imagination. I certainly didn't feel the acceleration, which is a good thing. It meant the inertial dampener was working as designed.

"Our estimated time to arrival at the pinnace's current location is one hour and twenty-six minutes."

"Thank you, Captain. Keep me informed of any developments."

I sat down at my desk and turned my attention to the vast collection of documents on my pad, all of them requiring some official response from me. Scrolling through the list, I made a mental note to hire a competent assistant to handle stuff like this. By the time I'd reached the end of the list, I decided three assistants were called for. Sighing audibly, I returned to the first document and opened it. I was still skimming through it when the comm beeped.

"My lady, the scanners show a starfighter in a slow orbit around the aft section. The bulk of the wreck hid it from our sensors until just now."

My heart jumped into my throat. Grabbing a portable comm, I said, "I'm on my way to the bridge. Can you tell if the fighter is threatening the pinnace?"

"Not yet, but I'd bet everything I own it is."

"So would I, Captain." My thoughts raced as I ran through the *Lady's* corridors. "I want an open line of communications with that pilot as soon as possible."

"You heard the Duchess, Barry?"

"Aye, Captain," the communications officer said. "I'm already working on it."

Barry was as good at his job as the rest of the bridge crew was at theirs. By the time I entered the bridge, he was in the middle of a conversation with someone.

"I already told you, *I* cannot negotiate with you. However—"

An irritated man's voice said, "Then why the hell are you even talking to me?"

Catching sight of me, Barry wordlessly handed his headset to me.

The irritated voice continued, "Either get me someone with a little authority or just—"

"This is Jeanine Langston, Duchess of Neert and Gaunner. Is that enough authority for you?"

The man was silent for a couple of seconds before, with a calculating tone, he answered. "Yes, you'll do just fine. Now, my terms are—"

"I don't care about your terms. *My* terms are as follows. First, you will eject from your starfighter. Second, you will surrender to whoever picks you up. Third, for the rest of this trip, you will do exactly what you're told to do when you're told to do it."

"Hold on, *my lady*," the pilot's voice dripped with derision when he spoke my title. "I'm the one calling the shots right now. And mentioning shots, I've got your little pinnace in my sights as we speak. You're going to do exactly as I say or else I'll blast that pinnace and what's left of our ship into little bitty pieces."

Great, a man with no grasp of the larger picture. "And what do you think will happen to you if you do that?"

"I'll die in a fiery explosion when you destroy my starfighter. I'm willing to die if I have to. Are you willing to lose everyone who was in the pinnace?"

In a cheerful voice, I said, "Ah, I see the problem. You think you'll get a quick, almost heroic death if you kill my people."

"What are you talking about, woman? What else are you going to do?"

"We'll disable your fighter—regardless of how much damage my ship takes while we do that. Then we'll bring you on board and bundle you into a spacesuit with enough oxygen to last for a full day. We won't give you any water or food. We'll disable the comm and bind your hands and feet. Then, with you unable to open your suit to space, I will personally shove you out of an airlock. You'll float through space for hours and hours, still perfectly healthy and perfectly aware, as you tumble through the void with no hope for rescue, less hope for survival, and with no company but yourself and the distant stars."

The bridge crew all watched me, their faces pale as they contemplated the horror I described.

I let my voice drop into a malevolent purr. "You'll be alive, but effectively already dead."

I let the pilot consider that for a second and then returned to my original, cheerful tone of voice. "Or you could just surrender and throw yourself on the mercies of the Ducal Court, aided by the good word I'll put in for you. What do you say?"

The comm was quiet for ten of the longest seconds of my life before the pilot, his voice cracking, said, "I, uh, surrender. Ejecting now."

Handing the comm headset back to Barry, I turned to the scanner station and said, "Sarah, did the pilot eject?"

Sarah tore her horrified gaze from me and checked her screens. "Um...Yes, my lady. He did just what he said he would do."

"What now, my lady?" Captain Tucci asked.

"We pick up the pilot and then dock with the pinnace when it leaves."

Barry said, "My lady, I've got Captain Haral on the comm. He's asking for you."

Taking the headset back, I said, "Drake? Are you okay?"

"We're all fine, Jeanine. We've got the hyperdrive and a few prisoners. Did you have something to do with the pilot ejecting from that starfighter?"

"A bit. We...came to an agreement."

"I can't wait to hear that story, babe."

"And I can't wait to tell it to you—in person."

An hour later, Drake was back on board the *Lady*, where he and the rescued starfighter pilot helped me negotiate with the other surviving starfighter pilots and the handful of survivors on the other two remaining pieces of the converted freighter.

By the time we'd picked up the last of the prisoners, Chief Mills had the hyperdrive installed and we were back in business.

"Everything checks out, my lady," the Chief reported. "I still want to get a new hyperdrive when we get to a spaceport, but this one will get us there just fine."

It did just that. Twenty-six hours later, we landed on Gaunner.

LADY THIEF

Jana

Growing up, I never really gave the Star Stone much thought. Sure, I learned about it in school like every other kid in the Star Kingdom, but that wasn't anything more than your basic royal propaganda dressed up as education.

We saw a vid of King Bernard's coronation, complete with a sonorous voice-over declaring, *"Prince Bernard places his hand upon the Star Stone and swears his oath to God and the subjects of the realm. God, acting through the Star Stone, envelops the prince in his crimson light and then withdraws it, leaving the newly Recognized king unharmed. This signifies King Bernard's divine mandate to rule wisely over us all."*

Every data pad produced for children came with *The Story of the Star Stone*, among others, preloaded. The story was a complete myth, of course. It told of a time when an imposter tried to usurp the rightful king of the People—yes, upper-case 'p' and everything. The usurper fooled many of the People with his silvery tongue and they flocked to follow him. The rightful king prayed for divine intervention and, with a clap of thunder and a bolt of lightning, God placed the Star Stone before the People. Then He spoke, *"Let all who lay claim to the throne place their hand upon the Star Stone so I may judge them."* The rightful king readily did as instructed. The usurper did so with reluctance and only because his followers demanded it of him. Both men spoke their oath and crimson light surrounded them. When it withdrew, the rightful king was unharmed while the usurper was burned to ashes.

My friends and I liked that story a lot, though it had more to do with the macabre death of the usurper than any deep love for kings or the Star Stone. But that's the level of material I had available to examine. And it's not like every book was written for children, either. There were plenty of mythological and historical studies on the Star Stone and its place in galactic civilization.

Read in rapid succession, those texts really pointed toward the one thing I couldn't find—a solidly scientific examination of the Star Stone. I couldn't even find any pseudoscience studies, with the exception of a few that came down firmly behind the royal rationale for the Stone.

I did find a few tantalizing hints that real studies might exist, including one proposal for such a study submitted to the royal family by the Royal Academy of Science. I didn't find a public response to the proposal nor did any of the hints lead to anything except dead ends. But those tidbits got me thinking.

If *my* continued wellbeing and that of my descendants depended on a big, glowing rock, I'd want to learn everything I could about the thing. Considering the reliable recorded history of the Star Stone goes back four thousand years, I felt certain at least one of those monarchs actually had the thing studied. It was probably done in secret by scientists sworn to secrecy and, equally probably, killed or imprisoned once they delivered their results.

Since I was at a dead end with my usual research methods, I chose to believe such research had taken place and that the royal family kept those results out of the public record and off the public networks. But the information *had* to be someplace where the current royal family could access it, if necessary. After all, knowledge is power and the royal family is all about power.

The good news from all of my digging and speculation was that I felt certain the information Jeanine wanted existed.

The bad news was that the information was almost certainly kept within the royal palace and well beyond the reach of common subjects.

I, however, was a very *un*common subject who wouldn't simply give up when a job got difficult. That's why I went searching for Mr. Dogan, the estate's security expert.

"What may I do for you, Miss Jana?" he asked when I tracked him down.

He always called me 'Miss Jana' no matter how many times I told him he could drop the honorific. He always smiled, nodded, and then kept on using it.

"Do you know how to get in touch with the lady thief who helped with the estate's security prior to Lady Evelyn's ball just before the royal wedding?"

"Of course, miss."

"Could you ask her to come around for a visit? I have a...business proposal for her."

"I don't suppose you'd like to tell me what that proposal is, would you, miss?"

"Not yet, Mr. Dogan." He frowned, though it looked more out of concern for me than annoyance at me. "If my proposal is possible—and that's a very big if—I promise I will tell you about it before the lady and I act upon it. Is that acceptable?"

He gave me a hard a look. "I have your word on that, Miss Jana? Lady Jeanine would be quite upset if anything happened to you."

"You have my word, Mr. Dogan."

"Very well, miss. I'll see what I can arrange."

An hour later, Mr. Dogan told me I'd have a guest joining me for dinner. After thanking him, I withdrew to my suite to prepare my pitch to the thief. Even a thief as talented as this lady would almost certainly balk at the idea of breaking into the royal palace—especially since she'd be taking me with her.

I didn't meet the lady thief when she visited the first time, back before Jeanine's Recognition, and wondered what she would be like. I imagined an exotically beautiful, slender woman of extreme grace and poise. For once, reality lived up to my imagination. The thief was just a bit taller than Jeanine, with light-bronze skin, dark eyes, and hair the color of midnight. Her movements appeared languid, but I sensed energy coiled inside of her, ready to burst out if needed. In that respect, she reminded me of Jeanine.

I led her to my suite, where the servants had set a table. Mom always taught me to keep business away from the dinner table, so I tried to keep the talk light while Lady Smythe-Warrington, thief extraordinaire, and I ate. She even insisted on a far less formal form of address the first time I used her official title, which is where my mother's training went awry.

"Please, Miss Ward—"

"Jana."

"Jana, it is," she smiled. "But only if you call me Tilly. All that 'lady' this and 'lady' that makes me want to look around for my great grandmother. My grandmother married a commoner and so did my mother. I'm twenty-five percent noble by birth, but one hundred percent commoner by inclination."

"And even more so by profession?"

Tilly grinned at me. "Good heavens, no, Jana. I am very definitely among the elite—the nobility, if you prefer—of my profession."

"There's that modesty you nobles are so famous for," I said, grinning to show I wasn't serious.

"Yes..." Tilly eyed me over her glass of wine. "Mentioning modesty, are you as good a slicer as I think you must be?"

I never told Tilly I was anything but one of Jeanine's many assistants. Try though I did to keep my expression neutral, I must have done something that gave away my surprise at her revelation.

"I have some excellent sources of information, Jana. They're vital in my line of work. I know Lady Jeanine had access to very talented slicer before her Recognition. I bet you're the slicer—but are you as good as my sources suggest?"

I shrugged, "Chances are that I'm better than you've heard. Depending on your source, I might be a little better or a lot better. I don't suppose you'd be willing to tell me who your source was?"

"No more than you would be, if our positions were reversed." I nodded in understanding and Tilly added, "But perhaps you could offer some qualitative assessment of your abilities?"

"I'd put myself in the top ten—top five, if the job involves intrusion and data theft."

Tilly's eyebrows rose in appreciation of my abilities—or maybe surprise at my audacity. "On all of Xapreathea? That's impressive."

"Your sources information must be woefully out of date if that's your interpretation of my qualification." I met Tilly's gaze boldly and said, "I meant I was among the top ten slicers in the Star Kingdom."

This time, I was certain Tilly's raised eyebrows represented surprise. "Now who needs lessons in modesty? If you're as good as you say you are, you must be counted as royalty among the slicer underground—and I'm sure I'd recognize your avatar name."

That last bit was a challenge. I got the idea that Tilly believed that *I* believed I was as good as I said. Since the galaxy is full of people who believe they are far more talented at their chosen profession than they truly are, she wasn't quite ready to simply take my word for it. Tilly didn't have to prove anything to me since I'm the one who approached her. I, on the other hand, had much to prove to Tilly—especially if I was going to convince her to help me.

"You realize it goes against my slicer nature to reveal my working name like this?"

"You know my real name and profession, Jana. Don't you think turnabout is fair play?"

Sighing, I nodded. "I'm Dreamwalker."

Tilly's eyes went wide and her mouth dropped open. Honestly, I couldn't have asked for a better response.

After watching Tilly's mouth open and close a couple of times, I said, "I guess you've heard of me?"

My comment snapped Tilly out of her shocked surprise. With a low chuckle, she said, "Yes, Dreamwalker, I've heard of you. But—"

"Anyone can give a name, right?" My interruption drew a cautious nod from Tilly. I continued, "After dinner, you can give me a data-retrieval quest. Pick anything you like. As long as the data is accessible from the net, I'll get it. Will that suffice?"

"Yes."

"Good. Now, I think that's more than enough business talk during the meal. My mother would say it was far too much."

"My mother would say the same thing," Tilly said, laughing.

We took our time finishing the meal, savoring the excellent food and the superb wine. But what really made dinner special was knowing we each shared the table with another woman of exceptional ability. This kind of thing happens to me so rarely— Jeanine is the only other one I've ever met—that I found myself wishing the dinner wouldn't end.

But, it did end.

After we drained our wine glasses, I said, "Much as I hate to return to business, it's time for me to prove I am Dreamwalker."

"I hate returning to business, as well. You are a truly fascinating dinner companion, Jana. Regardless of what happens in our business dealings, I do hope we can be friends."

"I'd like that, Tilly."

"Good. During dinner, I tried to think of a sufficient challenge for your abilities. I toyed with stuff like breaking into some royal database or other, but you did that months ago when you got Lady Jeanine's DNA test results."

I inclined my head in acknowledgment.

"How about a timed challenge? Say, thirty minutes to find a file on someone's data pad. I'll only give you their name. I won't even tell you what planet they're on. This estate does have a subspace connection, doesn't it?"

"Of course. And I accept your challenge. What's the name?"

"The timer starts as soon as I give you the name, Jana."

"Agreed."

"Don't you want to connect to your system first, so you don't waste any of the time?"

I waved my hand. "Pffft. Give me the name and start the timer."

Tilly smiled at my nonchalance, opened a timer on her portable pad, and said, "Jordan Barton."

"Spelled exactly as it sounds?"

"Yes."

"Have another glass of wine and relax, Tilly. I'll go get a file from his data pad."

Twenty-three minutes later, I returned. A file from Jordan Barton's system showed on my pad's display.

Tilly's eyes narrowed when she saw what the file was.

"That bastard!"

"You didn't know he was recording your, um, intimate time together?"

"I most certainly did not!"

"I figured as much. Don't worry, I completely wiped every file, tracked down his backups on the network, and wiped them, too. The one you're looking at is all that's left."

"You did all of that in twenty-three minutes?"

"Oh, no, that only took ten or eleven minutes. I spent the rest of the time identifying the other women he recorded, forwarding a single recording to each of them, and then wiping all those files, too." I smiled brightly at Tilly. "Us girls have got to stick together, after all."

Tilly regarded me for a moment before saying, "I'm

impressed, Jana. Really impressed. And I owe you for finding and wiping those recordings. Whatever it is you need, I'll do it if it's within my power."

"You might want to hear what I need before you say something like that, Tilly."

She waved off my warning. "Anything. Just name it."

Taking a deep breath, I said, "I want you to get me into the royal palace so I can find out what the royal family knows about the Star Stone."

Tilly stared at me for ten long seconds. "Is that all? I mean, you don't want me to get you Recognized as Queen of the Realm while we're at it?"

I chose to ignore the sarcastic tone. "Nope. Just break me in, help me find one of the royal family's most closely guarded secrets, and then get me out again. If it helps, we really just need to find a way for me to connect to the palace's internal network."

"So, you don't need to grab a book from King Bernard's personal library or anything?"

"I hope not, but I also can't promise anything."

"Right..."

"Think about the boost to your reputation, Tilly. You could go from thieving nobility to thieving royalty with one job."

"Do you really think we can do this, Jana?"

"I'm not saying it will be easy and it's going to take a lot of advance preparation, but I wouldn't have proposed it if I didn't think it was possible."

Tilly scrubbed her face with both hands. When she pulled them down, she wore a wide grin. "What the hell, Jana. Let's do it!"

WELCOME TO GAUNNER

Jeanine

Drake and I caught up on our sleep after the events in the Vollec system. I felt certain neither of us would have many opportunities for such luxuries once we reached Gaunner. We were as well-rested as possible when Captain Tucci guided the *Lady of Neert* to her first-ever landing on Gaunner. Before debarking, I gave final orders to Captain Tucci and Chief Engineer Mills.

"Chief, the hyperdrive is your top priority. If any of the locals show recalcitrance, feel free to invoke my name and direct them to call my office."

"As you say, my lady," the Chief said. "I'll have my people do all of the actual work on the *Lady*, of course."

I shook my head, "No, I want you to hire the best local crew you can find and let them install the hyperdrive."

"I must protest, my lady!" Captain Pennington said. "We can't trust *Gaunnerians* with this work. They could easily sabotage the ship while pretending to do the work."

Chief Mills nodded emphatically, "Exactly. We can't—"

"Convince the people of the Duchy of Gaunner they can trust *us* unless we're willing to trust *them*," I said. "I appreciate your concerns, gentlemen, but this is the perfect opportunity to begin mending the schism between Neert and Gaunner."

"Will you at least allow my people to supervise the work and perform a private inspection once it's done?" the Chief asked.

"If it will make you and Captain Pennington feel better, Chief, go ahead," I said. Both men nodded in relief, so I turned to Captain Tucci and said, "To show these gentlemen that I'm not ignorant of the possible dangers ahead of me, I want all of the *Lady's* stations manned at all times. If you detect any threats to the ship, take off and *then* call Drake or me."

Captain Tucci was no more pleased with her orders than the Chief had been. "And abandon you, my lady? Surely—"

"I appreciate your concern, Captain, but those are your orders. Once you're outside of the atmosphere, place a subspace call to Neert and the nearest Royal Navy base and summon help."

Tucci said, "I will do as you order, my lady. But what if *you* are threatened?"

"I'll have Drake, Captain Pennington, and his guardsmen protecting me." Seeing everyone opening their mouths to protest, including Drake, I hurriedly added, "*But* we will call the ship if we need immediate extraction. If we do call, come and get us—wherever we are and whatever you have to smash through to reach us."

"While also calling Neert and the Royal Navy," Drake added.

"Yes," I agreed.

"What if—?"

"I can't leave orders for every eventuality, Captain," I interrupted. "In any other emergency, use your best judgment and act accordingly. You have my full trust."

With that, Drake, my guards, and I exited the *Lady*. A stiffly proper man in the uniform of the Duchy of Gaunner waited for us at the bottom of the ramp. He saluted and, between us and several ground cars, a squad of ducal guards snapped to attention and presented their arms.

"On behalf of your new subjects, welcome to Gaunner, my lady."

I checked his rank insignia and said, "Thank you, Captain...?"

"Reel, my lady. Bryan Reel, Commander of the Duchess's Guard." His eyes flicked over my shoulder to Captain Pennington and the dozen guardsmen under his command. "Where are the rest of your personal guards, my lady?"

Without looking, I could picture the pained expression Captain Pennington was giving to Captain Reel. I'd seen it many times since I told the Captain he could bring no more than a dozen guardsmen. To be fair to Captain Pennington, I'd also seen that same expression on Drake's face many times, as well. I gave Captain Reel the same explanation I'd given back on Neert.

"A dozen dedicated guardsmen, plus the fine gentlemen lined up behind you, should be more than sufficient to protect me from any normal threats."

"But, my lady," Reel said, "a large and determined force could overwhelm our combined forces and capture or kill you."

Captain Pennington muttered, "That's exactly what I said."

Ignoring the comment from behind me, I asked, "Do you have any idea how many people live in the Duchy of Gaunner, Captain Reel?"

The question took him by surprise. "I, um... Not right offhand, my lady."

"At the last census, it was close to fifty billion people living on the duchy's eleven planets. Gaunner, alone, holds almost a quarter of that population. If even a fraction of those people rose up against me, could the entirety of Gaunner's military stand against them?"

"Not if they were truly determined, my lady."

"Exactly. Ducal guards exist to stop *small* bands of attackers. Between your guards and Captain Pennington's guards, I have three dozen highly-trained and, most importantly, *loyal* guards watching my back."

"Not that my lady's assessment is incorrect, but may I ask why you think my men and I are loyal?"

"Because I'm not dead. You could have killed us all in the blink of an eye, had you wished to do so. You must have worked closely with my predecessor before she married into the royal family. Had you reached out to her, I have no doubt Her Highness would have arranged for immunity from justice and a quite lavish retirement for the men who ended my life."

Captain Reel gave a thoughtful nod. "I see your point, my lady."

"Good. May I assume you have plans to brief Captain Pennington on all security matters after we reach the palace?"

"I do."

"Excellent. Then let's get going."

The ride from the spaceport to the palace was...strange. Though I'd specifically forbidden any kind of a procession or parade for me and even kept my arrival time vague to avoid any such disruptions, word got out. Our little convoy of cars drove through streets lined with people.

Faces impassive and voices silent, they watched us pass. There were no welcoming calls. There were no hateful denunciations. The mute reception quickly went from strange to unsettling. And, finally, it was too much for me.

"Stop the car."

"*What?*" Captains Pennington and Reel said.

Speaking to our driver, Captain Reel added, "Corporal, do not stop this vehicle."

Glaring at Reel, I said, "Corporal, the Duchess of Gaunner commands you to stop the car. *Now*."

The car was already slowing when Reel said, "Do as her ladyship commands, of course."

Pennington, perhaps hoping to invoke a higher power, said, "Captain Haral, could you convince the duchess that whatever she is doing is...hasty?"

"Don't you think we should find out what she's planning before we pass judgment, Captain?" Drake asked.

"I will have to address my subjects at some point," I said. "Why not get a head start on it and do so now?"

"You'll let the captains deploy their guards around the car before you get out?" Drake's voice was not very hopeful.

"Good God, no! I'm not a conqueror come to lord over the vanquished. I'm just going to talk for a bit and then we'll continue on our way." I turned my attention to Captain Reel. "You know these people, Captain. Do you honestly think I'll be in any real danger? If you do, I will order the Corporal to drive on."

Captain Reel obviously wanted to claim such danger existed, but he couldn't bring himself to lie. "I doubt it, my lady, though I cannot rule out the possibility of someone acting unexpectedly."

"I understand, Captain. Will it make you feel better if I allow you and Captain Pennington to accompany me?"

As both captains nodded, Drake said, "And me. You're not putting one foot outside of this car unless I go, too."

"Of course, dear. I expected nothing else."

Drake opened the door and climbed out of the car. I came next and, as the two captains followed, walked toward the crowd. Smiling broadly and hoping no one else could hear my hammering heart, I stopped before a woman about my own age. She held a very young boy in her arms while a girl, no older than three or four, clutched her skirt.

I said, "Hello. I'm Jeanine Langston, Duchess of Neert and Gaunner."

The mother gaped at me for two long seconds, as did everyone else in my field of vision. Then she paled and did her best to curtsy while holding the toddler and trying to keep her daughter close. Seeing the panic flaring in the woman's eyes, I mentally cursed myself for being so impulsive. I can't imagine surprise meetings with some of my predecessors went well for the commoner so 'honored.'

"Please, ma'am," I said, "there's no need to curtsy—especially while you're holding a child."

The poor mother froze in the middle of her obeisance, looking all the world like a terrified rabbit caught in a spotlight. Her eyes darted right and left as if she was looking for an avenue of escape.

All of the anticipation and excitement drained out of me. "I didn't mean to frighten you, ma'am. I just—"

"Come back to the car, Jeanine." Drake caught my arm and pulled me away. With his free hand, he gave a friendly wave to the crowd and called, "Sorry for the disruption, folks. We'll be on our way."

The young girl chose that moment to get over her shyness. In a loud voice, she said, "You scared my mommy and should tell her you're sorry!"

A nervous titter ran through the crowd around us and the terrified mother whispered, "Hush, Sasha!"

Pulling out of Drake's grasp, I turned around and looked at Sasha. One hand still firmly clutched her mother's skirt but the other was propped against her hip and she glared at me with a level of defiance only seen in the very young. Putting on the friendliest smile I could muster, I went down on one knee and met Sasha's gaze.

"*Please* pardon her, my lady," Sasha's mother said. "I'll punish her quite severely when we get home. There's no need for you to sully your hands with the likes of her."

Sully my hands? Good God, was everyone else on Gaunner as terrified of me as this woman was? Probably not, but this truly showed how far I had to go to convince these people I wasn't a monster. They all knew how Olivia would have treated Neert if she had gained control of it and, obviously, they assumed I'd treat them as badly.

As the mother's entreaties washed over me, the crowd around joined her in begging pardon for little Sasha. I hung my head to hide the tears that welled up in my eyes. This had all gone so wrong, so quickly, and in ways I'd never have guessed. Surreptitiously, I tried wiping away the tears. I had no idea how the crowd would react to them, and was no longer willing to risk another misinterpretation of my intentions.

Sasha had other ideas. Being the only one on my level, she saw my tears, saw me wiping at them, and asked, "Why are you crying?"

Still blinking furiously, I raised my head and looked through the tears at the little girl. "Because this went so wrong and I'm so very sorry it did. I just wanted to meet some of the people of Gaunner. Instead, I scared your mommy and all the people around her."

Sasha gave this some thought. "You're saying 'sorry' to everyone?"

"Yes, Sasha, that's what I'm saying."

"That's okay, then." She cocked her head, regarding me carefully. "You're very pretty."

An honest laugh bubbled up through my tears. "Thank you, Sasha. You're very pretty, too. And I love your dress."

Sasha looked down at her dress and, obviously mimicking her mother, said, "This old thing?"

A few actual laughs sounded around us. I reached out a finger and tapped Sasha's nose.

"Old or not, *I* like it." Standing, I met the uncertain gaze of Sasha's mother. "She's adorable, as is the little man in your arms. Please, please, believe me when I say it was never my intention to upset or frighten you."

The woman's head jerked back and forth in negation. "I'm fine, my lady. Really!"

"That's very kind of you to say...I'm afraid I don't know your name and Sasha's Mommy seems a bit juvenile for a conversation between adults."

"Carol, my lady. Carol Holder."

"I'm very pleased to meet you, Carol. May I call you Carol?"

"Of course, my lady."

"Carol, you may always be honest with me. I know many members of the nobility can be complete..." Remembering the young ears listening to me, I stopped short of saying 'assholes' and searched for a more acceptable alternative. "Twits. I've only been one of them for a month or so. Before my Recognition, my life was much like yours."

"I'll try to remember that, my lady."

"Thank you, Carol. And I am truly sorry for the fright I caused. Is there anything I can do to make up for it?"

Carol silently shook her head but Sasha said, "Mommy and Daddy need a babysitter so they can go to Annie's versary. Mommy says she's commed everyone."

"Sasha!" Carol cried, blushing furiously.

I look at the little girl. "Well, that is a serious problem. Do you know when their anniversary is?"

"Ask Mommy."

I looked at Carol and cocked on eyebrow in inquiry. Her blush, just subsiding, flared anew.

"Pay no attention to Sasha, my lady. Everything is fine."

"I just finished asking you to be honest with me, Carol. When is your anniversary and—tell me truly—do you have a sitter for the children?"

"Tomorrow night, my lady, and not yet. But I'm certain I'll find someone."

"I'm certain, too, because you just have." I pulled Drake up next to me. "The two of us will be honored to babysit your children while you and your husband celebrate. Would you allow the children to visit with us at the palace? It will please those two large gentlemen behind me if they don't have to worry about securing a private home. I could send a car to pick up all four of you and then let you and your husband have the car and driver for the rest of the evening."

Sasha's eyes went round. "You live in a palace?"

"Yes, we do," Drake said. "So, you can pretend you're a princess all evening."

Sasha eyed Drake dubiously. "How do you know about playing princess?"

"Because, long ago, I had a little girl just as beautiful as you. She and her mother live with the angels, now, so I haven't been able to play princess in a very long time."

"Oh." Sasha thought this over for a second. "Do you remember how to play?"

Drake bowed deeply to Sasha. "A gentleman *never* forgets how to play princess, your highness."

Sasha grinned at him and then looked up at her mother. "Can we, Mommy? Can we, please?"

"I don't know, Sasha. Lady Jeanine is a very busy woman and Captain Haral might not want certain...reminders."

I took Carol's free hand. "I won't insist, of course, and won't be offended if you don't accept our offer. But I know Drake and I would both truly enjoy having the children visit. Besides, it will give me a taste of what to expect when we have children of our own."

The entire crowd around us was silent, waiting for Carol's answer. She looked down at her daughter. When she looked back at me, she wore a shy smile.

"Of course, we'll accept your kind offer, my lady."

The crowd around her burst into cheers. Startled at the sudden noise, the toddler wrapped his arms around Carol's neck. Sasha, on the other hand, jumped up and down, clapping her hands. We got the Holder family's address and comm codes. I had Captain Reel give Carol a code guaranteed to reach someone who could bring the call to Drake or me.

With a small wave to Sasha and a bigger wave to the crowd, we got back into the car and drove on. News of our short visit with Carol and her children raced ahead of us by word of mouth. People must not have garbled the message too much because we were met with smiles, waves, and even a few cheers along the rest of the route.

As we pulled up in front of the same palace where I was held prisoner mere months ago, we found a much more formal reception waiting for us. Guards formed up and top-level servants and assistants were gathered to meet us.

Before getting out, Captain Reel asked, "May I assume today was atypical of your usual behavior around hostile crowds, my lady?"

Drake answered before I could. "I'm afraid not, Captain. Jeanine can be quite..."

"Choose your next words very carefully, Drake," I growled.

"Um...unexpectedly outgoing?" He gave me an inquiring look. I nodded my acceptance of the phrase, so he continued, "She'll be the picture of introversion for hours on end. Then, just as you allow yourself to relax, she'll suddenly become an extrovert."

"Ah," Reel said. "Thank you for the warning, sir, though it comes somewhat late for today."

Drake offered an unapologetic shrug. "Everyone's life gets more interesting after they meet Jeanine, Captain Reel. Accepting that *now* will do wonders for your blood pressure."

ROYAL SUMMONS

Olivia

"Her Majesty, Queen Charlotte, requests your presence, Your Highness."

William and I had just returned from some dreary public affair, one simply packed with commoners desperate to get a glimpse of their betters. Despite myself, I spent most of the event wondering how dreary common lives must be if simply being in the same room with us lent them some form of imagined glamor.

When I was a child, my father swore to me that we were little different from commoners. We had more and finer possessions and our words often carried the weight of law—though not as often as some of his peers wished—but we all loved, lived, ate, slept and relieved ourselves. He added that last bit just to see my face screw up and listen to me squeal, "Ew! That's gross, Daddy."

The queen's summons wiped the nostalgic smile from my lips. William, no doubt more used to his mother's moods, sighed.

"May we have a moment to freshen up, first, Matilda?" he asked.

The queen's personal assistant curtsied and said, "Please forgive me for my lack of specificity, Prince William. Queen Charlotte's summons is intended for Princess Olivia, alone."

"There's nothing to forgive, Matilda." William tried to suppress his relieved smile and failed. Kissing me lightly, he whispered, "Join me when Mother dismisses you. We can wash the scent of the masses from each other."

Since the queen had never summoned me like this before, I doubted I'd be in a particularly good mood when she released me. Then again, the kingdom had certain expectations from me, ones I couldn't meet if I kept my legs closed simply because I didn't feel romantic.

"That sounds marvelous, dear," I whispered back. Turning to Matilda, I said, "Lead on."

My trepidation increased when Matilda took me to the queen's office rather than her personal quarters. I'd been to her office before, of course, but only with advance knowledge of the meeting and the reason behind it.

One of the guards opened the door, allowing Matilda and me to sweep into the office without slowing down. Matilda stepped to one side, leaving me framed in the doorway. Queen Charlotte sat at her desk, a pad in one hand and a stylus in the other. Her eyes slid across the screen, never once glancing at us.

Matilda said, "Princess Olivia, as you requested, Your Majesty."

Still not looking up, Queen Charlotte said, "Thank you, Matilda. That will be all."

Matilda curtsied and left through the still-open door. It closed behind her.

I stood as patiently as possible, waiting for Charlotte to turn her attention upon me. She kept reading. It's an ancient technique designed to establish control for the summoner and remind the summoned of their place in the hierarchy. I used it all the time during my years as Duchess of Gaunner and found it disconcerting being on the receiving end.

After a couple of minutes, Charlotte signed whatever she was reading. Setting the pad and the stylus on her desk, she looked at me for the first time and waved to one of the seats before her desk.

I bobbed a quick curtsy before sitting. "Thank you, Your Majesty."

The queen gave the barest hint of a nod. Was she simply acknowledging my thanks or showing approval at my formal tone? I couldn't tell.

"You know why I summoned you, Olivia."

My mind whirled with possibilities, each more outlandish than the last. Forcing myself to concentrate, I carefully sifted through everything I'd done since my last conversation with the queen. Nothing even remotely stood out.

"I humbly beg your pardon, Your Majesty, but I do not."

Charlotte's eyes hardened. "Don't play stupid with me, Olivia. I've got the external situation under control—no thanks to you—but it's apparent I haven't been vigilant with the internal situation."

I quelled a surge of panic and wracked my brain for anything I'd done that might require the queen's personal attention. Once again, nothing came to mind. I carefully composed my face and my thoughts before meeting her gaze.

"I swear to you, I have no idea what situation you are referring to."

Charlotte's eyes flashed with the first true anger I'd seen in them. "We hardly have time for games, *girl*, but I'll humor you. I'm talking about the attack on the *Lady of Neert* in the Vollec system."

"Was it pirates? If so, it's a pity they didn't get the bitch, but I don't see what any of that has to do with us."

The anger in Charlotte's eyes faded a bit, replaced by surprise. "Are you saying you didn't hire the mercenaries to stage the attack?"

"What? Of course, not. Actually staging an attack like that would be sheer stupidity!"

Charlotte drummed her fingers on her desk. "Why?"

"How many reasons do you want? None of us knew Lady Jeanine was coming to Xapreathea until she waltzed into my ball. Staging an attack on a route no one ever expected her to use would draw unwanted attention to the attack. Furthermore, orchestrating the attack on such short notice would almost certainly leave tracks leading right back to the orchestrator. Plus—"

"There's no need to continue, Olivia." Charlotte looked down and rubbed her temples. "I now believe you had nothing to do with the attack, though I find myself wishing otherwise."

"You mean it wasn't simply a chance encounter with pirates? And why would you wish I *was* involved?"

"The answer to both of your questions is the same. When I first heard of the attack on Lady Jeanine, I initiated a very quiet investigation into the matter. My staff found a very obvious financial trail leading back to accounts owned by William and, since the wedding, you." Without looking up, Charlotte asked, "Did anything happen between you and William after your ball ended a few nights ago?"

"It would be more appropriate to say something did *not* happen after our ball." At my mother-in-law's sharp look, I hastened to add, "Fear not, I did my royal duty. I just wasn't as... enthusiastic...as I'd hinted I would be when we were dressing for the ball."

"And William noticed?"

"Of course, he noticed. He is *extremely* observant when it comes to sex. He was really quite a dear, too, kissing and massaging me until I relaxed enough to at least enjoy myself." I smiled, remembering how loving he'd been. Then the memory extended beyond our love-making and the smile faded. "Oh damn. He didn't! Did he?"

"Would you care to elaborate on that, Olivia?"

"Afterward, when he was holding me and still doing his best to comfort me, William asked if there was anything else he could do for me. Without thinking, I said 'Rid me of that bitch.' We fell asleep in each other's arms and I didn't give it a second thought—until now." It was my turn to rub my temples. "I will, of course, claim sole responsibility and face the consequences. Just..." My breath caught and my vision blurred. "Charlotte, promise me you'll help William get over me and will find another woman who will make him happy."

"Don't be so melodramatic, dear." For the first time since I arrived, Charlotte's tone was warm. "My staff has already scrubbed the financial records and replaced them with false ones leading to someone else. It won't stand up to serious scrutiny, but there are only a handful of slicers in the entire Star Kingdom capable of uncovering the truth, now."

Then Her Majesty, Queen Charlotte did something she'd never done before. She came around her desk, pulled me to my feet, and then enveloped me in a maternal hug.

"Thank you for your willingness to put William's needs ahead of your own, Olivia. I knew I'd done well when I selected you, but until just now I had no idea *how* well. You truly are the daughter I never had."

Charlotte gently pulled my head down and kissed my forehead. "Leave everything about this situation to me—including admonishing William."

She spun me about and gave me a gentle shove toward the door. "Why don't you go tend to that foolish son of mine? Be as enthusiastic and adventurous as you wish. I have everything under control."

I stopped at the door and looked back at Charlotte. "I've so terribly missed being a daughter. Ever since my parents died... Did you truly mean that—about me being the daughter you never had?"

The smile that softened the queen's face was so gentle and loving I could not doubt her when she said, "With all my heart, dear. Would a mother ever lie to her daughter about something so important?"

"No, most definitely not." I found my eyes blinking away a sudden rush of tears. "I love you, too, Mother."

With a light heart and a delighted smile, I all but floated down the hallway to my suite. Once the door closed behind me, I treated William to a very enthusiastic and daringly adventurous night.

THE GREATER GOOD

Jeanine

The cars swept up the drive toward the ducal palace. It looked as if the entire staff was gathered outside in extremely well-ordered rows. The senior members of the staff formed a small delegation at the end of a very red carpet. A man who could only be Daniel Colin, former personal assistant to Olivia, stood slightly apart from everyone else.

It was my first time seeing Colin in person and I found his appearance impressive. He was entering his senior years, but age lent him a dignity no younger man could match. Without looking into them, I felt certain his eyes would convey gentle wisdom and serene confidence—the same things I found looking into Grandfather's eyes when he still lived. Colin had served House Kahn his entire life, working directly with Olivia and her three predecessors. How, I wondered, would he react to the sudden turn of fortune that put House Kahn under the rule of its ancient rival, House Wilkinson?

My mind hopped subjects and I found myself wondering if either of those houses even existed anymore? Olivia, the last member of House Kahn, was a member of the royal family, now. And was I ever really a member of House Wilkinson? Was I forming House Langston, the newest great house? Or, should that be House Haral, since I had married Drake?

I gave myself a mental shake. If our planned revolution succeeded, the great houses would be swept aside, anyway. If it failed, I doubted anyone would worry about what house I belonged to.

As the car stopped, Colin opened the door. Stepping back, he bowed low. Behind him, all of the men bowed in unison. The women curtsied with the same precision timing.

Holding out a helping hand, Colin said, "Lady Jeanine, welcome to Gaunner."

Accepting the proffered hand, I slid out of the car. "Thank you, Colin. May I present my husband, Captain Drake Haral?"

Colin straightened and, again in unison, the rest of the staff did the same. He shook Drake's hand. "Welcome, sir. Your sterling reputation precedes you."

Drake smiled, "Sterling reputation? Could I get that in writing, please? Several of my former commanding officers won't believe it coming from me."

Colin laughed and it sounded warm and genuine, as if he was truly amused by Drake's lame joke. "I am at your service, sir."

Drake stood aside so the two captains could follow us. Motioning to them, I said, "You know Captain Reel, of course, but this other gentleman is Captain James Pennington, commander of the House Wilkinson ducal guards. Captain Pennington's commands carry the same weight as Captain Reel's."

Colin nodded to both men, but spoke to me. "As you wish, my lady. Now, if you'll permit me, I'll introduce you to the rest of the senior staff."

"By all means, Colin."

Before Colin could speak, Drake quietly said, "Babysitting advice, babe?"

"Oh, thank you, dear." I turned toward the gathered staff and raised my voice. "If any of you have recent experience dealing with young children—in this case, a four-year-old girl and a one-year-old boy—would you please come by my office in two hours?"

The staff exchanged uncertain glances and Colin's expression faltered for just a second. As quickly as word of my impromptu meeting with Carol Holder swept through the crowded streets, apparently that same word swept around the palace without crossing into it. That was interesting.

Attempting to quell the confusion, I added, "I stopped and spoke to some of the people on the ride to the palace. Drake and I have agreed to watch two children tomorrow night so their parents can enjoy an anniversary celebration. I'm simply looking for suggestions for dinner, snacks, and entertainment."

The buzz of conversation rose in the wake of my announcement. I saw Colin's face darken and felt certain he was preparing a rebuke.

Speaking before Colin could, I called, "Thank you for such a fine welcome but, please, go on about your business. It's much too cold to stand around watching me get introduced to the senior staff."

A few people turned away, as if heading inside, only to stop short when they realized most of the staff were still standing there. Those few turned back, trepidation etched on their faces. What the hell?

"Really, it's okay to leave," I called. "Go. Shoo."

Those few who originally turned away did so again. This time, most of them kept going. That still left ninety percent of the staff milling around in confusion.

I looked at Colin and raised an eyebrow. "Care to tell me what's going on?"

Looking uncomfortable, Colin said, "Lord Robert, Princess Olivia's late brother—"

"Yes, I know who he is. Or was, to be more precise," I said.

"He had certain...expectations...for the staff. Among those was that the staff should remain attentive until he said 'staff dismissed.' He tested them often, using phrases such as you did, and punished those who left before he gave the correct order. Lady Olivia maintained the practice out of respect for her brother."

"So, if I call 'staff dismissed,' everyone will leave?"

"Indeed, my lady."

"Screw that." I turned back to the staff. "Listen up, everyone. I'm not Lord Robert. I'm the reason the Star Stone turned him into a pile of ashes. I'm not Lady Olivia. I'm the one who blew up her wedding. I refuse to play word games with you. If I tell you you're free to go, I mean exactly that. I will not use Lord Robert's catch phrase. Now, go inside and get warm."

This time, everyone went inside. Some were obviously reluctant—perhaps they were ones Robert had punished—but they all went.

"Don't worry, my lady," Colin said, "I'll address the issue with the staff."

"You most assuredly will not. I will not have this tenuous beginning ruined by a stern lecture from you or any other member of the staff." My gaze swept over the senior staff still waiting for an introduction. "Is that clear?"

Heads bobbed and voices said, "Yes, my lady."

"Good." I dropped the glare and called up my best professional smile. "Colin, please begin the introductions."

Fifteen minutes later, the senior staff filed inside behind Drake and me. A shy maid who looked no older than sixteen met me with a bobbing curtsy.

"May I take your coat, my lady?"

As I was already shrugging out of the coat, the girl rushed to help me. Smiling over my shoulder at her, I said, "Thank you...?"

"Mary, if you please, my lady."

With the all-too-recent reminder that life in the Gaunner palace had little in common with life in the Neert palace, I broadened my smile before speaking. "Thank you, Mary. May I ask your age?"

Apparently, duchesses didn't request permission from mere maids, because Mary's cheeks colored and her eyes darted to Colin before returning to me. "Of course, my lady. I am sixteen and yours to command."

"You're a free citizen of Gaunner, Mary, and belong to no one but yourself." As the girl's eyes widened, I added, "Shouldn't you be in school right now?"

Fear filled Mary's eyes. "I...That is, um—"

"That will be all, Mary," Colin said, his tone stern.

All of the color drained out of Mary's face. "Yes, sir."

Turning quickly, Mary all but ran from us. I thought about ordering her to return, but that would only further terrify the girl.

"Captain Reel?"

"Yes, my lady?"

"Do you have a guardsman who is particularly popular with the young, female members of the staff? One who is handsome and gentle, who can coax young Mary to willingly meet with me?"

"I know just the man for the job, my lady. Shall I summon him?"

"There's no need, Captain," Colin said. "I'll speak to Mary, myself."

"Ignore Colin, Captain Reel. Send for your man. I want to speak with him before he goes after Mary."

"Really, my lady," Colin said, "you needn't concern yourself with minor staffing problems. Until you're more familiar with the staff and their issues, I strongly encourage you to leave such matters to the senior staff and me."

"Captain Reel, please also summon a squad of armed guards, if you please."

"That is a sensible precaution, my lady," Colin said. "I must admit I was surprised when you left your most fearsome protector, Sir Phillip, on Neert."

"I left Sir Phillip on Neert so I wouldn't look like a

redheaded version of Olivia. A heavily armed knight who glares at everyone around me won't exactly make me appear approachable, after all."

Colin assayed a smile. "I hope you won't consider it presumptuous of me to note that it's not a duchess's job to appear approachable. Effective ruling, after all, requires a certain distance and detachment."

I turned a white-hot glare on Colin and was gratified when he took a step back. "I consider it extremely presumptuous of you, Colin."

Colin bowed, "Then I humbly beg your pardon, my lady."

"Not granted."

Colin jerked upright, shock replacing his studied calm. "My lady—"

"You know, I asked Sir Phillip all about you and the rest of the senior staff. My only order was for him to be truthful. He had quite a lot to say about all of you." I crossed my arms and let my gaze sweep over the entire senior staff. "You should all be happy Recognized knights cannot testify in royal court, otherwise you'd be facing some very serious charges."

Anger flowed into Colin's eyes. "I but did my duty to my duchess and my duchy."

"By breaking both royal and ducal laws whenever it suited you."

"When I believed the greater good required it. And for which, by your own admission, you have no proof," Colin said.

"That's very true, Colin. I can't send you to the royal courts without proof. Considering your close connection with the new princess of the realm, I expect you'd receive a royal pardon, anyway." Colin's look of triumph at my admission made my next words all the more satisfying. "*But* centuries of rule by House Kahn have established certain legal precedents, one of which is about to bite you in the ass."

Colin figured it out before the rest of the senior staff did. "By tradition, the senior staff are not held to that standard, my lady."

"Yeah, well, traditions change, Colin." Looking past him to the rest of the senior staff, "What Colin remembers and you don't, is that the duchess's merest whim has the force of law on Gaunner. I don't *need* proof or charges or even a trial. If I say you're guilty, you *are* guilty."

Captain Reel's guards marched in at that exact moment.

"Captain, does the palace have a dungeon?"

His face a mask of studied indifference, Reel said, "No, my lady."

"How about cells of some kind?"

"Again, no, my lady."

"What about some particularly cramped, uncomfortable, and generally crappy rooms?"

A tight smile appeared on the captain's face. "Those, we have in abundance, my lady."

I waved at hand at Colin and the rest of the senior staff. "These...people...are under arrest. Place them in the least comfortable, most cramped rooms you can find. Keep them under armed guard at all times. For the time being, have the guards set their blasters to stun."

"As you command, my lady. How long should I plan on keeping them under guard?"

"I don't know, Captain Reel. Until I decide what to do with them, I guess."

Captain Reel snapped off a salute. "You heard our duchess, men. Take them away. Put them in the unused servant quarters in the west wing for now."

As the guards hustled the stunned former senior staff away, Reel gave Drake a wry smile. "You were quite right, sir. Things do get interesting with Lady Jeanine around."

Without exchanging any words, Captain Reel entered my office ahead of Drake and me, waving the receptionist back into his seat, while Captain Pennington took the rearguard position. Neither man offered to help with my coat—entirely appropriate behavior for bodyguards—nor spoke while Drake shut the inner office door. I settled into the seat behind the desk.

Watching their studied calm, I sighed, "Go ahead, gentlemen. You may speak freely."

Caught off guard by my offer—a rather amusing thought, since guarding is the essence of their jobs—Reel and Pennington exchanged glances as if they were telepathically discussing who should scold me first. Their hesitation let Drake beat them to the punch.

"I thought you were going to handle this situation *quietly*, Jeanine. Wait until you had the senior staff here in your office, lay out your findings, give them one chance to defend themselves, and then simply release them from employment." His voice was level but held an intensity of emotion I hadn't heard since he first told me of his wife and daughter. "Why didn't you tell me you changed your mind?"

Apparently, Pennington and Reel came to an unspoken agreement because Captain Pennington said, "Captain Reel and I concur with Captain Haral, my lady. Your actions stunned the senior staff, otherwise, I'm not certain events would have gone so smoothly."

"I share my fellow captains' opinions, my lady," Reel said. "No one left in the duchy instills as much fear as Colin. He knows where every noble body is buried and which noble closets hide skeletons. Arresting him and his cronies will arouse Gaunner's lesser noble houses and may very well excite them to injudicious actions."

I met all three stern gazes with an equanimity I didn't feel. "Good."

"*Good?*" Drake shouted. He visibly restrained his emotions and said, "Please explain what you mean by that, babe. While you're at it, please explain why I shouldn't feel blindsided by your actions."

I sighed, "My plans for Colin and his friends changed a split second before I asked Captain Reel to send for a squad of guards. Up until that point, I was willing to keep things quiet and allow the senior staff to officially resign their posts and leave with their dignity intact. Hell, I'd even have issued a proclamation thanking them for their fine service and explained their departure was nothing more than the fallout from a change in ruling houses."

The ghost of a smile flitted across Captain Reel's face. "You were not prepared for the full effect of Mr. Colin's personality, my lady."

It wasn't a question and Reel didn't expect an answer, but I gave him one anyway. "I confess, I was not. In my foolishly optimistic way, I assumed the man would be deferential in public, at the very least."

"If you had spoken to me of your plans, my lady, I could have disabused you of that notion," Reel said.

"Why, Captain Reel, I don't believe I've ever been called an idiot quite so politely!"

"That was not my intention, my lady! I—"

"That was a joke, Captain," I said.

As if unwilling to take my word for it, Reel glanced at Captain Pennington. Reel only relaxed when Pennington gave a slight nod.

"I'm sure you'll get used to my peculiar sense of humor," I added.

Once again Reel looked to Pennington, who shook his head this time.

"As for confiding in you, Captain Reel... How shall I put this?"

"You weren't certain you could trust me, my lady."

"If it helps, I was *almost* certain I could trust you. Sir Phillip certainly has a high opinion of you. I had not planned quite such a trial by fire for you, though."

"But you also didn't count on Colin being so thoroughly himself."

"Quite right, Captain. Perhaps he thought he was being

clever, ordering the staff to wait for the 'official dismissal phrase', and I was willing to overlook it in public." All three men raised their eyebrows in surprise, so I added, "It's a textbook power play, making me use House Kahn's methods during my first meeting with the staff. It would align me with the old way of doing things and make winning the staff's hearts all the harder. I avoided Colin's little trap and was content to leave it at that. Colin had other ideas."

Drake's eyes narrowed. "Are you saying his handling of the young maid was his attempt to put you in your place? If so, he doesn't know you at all."

Reel said, "When alone with the senior staff, Colin was rather contemptuous of you, my lady. He claimed you were an even greater fool than Lord Lockridge and, if left without the benefit of proper guidance, would end up giving commoners the same rights granted to the aristocracy. He assured his friends that you were in over your head and would secretly welcome his firm guidance."

I raised a single eyebrow. "If Colin was alone with the senior staff, how do you know what he said?"

Without batting an eye, Reel said, "It is my duty to protect you, my lady. I bugged his quarters, offices, and meeting rooms."

"Surely, Colin had those rooms swept for bugs?"

"Twice daily, my lady. But he asked my men to perform the sweeps." I must have shown incredulity, because Reel added, "My family has guarded the dukes and duchesses of Gaunner for over a century. Colin believed my loyalty lay absolutely with House Kahn rather than with the duchy."

"You don't feel any personal loyalty to Lady Olivia?" Drake asked.

"She is no longer my duchess, so that is a moot question. Lady Jeanine is the Duchess of Gaunner now. I am hers to command as long as she holds the title."

Drake smiled, "Well said, Captain."

"Does this suitably answer the question of loyalty, my lady?"

I nodded, "It does."

"Then please confide your plans to me so I may provide you with the best protection available."

"Of course." I took a moment and ordered my thoughts. "Am I correct in assuming the cream of the duchy's aristocracy is here on Gaunner?"

"They are, my lady. They want to observe you closely and get a feel for your mettle."

"And stand ready to drive a dagger into my back if I falter, no doubt."

"I hope you mean that figuratively, my lady. Though a few of them would happily stab you, literally. What are your plans?"

"I want to address all of the nobles, openly and in public, two days from now." I gave the captain a faint smile. "I'm afraid they won't like what I have to say."

"I don't suppose you would share your surprise announcements with your captains of the guard, my lady?" Captain Pennington asked.

A knock sounded on the door before I could answer. Guessing what was behind the knock, I called, "Come in."

My receptionist opened the door and stuck his head into the room. "One of the guards is here to see you. He, um, brought a maid and claims you asked to see her?"

"I did. Please show her in." I turned my attention back to the captains. "I will share everything with you, but I need to see the maid, first. I don't want to give poor Mary time to let her imagination run wild and get herself all worked up. I'd also like to meet with her privately."

Both guardsmen saluted, "Yes, my lady."

As they headed for the door, Drake gave me an inquiring look. After a second, I nodded and he followed them out of the office.

The handsome guard led Mary into the office and saluted. Mary immediately dropped into a deep curtsy and held it.

I stood and came around the desk. "Thank you, Corporal...?"

"Ivanov, my lady."

"You're dismissed, Corporal." The man snapped his hand out and down, spun about, and almost marched out of the office. I made sure I had a friendly smile on my lips and then said, "Please rise, Mary. There's no need to be nervous. You've done nothing wrong."

A brief smile flashed across Mary's face before her uncertain expression returned. "If you say so, my lady."

I caught both of the girl's hands in mine and looked her in the eye. "I just wanted an opportunity to finish the conversation that Colin so rudely interrupted."

"Did you really—" Mary's eyes widened and she clapped both hands over her mouth.

Resisting the urge to sigh, I gently pried Mary's hands away from her mouth. "It's perfectly fine to ask me questions."

Mary's mouth opened and closed twice before she finally said, "Did you really have Colin arrested?"

"Yes."

"For what he said to *me*?"

"Not entirely, Mary. Not even mostly, but his treatment of you was the final straw." As Mary took this in, I added, "Now that we've got that out of the way, would you please tell me why you weren't in school today?"

Too stunned by my admission, Mary forgot to be nervous. "I don't go to school, my lady."

"Since when?"

"Since last summer when my father was thrown into debtor's prison. The courts assigned my younger sister and me to the palace because we're pretty. They put my little brother on the street cleaning crew and Mom kept her regular job."

Though I was afraid I knew the answer to my next question, I asked it anyway. "Why did the court do that? What's the point?"

"So we can earn the money to pay Dad's debts, my lady."

"That is *barbaric*!" I growled. Mary shrank away from me, fear returning to her eyes. Forcing my smile back into place, I said, "I'm not angry at you, Mary. You truly have nothing to fear. In fact, I'm going to personally review your family's case and make sure you and your siblings are put back in school."

"But my father—"

"Don't worry, Mary." I pulled her into a quick hug. "I won't leave him to rot in prison."

A few minutes later, I showed a much more animated sixteen-year-old out of my office. As she all but skipped through the outer office, I motioned the three men back inside.

Life in the Duchy of Gaunner was far worse than I'd imagined—and that meant my sweeping changes would face far more opposition than even Evelyn or I imagined.

UNEXPECTED DEVELOPMENTS

Olivia

I kept my pace measured but purposeful as I strode toward Mother's office. My expression said 'busy princess, stay away' to all who saw me. That's what I was aiming for, at least. Based on the looks I drew from the palace staff, I nailed the 'stay away' part. 'Busy princess' might have come closer to 'pissed off princess' or, worse, 'worried princess.' The important thing is that no one asked me where to seat Lord Blowhard or Lady Spiteful at the next Royal Banquet.

Matilda looked up from her pad when I entered Mother's outer office. Whatever my expression truly said, it spoke volumes to the observant woman. Without a word from me, she tapped the comm in her ear.

"Princess Olivia is here to see you, Your Majesty. It is important." Matilda listened for a few seconds, then said, "Yes, ma'am, I will."

Tapping her comm again, she motioned to a chair outside Mother's office. "Her Majesty will be with you in just a moment."

I squashed the irrational inclination to simply storm into Mother's office and settled into the chair. My comm buzzed as I settled into the chair, but I ignored it.

After a minute, the door to Mother's office opened. She showed out a man and a woman I didn't recognize.

"I'll arrange another meeting for this afternoon," she said.

"We are at your service, Your Majesty," the woman said.

They both nodded respectfully—the closest thing Mother allowed to bowing and curtsying when she was away from formal occasions—and left.

Mother smiled at me. "Come in, dear."

As soon as the door closed behind me, I opened my mouth to speak. Mother put a gentle finger to my lips.

"Not yet, Olivia. Your brain is whirling so fast it's making me dizzy. Sit down, take a deep breath, and order your thoughts. *Then* speak."

Nodding, I sat. I almost skipped the deep breath, but Mother was watching me closely. I slowly filled my lungs, feeling my shoulders pull back and my posture straighten. I released the breath and my anxiety flowed out with it. Without conscious effort, my thoughts fell into order.

"Very good, dear. Now, what news do you bring?"

My comm buzzed before I could speak. I didn't have time for such trivial interruptions and turned it off.

"You may answer the comm, if you wish, Olivia."

"Thank you, Mother, but no. If it was an emergency, we'd have a squad of guards surrounding us right now. The comm can wait. My news, on the other hand, may require a faster response."

"You have my undivided attention, dear."

"The bit...excuse me, Mother, I mean *Lady Jeanine* has arrested Colin and the rest of the palace senior staff."

Mother frowned, "I haven't received word of this."

"Gaunner was *my* duchy, Mother. It cannot come as a surprise that I still have people loyal to me within the palace."

Mother inclined her head in acknowledgment. "When did this happen?"

"Four hours ago."

"Your loyal source used a *subspace* call to alert you? My God, Olivia, every one of those calls route through a single orbital relay! You've jeopardized your source and—"

It's rarely a good idea to interrupt a monarch, but I did it anyway. Considering the situation, I felt I had the right this time.

"My source called his cousin, who works in the Gaunner embassy here on Xapreathea. The news is of sufficient importance that no one will consider it unusual. The cousin and I each have single-use comms so she can contact me in situations such as this one."

"What did you do with those comms?"

"Destroyed them, of course. And the cousin is a long-time friend from school. We comm each other several times each week, so no one should suspect a thing."

"Very good, dear. I retract my objections. You say Lady Jeanine arrested your former assistant and the rest of the senior staff?"

"Yes, Mother."

"Does she have grounds for the arrests?"

"If she questioned Sir Philip—she's no fool, so I assume she did—she'll have ample reasons to arrest all of them. But she won't have any court-admissible evidence."

Mother shook her head in admonition. "She won't have any evidence admissible in the royal courts, dear, but didn't your predecessors structure Gaunner's ducal laws rather differently?"

God above, I'd forgotten just how easy it was to manipulate the Gaunner legal system. "I'd...forgotten about that 'feature' of the system."

"That's because you were a careful and thorough duchess, dear. You found ways to achieve your ends without resorting to such crass means. Your father did the same and I assume you learned it from him. Robert, unfortunately..."

I bristled at the queen's insinuation. A hot retort died on my lips, though. Mother was adept at finding a person's buttons and pushing them at just the right moment to get the result she desired. She also did it as a test, which was probably her intention this time. Pushing aside my irritation, I did something I had done far too rarely—I called forth my memories of Robert and viewed them as objectively as possible.

My brother did not fare well under the unforgiving light of logic and reason.

Sighing, I said, "You're right, of course, but he is my brother. *Was* my brother—until Lady Jeanine killed him."

Mother's lips compressed and her eyes hardened. She didn't say anything, but her expression spoke volumes.

Shrugging, I said, "I concede your point, Mother."

"What point is that, dear?"

She was going to make me say it.

I took another deep breath, straightened my shoulders, and said, "Robert killed himself with a combination of ambition and overconfidence. Lady Jeanine had no knowledge of her ancestry, so it is unreasonable for me to blame her for Robert's death."

"I'm proud of you, dear. I know how desperately you wanted to hold onto your false image of Robert as a brave crusader. In truth, he was the butcher everyone said, and terrified every noble in the kingdom. Even Bernard and I were wary of him." Mother captured my gaze with hers. "Before Robert's rather timely demise, more than one of the great houses tentatively suggested it was past time for us to remove him. And I would have pushed Bernard to accede to their requests."

I blinked several times, trying to come to grips with Mother's statement. Then I blurted the only response I could think of.

"Why?"

"To protect you, dear."

"Me? But—"

"If one of the other houses assassinated Robert, they'd have killed you, too. A dead woman can't take revenge for her brother's murder, after all. I already had my eye on you and didn't want anything happening to my prospective daughter-in-law."

"Why didn't you make your interest known to me? I was already in my mid-twenties by then. We could have moved ahead with marriage plans easily enough."

"Olivia, why were you so sexually inexperienced when you married William?"

"Because men simply didn't find me...attractive."

"Nonsense, dear. You're a naturally beautiful woman and you'd be surprised just how many men *want* an intelligent lover. No, it wasn't *you* who drove men away. It was Robert. I know of four men he almost beat to death when they showed an interest in you. Much as I wanted William to marry you, I wasn't willing to risk his life to get you."

"I didn't know Robert was doing that. But, once Robert was out of the way, why did you wait another three years to contact me?" Before Mother responded, the answer came to me. "Of course, you were watching to see how I reacted to Robert's death and how well I ruled Gaunner."

"Yes, which brings us back around to the new Duchess of Gaunner and her rather unexpected actions. What do you think we should do about her?"

"If we simply wait for a few days, I expect the Gaunner aristocracy will take the decision out of our hands. It's possible they'll just assassinate Colin and his friends. It's probable they'll kill Lady Jeanine." Mother nodded, obviously waiting for me to go on. I thought through the implications and said, "We couldn't simply sit by and let them kill Lady Jeanine because it will look as if *I* was behind the assassination. And, by extension, my guilt will extend to the royal family."

"That just about sums it up, dear. The question is, what are we going to do about it?"

"We need to stop the aristocrats before they do something stupid." Slumping back in my chair, I said, "Honestly, the biggest problem is that Jeanine only sees the current situation in the duchy. She has no appreciation of the long history that led to that situation."

"I think your analysis is spot on, Olivia. I'm really quite impressed." Mother showed it by smiling broadly. "But what can we do to stop the chaos that would result from Lady Jeanine's assassination?"

"I...have to go to Gaunner, settle the aristocracy, and explain everything to Jeanine."

"What an excellent idea! I'm afraid you and William will have to leave today if you have any hope of quelling the situation."

"Yes, Mother. If you'll excuse me, I'll go oversee the packing."

"One last thing, dear. With your newfound insight into recent events, perhaps you can find a way to make friends with Lady Jeanine." I opened my mouth to protest, but Mother cut me off. "I know, it's a long shot, but she could prove a quite valuable ally. We already know she's a dangerous enemy and will become far more dangerous if can't bring her around to our way of thinking."

"What do you mean, Mother? What else can she do to us?"

"She's aligned herself with the budding revolution, dear. It's even likely she'll let them operate from within her territory."

"*What*? If we can prove that, why are we even having this discussion? Let the Gaunner aristocracy kill her and then expose her as the traitor she is!"

"Because we can't prove it, Olivia. And even if we had proof, I'd rather find a way to bring such a valuable asset around to our side than see her wasted—both literally and figuratively."

Before I could say anything else, Mother's comm buzzed. Frowning, Mother activated the comm.

"Yes, Matilda?"

"Please pardon the interruption, Your Majesty, but I have Dr. Edwards on another line. She's been trying to reach Her Highness with some news."

Mother gave me a look and I shrugged. "I had a routine physical the other day. I feel fine, though, so can't imagine what she wants."

"Put the royal physician through, Matilda."

Seconds later, Dr. Edwards' voice sounded. "Good morning, Your Majesty, Your Highness. It's just as well the two of you are together. Now, I won't have to make a second call."

"We're very busy, Dr. Edwards," Mother said. "Please come to the point. Does Olivia have some dread disease?"

"My apologies, Your Majesty, and most assuredly not. I bring nothing but good news and happy tidings. Congratulations, Princess Olivia. You're pregnant!"

YOU SHOULD TRY IT SOMETIME

Jana

"Really, Jana, this is standard procedure—all part of preparing for a big job."

I tried looking down into the open hole at my feet, but it was so dark I couldn't even see the hole, much less into it. Back alley odors assaulted my nose while strange, nearby rustling kicked my imagination into overdrive. Worse, fetid air rose from the hole I couldn't see.

A hand suddenly grabbed my shoulder and it took all of my self-control to keep from crying out. "Would you consider slicing a high-profile target—say, the Royal DNA Database—without jacking in and scouting its defenses ahead of time?"

"No, I wouldn't," I replied, "but I'd also be warm and comfy in my own home while I was doing it."

Tilly gave a low laugh. "That's not how burglary works. I have to get my hands dirty—and sometimes my knees and elbows and even my face. This time, you get to join in the fun."

"Yay, me," I murmured.

"Exactly. It's also good practice for you before the real break-in." I didn't even hear Tilly move, but her voice came from near my feet. "Wait ten seconds, then feel your way down and into the hole. I've positioned you right in front of the ladder. We're not in any rush right now, so move at whatever speed makes you comfortable. We won't use any of our fancy equipment until you pull the cover back over the hole, though. Got it?"

"Got it."

I squatted down and felt around for the edge of the hole. It was right where Tilly said it would be, as was the ladder. With exaggerated caution, I put a foot into the hole and felt for the top rung on the ladder. Once I had my foot on that, I picked up the pace. Soon enough, I was entirely inside the hole. I grabbed the cover and pulled it into place above me.

"Okay, I've closed the cover, Tilly."

A dim light sprang into life below me, barely illuminating Tilly's face. After pure darkness, it was so welcome that I couldn't take my eyes off of it.

"Don't look directly at the light, Jana. You'll ruin your night vision."

Crap. Tilly had already told me that a dozen times today. She repeated it so often, I actually got angry and told her I wasn't an idiot and she could stop repeating the same simple instructions.

So, when I got to the bottom of the ladder, I looked at the ground and muttered, "I guess I *am* an idiot, after all."

Tilly was supposed to be all supportive and explain how it was just nerves and that I shouldn't worry about it. As I was learning, Tilly is not that kind of friend.

"Yep, you sure are."

I tried glaring at her, but my glare was blocked by her infectious grin. Giving in, I grinned back.

"Now, I want to take you on a slicing run sometime, so I can turn the tables on you."

"And run the risk of having my brain blown up?" Tilly handed me a backpack and headed off into the darkness. "No, thank you!"

I fell in behind her. "It's better than getting your hands dirty."

"I can survive getting gunk on my hands. You can't say the same about having your head explode."

"Now I *have* to take you with me next time I break into the Royal Center for Disease Control's database. If you had any idea how many nasty bugs can get into your system through contact with your hands, you'd never stop washing them."

"I'll pass, if it's all the same to you."

"Coward."

"Considering our current situation, I won't dignify that with an answer. We're also getting close to the royal palace grounds, so please restrict yourself to hand signals until further notice."

For the next twenty minutes, I did exactly as Tilly had taught me. I put my feet where she put her feet. I only touched what she touched. I ducked, crouched, waddled, crawled, and even slithered—always following her impossibly graceful form. All in all, it was one of the least enjoyable things I'd ever done. But, finally, Tilly took a side tunnel that sloped up.

Five minutes in that tunnel led us to a long-disused room. My best guess is that it was originally designed so workers could take a break from the tunnels and stand fully erect. God knows, I was happy to have the chance to do that. Once again, I followed Tilly's lead, working my shoulders like she did and arching my back to work the kinks out of it.

And that's when I spotted something that was out of place.

It wasn't much, just a minor discoloration. My eyes automatically tracked it. I didn't give it much thought until I realized the discoloration began with a small, though very precise, hole at the apex of the domed ceiling and went straight down the side of the dome to another precise hole. Everything was so well hidden, if I hadn't noticed the discoloration, I'd never have noticed the holes.

Nudging Tilly, I pointed up at my discovery. She didn't know what I was pointing at until I used a laser pointer to trace from one hole to the next. She delved into my backpack, sorted through the implements she stored in it, and came out with a flat-ended tool of some kind. She had no luck scraping away the discolored material, so changed tactics. She dug away at the original dome material. It flaked away pretty easily. After a couple of minutes, she uncovered a narrow cable. My eyes went wide when I recognized it.

Abandoning her own restriction against speaking, Tilly whispered, "What is it?"

"I've only seen images of it," I whispered back, "but it looks like an ancient network cable."

"Okay... What is a network cable?"

"It's how data pads used to communicate with each other and the net. Some networks still use cables, because they're more secure than a broadcast network, harder to disrupt, and—since you have to have physical access to the cable—harder to slice. But you only find cables on military bases and spaceships, these days—and they don't use ancient stuff like this."

"Do you have any idea what network this connects to?"

"How would I know? It's possible this cabling is so old it's no longer connected to anything." I grinned at Tilly. "But I'll bet it's some forgotten connection for the palace network."

"Can you connect to something this old?"

I twirled a finger, indicating Tilly should turn around. When she did, I dug into her backpack and pulled out my tools.

"Probably not, but I've got to try."

My initial guess was correct. None of the tools I'd brought were useful for splicing to something as old as this network cable. I was able to measure network activity traveling through the cable. To my surprise, not only was the cable active, it was *extremely* active.

"We might not have to go any further than this room, Tilly, though I won't know for sure until I can connect to the cable."

"Can you get the equipment you need? If this thing is as old as you say it is, does anyone even make what you need anymore?"

"Even if no one makes it, I know where we can get what we need. And when I say 'we' I really mean 'you'."

"What do you want me to break into now, Jana?"

"The Royal Museum of Technology."

Tilly gave a pretend yawn. "Couldn't you come up with something challenging?"

"You can break into it?"

"In my sleep."

"It might not be necessary, but it's good to know."

It proved necessary.

Tilly did the job the next night and in under an hour. I stayed home and didn't get my hands dirty—literally or figuratively.

I spent several days preparing to use the equipment Tilly stole for me.

I started by assuring myself I understood the basic functionality and then dove into the inner workings of the technology. Every piece of it was centuries out of date and I had to search the net extensively to find ways to connect my modern slicing tools to these museum pieces. Since the museum theft made the news, I assumed the authorities would be watching the net for just this kind of activity, which made all of my work even more difficult. Covering my digital tracks is second nature, but it's harder when you're sure large, royal agencies are watching for you.

Once I had the information I needed, I built the connectors and programmed the interface. It's very exacting work that proved more tedious than difficult. When I was finally satisfied everything was ready, I carefully packed it all into a backpack and grabbed a bottle of very good whiskey on my way back to my suite. There, I sank into a comfortable chair and poured myself a generous shot.

Tilly entered as I swallowed the shot. She grabbed a shot glass of her own and held it out to me. I filled hers just as generously as I filled mine.

"Brice told me you finally left the workshop." Holding her glass up, she asked, "Shall we toast to success or are you drowning our failure?"

Raising my glass, I said, "Success!"

"Success!" Tilly repeated.

In unison, we knocked back the whiskey and heaved great, contented sighs.

"What time is it?" I asked.

Pointedly looking at the chrono hanging on the wall to my right, Tilly said, "Two oh eight."

"Morning or afternoon?"

"Doesn't the sunlight streaming into your bedroom give you a clue?"

"I have not looked into my bedroom, yet." Mimicking one of those fake psychics you find in marketplaces all around the Star Kingdom, I put a hand to my head and added, "But the great spirits have come to my aid. I deduce it is two oh eight in the afternoon."

"The great spirits lied to you. Or maybe it was me. There's no sun shining through your bedroom, Jana."

I groaned and turned toward the bedroom. It was deeply dark. Now that I thought about it, the lights had come on when I entered the suite.

"You've ruined my faith in humanity, Tilly. I shall never believe another thing you tell me."

"Fine." Tilly held her glass out for a refill. Once both of our glasses were full, she raised her glass again. "One more drink, then we'll return to the tunnels while it's still dark."

"I'll drink to that!" After another contented sigh, I struggled to my feet. "Let's go."

"I thought you weren't going to believe anything I told you."

"Oh, yeah." I waved her objection away. "I forgive you."

"So, now you'll believe what I tell you?"

"Abso-damned-lutely."

"Good. You're exhausted. Go to sleep. We'll make our run once you're well-rested."

"I'm too keyed up to sleep, Tilly."

She grabbed the bottle of whiskey. "Well, I know how to fix *that* problem."

Twenty minutes later, she called Brice to help carry me to the bed.

When next I opened my eyes, late afternoon sunlight streamed through my bedroom windows. I blinked, shielding my eyes from the sudden onslaught of photons, and made out a barely discernible figure next to the window controls.

"Awaken and arise, sleeping beauty!" Tilly sang.

Groaning, I turned away from the window and buried my face in the pillow. "There are laws against this kind of assault."

"No, there aren't."

"Then there ought to be. Remind me to talk to Jeanine about it next time I see her."

"You want to hear the short version of what you just said, Jana?"

"Not really."

"Too bad. Everything you've said so far translates as 'wah.' It's really quite unbecoming for a woman of your talents."

"It's not my fault I'm not a morning person."

"It's nearly dusk."

"It's not my fault I'm not a *virtual* morning person."

Something landed on top of me. Cracking one eye open, I saw the burgling clothes I'd worn a few nights ago.

"You were raring to go burgling fourteen hours ago, when you desperately needed sleep. Now, all you want to do is lay about in bed? I don't think so!" She clapped her hands right in front of my face and yanked the covers away. "Let's go, recruit. Get your butt out of bed and into the shower. I expect you dressed and ready for work in fifteen minutes."

I fumbled my way out of the bed and stumbled toward the bathroom. The dark clothes I'd left on the bed sailed over my head and landed in front of me. Instead of bending over and picking them up, I kicked them along ahead of me.

Just before slamming the door, I said, "I want breakfast—"

"Dinner."

"Whatever. Just make sure there's food waiting when I come out."

The aroma of delicious food welcomed me from the shower. I suddenly discovered I was ravenous and began shoveling food into my mouth before I even sat down. Tilly ate with greater decorum—no doubt because of the noble blood flowing through her veins—and filled me in on the latest news. I'd ignored all of that while working on the interfaces. One particular bit of news surprised and worried me.

"Wait, the prince and princess are going to Gaunner?"

Tilly nodded.

"Are they leading the Spinward Fleet along with a bunch of transports full of Royal Marines?"

"No, Jana. They've got their usual escorts, of course, but that's it. The newsies label this a state visit, allowing the previous Duchess of Gaunner to welcome the new Duchess of Gaunner."

"This *is* Princess Olivia they're talking about?"

"The kingdom only has one prince and princess, though there are rumors that Olivia is pregnant."

"Pregnant? What—?"

"Pregnancy is a condition known to occur as a result of sexual intercourse between members of the opposite sex." Tilly smirked, "Perhaps you should try it sometime."

"Pregnancy?"

"Sex."

I threw a roll at her. To my disgust, she caught it easily. To my further disgust, she hit me between the eyes when she returned it.

Carefully ignoring the subject of my sex life, I said, "Does anyone truly believe Olivia is just going to go make nice with Jeanine? I mean, she spent years trying to find and kill her. After Jeanine ruined Olivia's wedding in such spectacular fashion, I can't imagine Her Highness has any warm and fuzzy feelings for Jeanine."

"Probably not, but Olivia is not going to do anything to harm her on this trip. After all, the entire Star Kingdom is watching. If Olivia makes any kind of unjustified attack, every noble and most of the commoners will rise up against the royal house. You can bet Queen Charlotte understands that and has drilled it into her apprentice." Pointedly changing the subject, Tilly pointed at my empty plate. "Have you finished gorging yourself?"

"My hunger is sufficiently sated for the moment."

"Good. Let's get going."

Forty minutes later, we descended into the deep darkness again. This time, I didn't give the disgusting tunnels and their fetid air a second thought. My brain was running in overdrive, trying to figure out what I would find when I jacked into this network. Or if I even could jack in.

Finally, the long, squirming trip through the tunnels ended. Tilly took command of both backpacks, handing me equipment as I called for it. The first time I asked for one of my interfaces, she gave me a blank look.

"Everything is labeled, Tilly."

"Oh. I should have seen that." She handed a signal splitter to me. "Um, I don't see a signal booster. How are you going to jack in after we get back to the palace?"

"I'm going to connect right here, so won't need a booster. If tonight's test goes well, maybe we'll bring a booster next time."

"What happened to the woman who didn't want to get her hands dirty?"

"She found a mysterious network carrying unknown signals and wants to delve into the mystery as soon as possible. Besides, do you remember what I told you about network cables and security? Unlikely as it might be, palace security could detect a broadcast signal and track it."

"You're not worried about rival slicers intercepting the signal?"

I made a dismissive sound. "Another slicer *might* find the

signal, but the only ones who could crack my encryption aren't on this planet."

"Your confidence reminds me of a nugget of wisdom told to me by one of my mentors when I was first making a name for myself."

"Please, do share!"

"Don't get cocky, kid."

I burst out laughing. "Yeah, my first mentor told me the same thing. Her version was 'Prisons are full of slicers who thought they knew it all.' Consider that yet another good reason to make a direct connection down here."

I tightened two more fasteners and then carefully inspected my work. After five minutes, I leaned back and stretched.

"It's time to find out what we've got, here."

"Jana, what should I do if anything strange happens to you?"

"Strange?"

"You know, like you see in the vids. Your body starts jumping around or goes all rigid or—"

"My brain melts and leaks out of my ears?"

"No... Okay, yeah. Maybe."

"Tilly, do vids get anything right about breaking and entering?"

"God, no! As far as I can tell, they just make up all sorts of crap and figure no one will know any better."

"What makes you think they do anything different with slicing?"

Tilly looked thoughtful for a moment. "So, this is completely safe?"

"No, but my brain won't melt." She still looked unsure, so I added, "If you get worried, just disconnect the cable from my interface."

"That won't trap your mind in the net?" I stared at Tilly until she blushed. "Sorry, Jana, that was a silly question."

"Just settle back and relax. I might be out of it for a while."

I carefully plugged into my equipment and ran a few system

checks. Everything passed with flying colors, so I activated the connection to the ancient cable. My mind slid through the interface and dove into the unknown.

Finally connected to the strange network, I found myself hesitating on my side of the interface. A nanosecond passed, then another. Reluctance had replaced my previous impatience. I'm not sure why it did, but that's the human brain for you. Steeling my resolve, I gave myself a mental kick and pushed through the interface.

To my relief, I found myself in a typical data stream. At least, it appeared typical at first glance. Then I realized all of the data was flowing in one direction. That's not entirely unheard of, but it's definitely atypical. On top of that, the data was moving far faster and in far higher volume than I thought I would see given the age of the network cable.

With my curiosity aroused, I snagged a passing data packet and examined it. And that's when I got my second surprise. The packet encryption was completely unknown to me. That simple fact wouldn't have surprised the vast majority of people in the Star Kingdom. I'm in the teeny tiny extreme minority of the populace who know all of the encryption schemes. Okay, that's a bit of an exaggeration—I know most of the schemes. I can decrypt those I don't know because they're based on the schemes I do know.

But not this one. It was completely alien to me. Nothing I saw within the packet was recognizable. Nothing.

I have no words to describe just how shocked I was. The last time this happened to me, I was eleven years old and attempting my first interplanetary slice. But even then, I recognized a little of what I found. My conscious mind whirled at this alien discovery. An analytical bit of my subconscious suggested the strange encryption was what allowed the antique cable to handle the volume of data.

That one little fact rising from the back of my mind kicked my brain into gear. I released my captive packet and it vanished into the flow of data. I had no idea what I was facing, but I wasn't going to learn anything hanging around just beyond my interface. With a virtual shrug, I followed the stream.

I took things slowly and kept an eye out for traps and other counter-intrusion measures. I deployed leading and trailing bots and paid at least as much attention to their feedback as I did to my own surroundings. It took a full second for something to happen, but it scared the crap out of me when it did.

Without a warning, my lead bot vanished. One picosecond it was there the next picosecond it was gone. That had never happened to me before, either. Then another bot disappeared, and one more after that.

Confused, I called all of my remaining leading bots back to me. I had them hold me in place, keeping me from drifting with the data and allowing me to turn all of my attention toward solving the strange disappearances. The problem was, I didn't have anything to go on. I created another bot and modified its programming so it sent back everything it discovered. My bots usually filter out a lot of noise, but I was no longer certain what was noise and what was data. I launched the drone and gave it all of my attention.

It sent back vast amounts of data during that short trip. I tried sifting through it, hoping I would detect something, but I didn't. And then it vanished. No warning. No change in the data it was sending back. Nothing. It was there and then it wasn't there.

For the first time in my adult life as a slicer, I got scared. So I pulled out.

Tilly was leaning against the wall and watching me. She jumped slightly when I moved, but waited until I disconnected from the network before she said anything.

"That was fast. What did you learn?"

"Nothing good."

"Should we be running right now?"

"I don't think it's that kind of problem, but an orderly withdrawal is probably a good idea."

As we spoke, I began packing my equipment. Tilly helped, but kept asking questions while she worked.

"So, what kind of problem is it?"

"I don't know. And that is the real problem." I ran a hand through my hair, covering the jack built into the back of my neck. "I've got a lot of data I need to study before I can answer that question. *If* I can answer that question."

Tilly's eyebrows rose in surprise. "That really doesn't sound good."

"No, it very much doesn't sound good. There's something... strange on the other end of that network cable. Something like I've never run into before."

"Aren't you familiar with every kind of data system in the Star Kingdom?"

"I thought I was. Obviously, I was wrong."

Tilly led the way into the tunnels and, thirty minutes later, we emerged into the dark alley. I was getting familiar with the place, so started toward the street while Tilly closed the cover. I hadn't taken two steps when Tilly's hand snapped out and grabbed mine.

"What—"

"Shush," Tilly whispered.

She was standing completely still, concentrating on something. I did as I was told, and waited for her to fill me in. After a few seconds, she turned and pulled me deeper into the alley. She moved with such urgency, I squashed my questions and followed her.

The alley took a turn to the right and, once we were around the corner, Tilly pulled me up against a wall. Holding a finger against my lips, she put her mouth next to my ear.

"Someone is waiting at the front of the alley. Keep quiet and do exactly as I tell you."

I nodded my head to show I understood. Hardly making a

sound, Tilly began pulling equipment from my backpack. I tried to figure out what she was getting based on the sounds, but had absolutely no idea. Giving up on that, I directed my attention toward the other end of the alley and tried to hear what Tilly had heard. I'd make a lousy burglar because I couldn't hear anything. Tilly pulled me from my sad attempts to imitate her by putting her lips against my ear again.

"We're going to the rooftops. Are you afraid of heights?"

"Let's say I have a healthy respect for them."

"So, that's a yes. Don't worry, I'll be right there with you. Do as I say, without question, and I'll get you out of this."

"Yes, ma'am."

Tilly took two steps back from the wall and I barely discerned her pointing to something straight up. The something made a soft sound and Tilly just stood there waiting. After a few seconds, I heard a slight buzz, as if the thing in her hands had vibrated, and Tilly pulled me toward her. She quickly looped some kind of harness over and around me and then connected it to her own harness.

Tilly whispered, "Wrap your arms around me below my arms, hold on, and keep quiet. It might help if you close your eyes, too."

I did as she instructed, wondering what was going to happen. I didn't have to wonder for long. With a sudden jerk, we rose swiftly into the air. It all happened so fast, I'm pretty sure I left my stomach on the ground below. A few seconds later, it caught up with us, but we were still rising.

Remember that little analytical part of my subconscious that helped me out during my brief attempt to slice into the ancient network? It chose this moment to calculate our rate of ascent and tell me how high we were.

Five hundred meters.

I really didn't need to know that. Did my subconscious care about that? No. It even told me that, during that time I'd been having this little mental debate with my subconscious, we had risen another hundred meters.

My healthy respect for heights turned out to really be fear. Lucky me.

Below us, lights stabbed through the darkness, so bright I noticed them through closed eyes. Voices erupted. Unable to stop myself, I opened my eyes and looked down. Far, far below me, lights waved all around the alley below. Little bitty figures moved around in the light, looking for something—us, no doubt. The terrified part of my brain wished we were down there to be found. The rational part of my brain had me close my eyes again, bury my face in Tilly's chest, and softly whimper.

"Almost there, Jana."

And then our ascent stopped.

"Okay, Jana, this next bit is the tough part. The roof's edge is half a meter above us. You have to climb up there."

"Can't we climb together? So we can stay hooked to each other?"

"No, we'd be facing each other and unable to climb."

"Well, how about hooking me to the line that pulled us up? Can we both be connected to that?"

"We aren't connected to that line, Jana. I'm holding onto the handle."

"Oh. So if your grip slipped..."

"Splat."

"You couldn't find a gentler way of saying that, Tilly?"

"No offense, Jana, but my arms are getting tired. It's time to move."

"Right. Okay. I can do this. Yep. Just half a meter. Easy peasy."

"Stop psyching yourself up and start climbing."

I did as Tilly instructed. I didn't fall, but I will never do that again. Ever. Still, when I had to do it, I did it.

After that, walking along the edge of the rooftop was nothing. Five minutes later, Tilly found a door, picked the lock, and we had stairs. Blessed stairs. With walls around them. And railings. It was heaven.

We spent three hours wandering around the city. We bought new clothes. We incinerated our old clothes. Much to my distress, we did the same thing with my equipment. The sole exception was the data stick I recorded everything on. The minute we got back to the estate, you can bet I loaded the data stick into my pad and began studying.

And if you made that bet, you lose.

The data stick waited while Tilly and I split a bottle of whiskey. Then we split a second bottle. I don't remember much after that.

THE HAND OF FRIENDSHIP

Drake

I stood front and center at the landing field, squinting into the bright morning light. My breath fogged in the morning air but blew away quickly in the cool breeze. Far above, sunlight glinted off the Royal shuttle as it began its final approach. Behind me, rank after rank of Gaunner military personnel shuffled and stretched, getting in one last bit of movement before they had to snap to attention. To my right, some members of the band were running through random notes in preparation for the Royal anthem.

Captain Reel stepped up next to me. "Everything is ready for Their Highnesses' arrival."

"Thank you, Captain."

"Sir, permission to speak freely?"

"When it's just the two of us, you always have permanent permission to speak freely."

"Do you think it is wise for Her Grace to stay at the palace? After all, we are welcoming the heirs to the throne. Won't her absence be viewed as an insult?"

"It is intended as an insult." I looked away from the descending shuttle and met Captain Reel's surprised expression.

"And, considering how hard Princess Olivia tried to kill Jeanine, perhaps it's just as well she's not here."

"I had heard rumors, of course. Are you saying the rumors are true?"

"We don't have any proof, if that's what you mean. But, yes, the rumors are true. I was there for several of the attempts."

"Then, why would Her Highness come to one of Lady Jeanine's seats of power, effectively putting her life in Lady Jeanine's hands?"

"That is a damned good question, Captain."

We fell silent as the shuttle drew closer, the roar of its engines blocking further attempts at conversation. A moment later, the shuttle was safely on the ground. A hatch opened, a ramp telescoped out, and a squad of Royal guards marched down it. They formed up on the ground and waited. Seconds later, the Royal couple stepped through the hatch and gracefully descended the ramp as the band struck up the anthem. The guards encircled the Prince and Princess and escorted them to me.

Captain Reel and all of his troops snapped to attention. The captain of the honor guard did likewise.

"I am Captain Reel of Her Grace the Duchess of Gaunner's personal guard. With your permission, I will assume responsibility for the safety of his Royal Highness Prince William and her Royal Highness Princess Olivia."

"I am Captain Palmer of the Royal Guard. I accept your offer but request permission for my unit to join your guard detail."

"Permission granted, Captain. We look forward to working with you and your men."

Now that the military formalities were out of the way, it was time for the aristocratic formalities. The guards stepped to one side, opening the way between me and the Royal couple.

I bowed. "Prince William, Princess Olivia, welcome to Gaunner."

"Please rise," Prince William said, looking around him.

"Where is Lady Jeanine? I was quite looking forward to seeing her again."

I remembered how the Prince ogled my wife at the ball a week and a half ago. From the look on her face, Princess Olivia remembered it, also. Tempting as it was to make a snide comment along those lines, I stuck to the official script.

"I am afraid Jeanine is unavailable right now, what with all the work involved in unifying two duchies." Princess Olivia's eyes narrowed but I just smiled blandly back at her. "She hopes my presence will demonstrate her true respect for the royalty and aristocratic customs."

I have to admit, I really loved that line. It sounds so sincere and respectful, but it's really the exact opposite. I'm a commoner. I've never even been knighted. I've never been raised to the aristocracy. I've never been Recognized by the Star Stone. Sending a lowly commoner to meet the second highest ranking couple in the Star Kingdom is a dire insult.

At least, that's what Jeanine tells me. All of her advisers agree with her. It's all too complicated for me. I'd much rather settle this with blasters at twenty paces, but, apparently, this is How Things Are Done.

Prince William flashed a smile that never reached his eyes and gave a single nod. "Lady Jeanine's respect and devotion are obvious for all to see."

"Excellent. Now that we've got that out of the way, why don't we get out of this chilly morning air?" I stood to one side and motioned them along the red carpet toward a waiting ground car. "After you, Your Highnesses."

The Royal couple swept past me and into the waiting ground car. I joined them in the rear compartment, taking a seat opposite them. Captains Reel and Palmer sat in the front with the driver while their men divided up amongst the leading and following cars.

As we pulled away from the landing pad, I raised the privacy window between the front and rear compartments. "Now that we've satisfied protocol and are in private, how about we drop all the fancy titles and flowery language and talk plainly?"

Prince William bristled, "Is this how you would treat your future sovereigns?"

"No, it's how I treat the people who have tried, multiple times, to kill my wife and me."

"How dare—"

Princess Olivia put a finger against her husband's lips. "Hush, William. Please let me deal with this. After all, Gaunner was my duchy."

William kept glaring at me but gave a short nod. I offered Olivia a bland smile and motioned for her to carry on.

Olivia gave a tentative smile. "Thank you, Captain Haral. While I concede that relations between our two families are... strained, I assure you we are here to help Lady Jeanine settle into her role smoothly."

"You will, I hope, understand my reluctance to accept you at your word?"

"You're an intelligent man and must know the entire Star Kingdom is watching us. Some, undoubtedly, are hoping for verbal fireworks and literal bloodshed. Most are simply curious to see how Jeanine and I get along after our contentious history. The nobility can be counted among the latter, with the caveat that they will join forces against the Royal family if William or I lift my hand against Jeanine."

"Then why are you here, Olivia?"

The Princess ignored my familiarity and waved a hand at the window. Outside, the citizens of Gaunner went about their normal business, though most stopped and watched our procession drive by. "Not so long ago, I was their duchess. Their well-being was my primary concern. As a Princess, I still count citizens of Gaunner amongst my subjects. Their needs are still my concern. I cannot let my past with Jeanine interfere with my obligation to these people."

"What about your obligation to the people of Neert?"

"It is of equal importance, given my new role in the Star Kingdom, but I have no experience ruling Neert. Any advice I might offer for that duchy will be far less useful than the advice Jeanine already receives from Lady Evelyn."

"So you're here to extend the hand of peace all of a sudden?"

"Yes, Drake."

"And you expect us to believe you, after the ambush in the Vollec system?"

Olivia leaned forward, her eyes intent. "I was just as surprised by that as you were. It was not of my doing."

I stared into her eyes for several seconds. "Strangely enough, I believe you. I'm not saying you and your family are entirely innocent in the matter, but I do believe that you, personally, had nothing to do with the attack."

Olivia leaned back, her expression of cool composure returning. "Thank you, Drake. I won't claim I'm here to become best girlfriends with Jeanine. I think we can both agree that will never happen. But we must reach a point where we can tolerate each other because we're going to be dealing with each other for a long time to come."

This time, I didn't fully believe Olivia. Perhaps, because Olivia spent so much time and effort trying to kill Jeanine. Okay, there's no 'perhaps' about it. That's exactly why I didn't trust her or believe she was ready to accept Jeanine as the Duchess of Gaunner. But, I did believe she was here to help. This time.

And that was going to have to do for right now.

SMARTASS WOMEN

Jeanine

For the second time in just a few days, the staff was arrayed at the entrance to the ducal palace. Only those performing truly vital tasks—such as guarding my collection of high-ranking prisoners—weren't standing in silent ranks facing the driveway, tiny clouds of expelled breath giving mute testimony to the morning cold. This time, though, only one person stood front and center, ready to welcome the royal couple of the palace.

Me.

I was still considering replacements for the imprisoned senior staff, meaning there was no one to stand with me. Some of the section heads had quietly offered to represent their people by standing with me. I appreciated the gesture, but refused each one. Olivia was coming to confront me and I'd be damned if I was going to drag anyone else into her line of fire.

The small convoy swung onto the drive and swept around the long, curving drive. When the car came to a stop before me, I opened the door myself before stepping back and dropping into a deep curtsy. I heard the rustle of clothing as the staff followed my lead.

Prince William climbed from the car and then extended a hand to aid Princess Olivia. As they walked toward me, Drake stood and shut the car's door. It pulled away as the couple reached me. William, as handsome as a finely-wrought statue, offered a bright smile that didn't reach his eyes. Olivia, as beautiful as an ice sculpture glistening in the sun, gazed around her with...what? Fondness? Cold contempt? I couldn't read any emotion in her.

William gave a vague wave of his hand. "Rise, please, do rise."

"Welcome, Your Royal Highnesses, to my home away from home." If Olivia caught the subtle emphasis I placed on 'my'— and I'm certain she did—she hid it well. "You honor us with your visit."

"Just as you honored us by sending your husband to meet us," Olivia said.

Apparently, the knives were coming out early. Well, two could play at that game.

"I do so apologize for not being there, myself. This is my first visit to Gaunner and you can't imagine how much there is for me to do, what with my rather sudden Recognition as the duchess. When you add in the unexpected removal of the palace's entire senior staff, I'm so busy that I barely have time to eat and sleep."

"Of course." Olivia made no further comment about it and I thought that meant she was willing to let this skirmish end in a tie. Then she called, "Staff dismissed."

No one moved.

"Old habits die hard, don't they, Your Highness?" I smiled brightly at Olivia before turning toward the waiting staff. "Thank you. Please go about your business."

At once, the staff turned away and, in the typical disorder you get when a crowd disperses, returned to the palace. Some of the younger staff members waved shyly at me. I returned the waves with vigor and a grin.

Olivia watched their departure without expression. Once the steps were clear, she sniffed, "That's not how things are done in Gaunner."

"No, Olivia, that's not how things *were* done in Gaunner."

She gave me a brittle smile. "Quite."

Extending an arm toward the palace in invitation, I said, "Shall we go inside where it's warm?"

William immediately offered his arm to Olivia and they ascended the stairs. Drake did the same for me, giving me a concerned look as we followed the royal couple.

"Is it wise to taunt her like this, babe?" he hissed.

"Do you think she's going to try to kill me in retaliation, darling?" I widened my eyes as if I'd had a sudden realization. "Oh, that's right, she's already tried that!"

Drake shook his head in frustration. "Why am I so attracted to smartass women?"

I patted his arm. "Because you'd get bored with dumbass women."

As I'd hoped, he gave a soft laugh. "You've got me there, babe. Just promise me you'll tread carefully around Olivia."

I shrugged, "I will if she will."

Once we were inside, I said, "I've scheduled a reception and luncheon in your honor. Perhaps you'd like to retire to your suite and freshen up before Gaunner's nobility arrive?"

William was just inclining his head in acknowledgment, when Olivia said, "You go on without me, William. Jeanine and I have some things to discuss."

I felt Drake tense before he said, "Perhaps I should join you, since I bear some responsibility for the duchy, as well."

"And as the prince of the realm, I should—"

"Thank you, both," Olivia said, gently pulling free of William's arm and kissing him on the cheek. "This should just be between the duchess and the...former...duchess. You know, girl talk."

I admit, my curiosity was piqued. Following Olivia's lead, I gave Drake a quick peck and said, "Why don't you show Prince William around the palace. Her Highness and I will be in my office."

The men were obviously reluctant, but neither of them said

anything as Olivia and I walked away. For several minutes, the only sound was the clicking of our heels on the marble floor. Only when we neared my office did Olivia break the silence.

"Thank you for agreeing to the private meeting."

"Does a mere duchess have the choice of refusing a royal princess?"

"You know she does, Jeanine."

"I was just making sure you knew, also, Olivia."

"Ah."

Edward, the receptionist whose name I'd finally learned, leapt to his feet and bowed when Olivia and I entered. Behind us, our guards stationed themselves outside the door.

"I'll be here for several days, Edward," Olivia said. "You may dispense with the formalities."

"As you command, Your Highness," he replied as he opened the door into my capacious office.

"Thank you, Edward," I said as we swept past. "When Mary arrives with the tea, send her in. Otherwise, Princess Olivia and I are not to be disturbed for anything short of an actual emergency."

"As you command, my lady."

Olivia automatically headed for the seat behind the desk. With a start, she realized her error and swerved for one of the seats before the desk. I pretended I hadn't seen that and went to the more comfortable and casual sitting area on the opposite side of the room. Olivia raised an eyebrow, but followed me.

"I think the desk would form a barrier to 'girl talk', Olivia. Besides, we'll be more comfortable over here."

As we settled in our seats, Olivia said, "I heard you say Mary will be bringing tea. How is the girl doing?"

That was an unexpected question, especially since I could have sworn Olivia was actually interested in the answer. Giving her a level stare, I said, "She's doing fine now that she doesn't have to fend off inappropriate advances from the head of house-keeping."

Olivia's eyes darkened. "That bastard! He knows the members of the palace staff are off limits for advances—appropriate or not. By God, I'll have Fenton's balls on a platter for this!"

"No, Olivia, Fenton's punishment is up to *me*."

Her anger subsided just a bit. "Yes, of course. It's just... I had that girl and her sister assigned to the palace to *protect* them from things like that."

Before I could stop myself, I blurted, "You actually *care* about those girls?"

Hot anger ignited in her eyes. "Of course, I care. For God's sake, those girls are—were—my subjects. They aren't to blame for their father's stupidity."

"Really? Then why didn't you intervene in the sentencing? Or, better yet, change the stupid law so it doesn't affect children?"

"Do you know the history behind the law you so blithely call stupid?" When I shook my head, Olivia said, "My great grandfather was a foolish and imprudent ruler. He supported his extravagant lifestyle by plunging our family deeply into debt. The rest of the duchy followed his lead, both on a personal and a corporate level. Loan defaults were so prevalent they nearly destroyed the duchy's economy. When my grandfather took over, he instituted draconian financial regulations aimed at bringing everything under control. They helped, but there were still so many people walking away from loans that more stringent enforcement was needed. He created the debtor's prison and made entire families liable for one person's irresponsible debts."

"It's still barbaric."

"Perhaps, but it worked. Mary's father was one of only four cases during my three years as duchess."

"If that's so, why was the law still on the books?"

"It was on my list of things to take care of, but I got... distracted...by a certain development."

"Sir Philip found me and you turned all of your attention toward killing me."

"You weren't the only distraction, but—"

We heard the click of a door opening. We fell silent and turned toward the door, expecting to see Mary pushing a cart into the room. To our surprise, the office door was still shut.

A sigh sounded from my left, the side away from the office door. "I am very sorry to see you here, Your Highness."

Silhouetted in a hidden door stood Colin. Beside him stood one of my palace guards, a strange gun held in his hand.

"Tranquilize both of them," Colin said.

Before we could rise or even cry for help, the gun gave a pop, shifted from me to Olivia, and popped a second time. I felt a sharp sting on my neck and then everything faded to black.

YOU'RE WASTING TIME

Drake

Prince William and I watched our wives walk away from us. I'll admit that a part of me enjoyed watching the two tall, slender, and beautiful women depart. I doubt they intentionally matched strides, but the synchronized swing of their hips was mesmerizing. Then their guards fell in behind the pair, blocking our view.

"Damn," the prince muttered softly. At my raised eyebrow, he grinned, "Tell me you weren't thinking the same thing and I will offer a profuse apology."

"That won't be necessary, Your Highness."

"Call me William. After all, this is a private setting."

Dozens of staff members hurried back and forth through the hall and six guards—five of them members of the prince's personal guard—stood close by us. What kind of fishbowl life could make the man think *this* was a private setting? I'd already seen how different the lives of the nobility were from my old life before Jeanine's Recognition. This was my first glimpse at the gulf between the lives of the nobility and that of royalty.

"Thank you, William. I assume you don't need my permission to use my given name?"

"By custom, which I would not break, I do."

"Then, by all means, call me Drake." I looked around, trying to figure out what to show William. "If you've ever visited this palace, you probably know at least as much about it as I do. Is there something in particular you'd like to see?"

William looked uncomfortable for a moment and I wondered what form of debauchery he was contemplating. After all, the prince had quite the reputation as a womanizer and gossip writers often speculated whether he was stepping outside of the bounds of his marriage vows or not. That is why his request completely blindsided me.

"According to the newsies, you and Lady Jeanine took care of two children while their parents celebrated their anniversary. Are the stories accurate?"

"For the most part," I said, not sure where he was going with this.

"Could you show me the playroom you had set up for the children?"

I stared at William in utter shock, unable to find anything to say.

A knowing look came into his eyes. "You expected something more in line with my reputation as the Prince of Parties? Perhaps, a request to send for the best ladies of negotiable virtue available on Gaunner or something equally inappropriate?"

I felt my face redden. "Actually, yes."

"I have it on excellent authority that you were no less of a womanizer than I was prior to your marriage to Lady Jeanine. Is it so hard to believe that I, like you, was changed by the right woman?"

"No, William, it's not. And I owe you a very deep and very sincere apology."

William waved it off. "Some of my closest friends have trouble believing I've changed, Drake. I can hardly blame a man who's just met me for thinking the same thing."

I started in the direction of the playroom, where I spent the next twenty minutes showing William what the palace staff created on such short notice. The toys ranged from amazingly detailed toy horses the children could ride to a princess's palace playhouse, complete with a balcony from which Sasha issued an astounding number of royal proclamations.

"I've enjoyed showing off the playroom, William, but I'm still puzzled by this request."

William was silent for a few seconds, before casually saying, "We'll make the official announcement soon, but Olivia is pregnant."

"You have my most sincere congratulations, William. Children are...life changing."

"So I have been told, Drake. I want to be the father my child deserves, not the caricature found in the news stories."

"That's an admirable goal, William. May offer one bit of advice that will go a long way toward making you that man?"

"Certainly."

I tried to think of a non-confrontational way to say it. Failing, I just came out and said it. "Stop trying to kill Jeanine. That suggestion applies to Olivia and your mother, as well."

"Mother warned me you would be blunt about certain matters."

"I lost my first wife and my daughter because a noble house decided they were in the way." I stopped and gave the prince a hard stare. "I assume you know what happened to the men who actually did it?"

"Yes, nor do I blame you."

"Do you know what happened to the noble who ordered the attack?"

"Lord Robert worked the courts and escaped any real consequences."

"Exactly. Should something similar happen to Jeanine, rest assured I will take very direct and very lethal action against those responsible—even if that person is a member of the royal family."

I'd meant to keep my voice low, but it rose as I spoke.

William's guards drew their weapons the second they heard the word 'lethal.' My single guard drew his in response while putting himself between me and most of the guards.

"Lower your weapons," William said.

The commander of the squad said, "He threatened you, Your Highness. We cannot—"

Two dozen guards, led by Captains Reel and Pennington, ran into the playroom and surrounded us. The two guard commanders eyed the standoff with considerable unease.

"May I ask what's going on, sir? Your Highness?" Pennington asked.

"Captain Haral was simply explaining his position on a private matter. He was *very* clear on the matter," William said. He turned his glare on the commander of his guard squadron. "I gave you an order, Captain Palmer. Are you in the habit of ignoring direct orders from members of the royal family?"

Palmer lowered his weapon and motioned for his men to do the same. "Of course, not, Your Highness. My apologies."

It was only then that I gave our two captains a closer look. Both wore very grim expressions.

"What's happened?" I asked. "Is Jeanine all right?"

"I don't know, sir," Captain Reel responded. "She and Princess Olivia have vanished."

My blood ran cold when I heard Reel's words. It's the only reason I can think of that I didn't scream in pure rage and horror. I recognized the anger and fear inside of me, but stuffed them into a corner of my mind. The emotions were out of the way, where they couldn't interfere with the rational part of my brain, but readily available if I needed to draw on them for strength or, God help me, revenge.

In level tone, I asked, "What do you mean?"

"Olivia is missing?" William cried. Anger suffusing his face, William stepped toward Captain Reel with raised fists. "Why are you just standing there? Get—"

I stepped between the prince and the captain, grabbing both

of his fists in my hands. "Hitting people and screaming will not help, Your Highness."

"How dare you lay hands on me?" he snarled, his eyes still wild. "This imbecile has allowed one of *your* people to steal my wife and our child!"

"They took my wife, too, William."

"I don't give a damn about your—"

Releasing his left fist, I gave William a hard slap, followed by a harder backslap.

"You're wasting time with this tantrum, prince."

Once they recovered from their shock, William's guards surged toward me. My own guards rushed to meet them, both sides ignoring the shouts from Pennington and Reel. Fortunately, my slap had its desired effect on the prince.

"Stop," William commanded. "Captain Haral is correct. We don't have time for my reaction nor a scuffle between our guards. Captain Reel, would you please tell us what you know?"

Relieved a civil war wasn't breaking out before his eyes, Reel said, "Princess Olivia and Lady Jeanine retired to my lady's office to talk. The only way into the office is through an outer office, where my lady's receptionist sits. Four guards were stationed in the hallway just outside of that office door. Neither woman left the room through those doors. We only discovered they were gone when a servant brought tea for them."

"There must be another entrance to the office," I said.

"Obviously so, sir. I have a dozen men tearing up the walls, floor, and ceiling right now."

"Take us there," William said.

"Have you sent anyone to check on Colin and the rest of the senior staff?"

"That was the third order I issued after we discovered Lady Jeanine and Princess Olivia were gone, sir. My first order placed the palace on lockdown and stopped all spaceship departures. Finding the unknown entrance was my second order." The Captain's comm buzzed. He listened for a moment and then said, "I'm afraid the senior staff, along with two of my guards, are missing. The other two guards, both presumably loyal to Lady Jeanine, are dead."

"I care only for finding and rescuing Olivia," William declared. Perhaps suddenly remembering the situation, he hastily added, "And, it goes without saying, Lady Jeanine."

"Of course," I said. "If you'll follow me, Your Highness, I'll lead you to the office."

Captain Reel gave a signal and six of his men led the way out of the playroom. William and I came next, followed by his guards. Once we were out in the large hallway, the rest of the guards spread out to either side of us.

When we reached Jeanine's office, the guards entered ahead of us. As soon as they gave the all clear, the prince and I hurried through the outer office and into a scene of total destruction in Jeanine's office. Floorboards were pulled up and ceiling tiles pulled down. Men wielding hammers had smashed holes into every part of the walls and, obviously, found what they were looking for.

A well-concealed door stood open on the opposite side of the office. From the look of things, Jeanine and Olivia had been sitting near it when it opened. William and I both started for the hidden passage beyond. Captain Palmer and Captain Pennington stepped in front of us.

"Get out of the way," William commanded.

"Move," I growled."

"Leave this to the professionals, sir," Pennington said.

Palmer merely shook his head.

"I'll have you tried for treason if you don't let me pass," William said.

"I cannot do so, Your Highness. The situation is dangerous and, quite frankly, you and Captain Haral will only hamper the efforts of those already searching these passages."

William and I exchanged resigned glances and retreated to the outer office, staying nearby while also getting out of the way.

I found myself sharing a sofa with a pale-faced Mary. She was trembling uncontrollably and blinking back tears.

Taking her hand in both of mine, I said, "Don't worry. The guards know their stuff. We'll have Jeanine and Princess Olivia back before you know it."

Mary's head jerked up and down, showing she heard me, but she didn't relax. I turned her face toward me and gently wiped away the tears that had spilled out onto her cheeks.

"What's got you so scared, Mary?"

"It— It's all m-m-my f-f-f-fault!"

William looked up at that, though he didn't say anything.

"How can it be your fault?" I asked. "All you did was discover they were missing."

Her head shook violently. "N-not today. W-when you first got here. Lady Jeanine got angry at C-Colin because of me. If I hadn't been there, maybe this wouldn't have h-happened."

"Nonsense," William said. "Every member of the aristocracy knows what Colin is like. Well, every member except Olivia, who was practically raised by the man. I expect he's probably been planning Lady Jeanine's disappearance since she was first Recognized as Duchess of Gaunner."

I thought, but did not say, 'Like pseudo father, like pseudo daughter.' Somehow, I thought Jeanine would disapprove. Besides, William was having more success calming Mary than I was.

"You listen to what Captain Haral said. Mary, is it?"

Mary bobbed her head. "Yes, Your Highness."

"Well, Mary, rest assured neither Captain Haral nor I blame you for happened. Indeed, we are thankful you were so prompt delivering the tea. It might have taken hours for us to discover their disappearance, otherwise."

"Thank you, Your Highness."

Thinking she needed something to take her mind off of the situation, I asked, "Do you feel up to fetching some snacks for the guards? Who knows how long they'll be working and it's already lunchtime."

"Yes, sir, I can do that." With a timid smile to both of us, Mary rose and headed for the kitchen.

When she was outside of the office, I said, "That was very kind of you, William."

"I'm a prince, Drake, not an inhuman monster."

"In far too much of my experience, the nobility are both very human and quite monstrous." I thought of the things Sir Philip told us about Olivia, some of it fact and some speculation, and found myself tempted to enlighten William. I resisted, again knowing Jeanine wouldn't approve, and simply nodded. "Perhaps that doesn't apply to you. I will say our time together today has convinced me to maintain an open mind on the subject."

For a moment, I thought William was close to confessing something. He didn't, though, so I put it down to my imagination. Even that thought was swept from my mind when Captain Reel came out to speak with us.

"We haven't finished searching all of the passages—it seems the palace is riddled with them—but I think it's safe to say they are no longer on or under the palace grounds. We've found several old and dusty passages that go well beyond the outer wall. The dust has been disturbed recently and by many feet. I'm afraid they could be almost anywhere, by now."

"You've got people monitoring communications?" William asked.

"Of course, Your Highness."

"Have you got any slicers searching the net for information on Jeanine and Olivia?" I asked.

Captain Reel looked surprised at my question. "No, sir. Do you think it necessary?"

"I think it might be our best chance of finding them."

"If you believe there is value," Reel said, his expressions till doubtful, "I'll see if my people can find someone."

"You do that," I said. "Meanwhile, I know someone on Xapreathea who might be able to help."

"It's a three-day flight from the capital to Gaunner, sir."

"Not necessarily," William said. "Do you think this person really can help, Drake?"

I nodded. "She's one of the best slicers in the Star Kingdom."

"That's good enough for me. Where shall I have Mother send a car?"

"A car for what?" I couldn't keep suspicion out of my voice.

"I want Olivia back more than I want to arrest some slicer, no matter how good she is. If your friend will accept a bit of risk, I think we can have her here in twenty hours."

"So, the rumors of an experimental hyperdrive are true. Send the car to the Neert estate." Turning to Edward, Jeanine's receptionist, I said, "The prince and I both need subspace connections to Xapreathea. We have to make the most important calls of our lives."

BRYCE IS...PERTURBED

Jana

I spent the whole day analyzing the information on my data stick, searching for some clue as to the nature of the system at the end of the one-way network cable. Tilly tried distracting me a few times and even brought out maps to plan a different route to the cable. I had been trying to find a polite way to get her to leave me alone when she grabbed two glasses and a bottle of whiskey. While she poured shots, I humored her by looking more closely at the map she had on her pad. Something clicked.

"Of course," I said as we downed our shots. "It's so obvious I should have seen it sooner!"

"What are you talking about, Jana?"

"That ancient network feed—it goes to the Star Stone."

"Where did that idea come from?" asked Tilly, pouring again.

"Look at that map on your pad. Our tunnel runs directly under the Star Chamber." I raised my glass in a silent toast to Tilly. "Once I realized the Stone was right above us, everything odd about that network feed sort of fell into place."

"Just because you don't recognize the network encryption, it doesn't mean the network leads to the Star Stone."

"I'm not basing it solely on that."

Tilly snorted and threw back her third shot of whiskey. For a wordless retort, I thought it was pretty eloquent.

"Okay, Tilly, you're right. I am basing this almost entirely on the encryption. But it wouldn't have crossed my mind if you hadn't shown me we were almost directly beneath the Star Stone."

"Oh, so now it's my fault?"

Grinning, I shrugged. "I call 'em as I see 'em."

"Whatever," Tilly said. "But what would a big, pretty rock do with a data feed, anyway?"

"I don't know. How does the big, pretty rock Recognize nobles? How does it know when a family line has an unknown heir, like it knew about Jeanine?" I pushed my glass toward the center of the table. "I think a little more mental lubricant might help me figure it out."

Tilly, damn her soul, stoppered the bottle. "I think you're well enough lubricated, already—especially after our excesses last night and that wild theory about the Star Stone. Why don't you sleep on this idea and we'll continue the discussion in the morning?"

"Okay." Remembering our harrowing escape up the side of a building from the night before, I added, "If I'm sober enough to have nightmares where I fall forever, I'm going to blame you."

Tilly demonstrated the depth of her sympathy by laughing at me. "Poor Jana, do you need your mommy to tuck you in and sing you a lullaby?"

I searched for a cutting response.

"No." Obviously, I didn't find one. I stood and said, "Humph."

Pointing my nose into the air to show my disdain, I stalked toward my bedroom. My exit might have been more dignified if I hadn't tripped over an ottoman. Flailing for balance, I knocked over a lamp and fell into another chair. Tilly's laughter rang as I pulled myself back to my feet. I very conspicuously slammed my bedroom door. Just in case Tilly hadn't gotten the message, I opened it again, stuck my tongue out at her, and slammed it again.

And I *did* have falling nightmares. I was in mid-fall when someone began shaking me.

"Jana! Wake up!"

"Whaaa?"

I forced one eye open and saw Tilly bending over me.

"Come on, Jana. Something important is going on."

"Then why isn't Bryce the one waking me up?"

"He was going to do just that. When he realized you were sleeping naked, he came and got me."

"Oh. That's very gentlemanly of him." With a groan, I pushed myself up and out of the bed. "I don't suppose you did anything useful like find some clothes for me?"

"Look at the foot of your bed."

I began pulling on the clothes. "Any idea what's up?"

"No, but Bryce is...perturbed."

"You're kidding, right?"

"I wish I was, Jana."

"I've never even seen Bryce mildly miffed. This can't be good."

When I emerged from the bedroom, a look of absurd relief flooded Bryce's face. That worried me even more than him being perturbed.

"What's up?" I asked.

"Captain Haral is on the subspace communicator. He's asking for you and is most emphatic that time is of the essence."

Following Bryce out of my suite, I asked, "Then why did you go get Tilly to wake me up?"

Bryce actually looked offended. "You were unclothed, Miss Ward. It would not have been proper."

"Screw propriety," I said. "If the estate was on fire, would you let me die to protect my modesty?"

"Of course not, Miss."

"Well, that's something."

A moment later, I settled in front of the subspace communicator. Drake, his face haggard and lined with worry, turned his eyes toward Tilly.

"Do you trust the lady thief?" he asked.

"Quite literally, with my life. What's wrong?"

"Jeanine is been kidnapped. They took Olivia, too."

"Oh my God, Drake! I wish there was something I could do to help."

"There is. I want to bring you out here to monitor communications and help us find her."

"I'll do anything you need, of course, but it will take days to get to Gaunner."

"According to Prince William, who is on the subspace comm with his mother right now, the Royal Navy has an experimental hyperdrive. It's never been tested on a flight this long, but he says it can have you here in twenty hours." Drake rubbed his for head and refused to meet my eyes. "Assuming it doesn't overload or something and... I actually don't know what it might do, but it's not entirely safe."

"Nothing about a life like mine is safe. The risk is worth it, if it helps get Jeanine back."

"I can't thank you enough, Jana."

"This experimental spaceship," Tilly said. "Do you know how many passengers it can carry?"

"I can find out," Drake said. "Why?"

"If there's room, I'm coming, also."

"Why would we need a thief? It's not like we're robbing anybody."

"Drake!" I said.

"I'm not offended, Jana," Tilly said. "Captain Haral isn't himself right now, otherwise he'd realize he *is* robbing someone —the kidnappers."

"She's right, Drake. If we can find where they're holding Jeanine and Olivia, stealing them quietly will be much safer than an all-out attack."

"Fine. Let me ask William about available seating."

"Ask if there's a subspace communicator on the ship, as well," I said. "If there is, I can start working during the trip."

"If that will work, do you even need to come to Gaunner?" Drake asked.

"Yes. Subspace communications have a slight lag. It's not obvious during conversations and not a particularly big deal for data retrieval jobs, but it's huge for real-time work—things like monitoring worldwide communications networks."

I could tell from the expression on Drake's face that he didn't understand, but he accepted my word. With a nod, he turned away from us and spoke quietly. I assume he was talking to Prince William, but I couldn't see anybody in the screen. After a moment, he turned his attention back to me.

"There's room for your friend and the ship does have a subspace communicator. Test pilots insist on it, in case the experimental drive strands them far from the normal hyperspace lanes." Drake glanced at Tilly, "Are you sure you're willing to risk this?"

"I met Jeanine once, back when I discussed holes in this estate's security with the two of you. I liked what I saw, but not enough to take this kind of risk for her. Jana, though, knows Jeanine very well and I trust Jana's judgment."

"Thank you," Drake said. "William says a car is already on its way to pick you up, so grab what you're going to need. I'll see you in about twenty hours."

Tilly and I turned away from the screen and were both surprised to find Bryce standing there. I'd completely forgotten he was in the room with us.

"I'll send servants to handle your packing," he said. "You need only concentrate on selecting what you need."

"Thank you, Bryce."

"You're quite welcome, Miss Ward."

Ten minutes later, Bryce handed our luggage to the Queen's driver and then held the back door for us. "Do be as careful as possible, ladies. The staff and I have grown quite fond of the two of you. We would be despondent if anything were to happen to either of you."

Tilly flashed a thumbs up. I kissed Bryce on the cheek.

"We'll be back before you know it, Bryce," I said. "And I promise, we'll find Jeanine and bring her back safely, too."

"I have no doubt of that, Miss Ward."

Bryce shut the door and the car roared off toward the spaceport.

ESCAPE

Jeanine

I swam up to consciousness slowly. Rolling my head off of my shoulder, I felt a sharp pain in my neck. The stabbing agony eased somewhat with movement, so I kept rolling my head around. Stiff and sore shoulders announced themselves next, followed by numb hands that were somewhere above my head. I tried lowering my hands and found the rest of me rising slightly. More pain blossomed as manacles bit into my wrists. The slight movement also made my stomach roil. It was probably an after-effect of the tranquilizer. I stopped moving so it could settle.

"You're awake at last, my lady," a man's voice said.

I felt certain I should recognize the voice, but it wasn't that familiar to me. Shaking my head in an attempt to clear it, I forced my eyes open. It took several blinks before my eyesight cleared enough to make out details.

Colin, the owner of the voice, sat opposite me, swaying slightly. I shook my head again before I realized I was swaying, as well. We were moving.

With that knowledge, I gave my surroundings a more careful examination. We were in a small compartment, something appropriate for a local delivery vehicle of some kind. The back doors were to my right. I assumed the driver's compartment was just beyond the blank wall to the left. Colin sat on the floor, leaning casually against the wall opposite me. Two other men—both of them young, muscular, and armed—sat to Colin's left. Olivia was draped comfortably on a small pile of cast-off Gaunner palace guard uniforms, her head cradled in Colin's lap.

I was alone on my side of the compartment. My hands were manacled to a ring bolted to the side of the compartment. My feet were free, which gave me a lot of options, but only if both of the guards came within range of them. In the hopes of encouraging that level of careless from the two men, I let my head loll and my shoulders slump, as if the effort of looking around had overtaxed my strength.

"Why am I still alive?" I mumbled.

"Because I have great respect and affection for the title of Duchess of Gaunner, even if the titleholder does not command the same respect. It would have been vastly easier to assassinate you, but in that direction lies anarchy or, worse, *democracy*." Colin actually shuddered as he uttered that last bit. "There's also the very real chance that your death might turn you into a martyr, a symbol for the commoners to rally around."

"Not that I'm complaining, but I think you greatly overestimate the people's love for me. I've only been here a few days and I carry the 'taint of Neert.' That *is* the phrase you used after my Recognition, isn't?"

"Yes, it is, and it gained considerable traction in the vids and among the people. Then My Lady Babysitter arrived and, with one simple conversation, ruined all of my careful groundwork." Colin shook his head in obvious admiration. "Offering to take care of that woman's children truly was a masterstroke on your part, my lady. I wish I knew how your spies found her and then made sure she was present for your arrival. However they managed that, it was brilliantly done.

"Had my informants recognized the importance of that little drama and alerted me immediately, your arrival at the palace would have gone much differently. As it was, I treated you as a naive young woman who was in over her head rather than the trained manipulator you most obviously are."

Wow. That had to be the most ridiculous misinterpretation of an event I'd ever heard. I guess Colin never even considered that it was mere chance that we stopped near Carol Holder and her children, nor that I made my offer to her out of kindness. Of course, I wasn't about to admit that to Colin now. Better to keep him misinterpreting my intentions and capabilities for as long as possible.

"Your deductive skills are surprising, Colin."

Colin gave me a polite nod of acknowledgment, which would have been funny in other circumstances. "A man cannot survive long in my position without being able to spot the truth behind the act."

"Then I hope you will realize I am not acting now. I am a patient woman, Colin, but you are trying that patience in the extreme. If you turn this vehicle around and return Olivia and me to the palace, I will pardon everyone who was involved with this abduction. If you continue with this foolish action, I will destroy you."

Colin clapped slowly while saying, "Bravo, my lady. That was a brilliant performance, one worthy of a great actress, but we both know you're helpless."

"Strange, that's what Sir Philip thought when he and his team of assassins attacked my grandfather and me. Now, he answers to me."

"That was a most impressive escape on your part, my lady, but I have a much greater advantage over you than Sir Philip did. Or did you not notice the manacles?"

"I believe you're forgetting about my husband." I jerked my head toward Olivia. "Not to mention *her* husband."

"Of the two, I am far more concerned with Captain Haral than I am the prince. But neither of them knows where I'm taking you, so my level of concern is extremely low."

"I'm sure that's exactly what those false pirates thought after they slaughtered Drake's wife and child. How did that work out for them?" I cocked my head as if pondering my own question. "Oh, yes, they were all killed or captured by him and his crew."

"You forget, my lady, that I am not some mid-witted naval officer playing pirate. *I* am an advisor to every duke and duchess of Gaunner for the last seventy-eight years."

"No, Colin, you *were* an advisor. You most assuredly are *not* mine."

"A fair point, my lady, but one which I shall see rectified soon."

"If you kill me, Colin, the king will have no choice but to make an example of you. Every great house in the Star Kingdom will demand it."

"That, my lady, is why I'm *not* going to kill you. I said as much earlier. That is predicated on your cooperation, of course."

Olivia chose that moment to stir and groan. Colin immediately turned his attention away from me and toward Olivia and her recovery. He gently helped her sit up, gave her sips of water, and let her lean against him as she came around. He even held her hair back when she recovered enough to vomit.

In case you're wondering, princesses puke just like the rest of us. There's nothing dainty or dignified about it. I waited for Olivia to regain her composure and order us to forget that we'd ever seen her heave her guts out. Instead, she curled up in a ball, held her stomach, and wailed in agony.

If Olivia's distress hadn't been so horrible, I'd have laughed at the look on Colin's face.

"What is it, Your Highness?" he asked. "What's wrong?"

Olivia gasped, "The drug...must be...allergic."

"No, Your Highness," Colin said, his head shaking vigorously. "I checked your medical records as soon as we got out of the palace. The tranquilizer we used is benign to you."

"Then my...baby."

Colin's face contorted in confusion. "Baby?"

Olivia nodded, her eyes screwed shut. "I'm pregnant."

If I thought Colin's expression was comical before, his latest one was hysterical.

"P-pregnant?" he asked.

I couldn't resist needling the man. "Don't they teach about sexual intercourse, pregnancy, and childbirth in Gaunner schools? I realize 'sexual intercourse' may be outside of your experience, but—"

"Be silent, you irritating woman!" Colin snarled.

Smirking at the two guards, I said, "Do you think I hit a nerve, there?"

One guard's lips twitched up before he got control of himself. The other guard's lips turned down in a frown, so I guess my attempt to win the men over with humor was a wash.

Colin turned to nearer guard—the frowning one—and said, "Contact the support team. Order them to grab the best doctor they can find and bring him to the rendezvous location. Make certain they understand this is a matter of life and death."

The guard pulled out a comm and began speaking urgently into it. The guy was unnerved enough by Olivia's cries that he forgot basic communications protocol and referred to 'her Royal Highness' over an open comm channel. Colin was so caught up in taking care of Olivia that he didn't even notice.

Everyone says you should never interrupt your enemy when he's making a mistake. It's one of the simplest and oldest gems of strategic wisdom known to man. I'm pretty sure Colin's and Olivia's diagnosis qualified as one of those mistakes.

I seriously doubted Olivia's baby was in any danger. I was more or less certain that babies in the womb weren't susceptible to allergies, though they can obviously be affected if their mother has an allergic reaction. What Olivia interpreted as her baby in distress was almost certainly her own severe stomach cramps. They're an aftereffect of several tranquilizers, especially if the person recovering from them puts something in her stomach too soon after they regain consciousness. That's the reason I didn't ask for any water when I woke up.

How do I know that? About five years ago, Grandfather dosed me with some of the more common tranquilizers so I'd recognize their effects and know the best ways to recover from each of them. Yes, that's what my upbringing was like. Anyway, I ignored grandfather's advice one time and drank a glass of water right after I came to. I spent the next couple of hours curled up in extreme pain and misery from severe stomach cramps—just like Olivia was doing right now.

I'm told all expectant mothers worry about something happening to the child they're carrying. No doubt, I'll react the same way—assuming I survived this kidnapping, anyway. To my surprise, I wanted to tell Olivia that her suffering wasn't affecting the baby. I didn't do it, though. Instead, I played on the fear.

"Well, this situation is pretty much the epitome of being royally screwed. I mean, we've got Olivia, who was royally screwed in the literal sense. Then we've got you, Colin, who is royally screwed in the figurative sense." I paused for a second, as if following a train of logic. "Does anyone know what the penalty is for killing a royal baby in the womb? Whatever it is, I can't imagine it's particularly pleasant."

Colin glared at me. "Gag her."

The guard who almost grinned at my gibe turned to a box I hadn't noticed before. It turned out to be nothing more than a toolbox, but it was a well-stocked one. If I could get loose, it was full of all sorts of potential weapons. It also had tape, which the guard pulled out.

"You should free my hands, Colin. I can help with Olivia."

"Why would I trust *you* with Her Highness's life?"

"Because, unlike everyone else in this compartment, I don't blame an innocent child for the sins of her parents. Olivia and I will never be friends, but I will do everything in my power to protect her baby. I'm the only woman here and the only one with any experience being on the receiving end of tranquilizers."

I saw Colin waver a bit. No one likes that helpless feeling you get when someone you care about is suffering. Give them a chance to hand responsibility off to someone else and most people will jump at it. Would that temptation be enough to overcome Colin's natural distrust of me?

In a surprisingly short time, Colin decided it was. "If you harm Her Highness in anyway—"

"You'll shoot me and bury me in a shallow grave. Got it."

The guard holding the tape said, "Is this wise, sir?"

"Probably not, but I don't have any other choice," Colin responded. "That's why you are to watch her like a hawk."

The guard shrugged and pulled a key from his pocket. He slid the key into the lock for the manacles and then stepped back out of reach. "Unlock them yourself."

Damn, I had a smart guard on my hands. If he'd stuck around and turned the key, I'd have had the manacle chain around his throat and been choking him before he knew what happened.

I turned the key and, rubbing my wrists to restore circulation, dropped to my knees next to Olivia. "Back off, Colin, and give me room to work with her."

I made a show of examining Olivia, poking and prodding her stomach. From experience, I knew just where her pain was the worst and probed there. Her Highness arched her back and screamed in pain, drawing alarmed looks from all three men.

"She's badly dehydrated."

It was absolutely true and completely irrelevant, but Colin immediately extended a bottle of water to me.

"In her condition, Olivia can't handle a mouthful of water all at once," I said. "We need to rehydrate her gradually. Let me see..."

Acting as if an idea suddenly occurred to me, I lifted Olivia and looked at the castoff guard uniforms piled beneath her. I pulled out one of the shirts and tossed it to Colin.

"Tear that into small strips."

Colin looked at the shirt without comprehension. "Why?"

"So you can soak them in water. I'll let Olivia suck the moisture out of them. It will let me rehydrate her at a gentle pace."

Colin continued staring at me, so I added, "Don't you know anything about desert survival?"

As I'd hoped, invoking a source for my request spurred Colin to action. That action proved futile when Colin couldn't tear the fabric at all. Not surprising, considering the uniforms are made of tough material. Besides, Colin was getting on in years and not in anything resembling peak condition.

He turned to the two guards. "Is there a knife in that toolbox?"

Frowning guard immediately turned and looked at the toolbox. Smart guard held out his hand for the shirt.

"I'll cut it up, sir. We don't want to have a knife that close to the prisoner."

"Good point, Corporal."

Colin leaned forward and around the frowning guard, holding out the shirt. Smart guard leaned forward to take the shirt. For a second, everyone was off balance and no one was looking at me.

I levered my legs into the air, balancing on my hands, and kicked backward at the two guards. My right foot smashed into the back of frowning guard's head, sending him face first into the toolbox. My left foot crushed smart guard's windpipe, sending him tumbling against the back door. His hands clawed at his throat, futilely trying to find a way to clear his airway.

Colin was just turning back toward me, his eyes wide with surprise and fear, when I grabbed his head and slammed it against the wall. His expression slackened and he slid to the floor, unconscious.

I realized frowning guard's body was quivering. Pulling his head out of the toolbox, I discovered why. Someone hadn't put the tools away properly, leaving a screwdriver with its blade pointing up. By sheer luck—good for me, bad for the guard—the man impaled his left eye on the tool. That luck abandoned me when it came to the man's comm. It lay in pieces around the toolbox.

I turned a dispassionate gaze on smart guard, whose face was turning red as he tried in vain to breathe. He held out an imploring hand.

I said, "You backed the wrong side, but I'm not cruel enough to let you die like that."

Hope flared in the guard's eyes. Then I rammed the knife from toolbox up under his ribcage and into his heart.

"I'm also not stupid enough to let a traitorous, trained warrior like you live."

As the life flowed out of the guard—who, in the end, wasn't so smart—I realized the vehicle was slowing down. All of the banging from the fight must have alerted the driver that something was wrong in the compartment. With no idea how many people I'd have to face or how well-armed they'd be, I decided retreat was the smartest course of action.

I opened the back door and discovered the vehicle was driving down a dark forest lane. I'd been unconscious the entire day! For reasons I can't fully explain even now, I hoisted Olivia over my shoulder. I took a second to steady myself and then jumped.

I'VE GOT SOMETHING

Jana

Slicing Gaunner's planetary net over a subspace comm line from a ship traveling in hyperspace proved more frustrating than I expected. Besides the normal subspace delay, which made real-time work like my communication search vastly more difficult, hyperspace caused unexpected distortions in the signal. Unlike the delay, you can actually hear the distortion when you're speaking with someone over the comm. Of course, I'd never spoken on the subspace comm from hyperspace before and I doubted anyone in the Star Kingdom had ever tried slicing under these conditions.

The distortion wasn't the only surprise I got on the trip. It turns out I suffer from hyperspace sickness. Tilly suffers from it, too, but nowhere near as badly as I do. The thing is, I have made a dozen interstellar trips in my life and never once had a problem. It's this damned new hyperspace drive—it never leaves hyperspace.

The drive isn't really what's new, though the pilot insists it has some improvements—ones only a pilot could love, I suspect. The new part is the navigation controls, and the changes in them really make a huge difference. In the past, ships entered hyperspace and stayed on the same vector until they popped back out of hyperspace. It was all straight-line travel, with the course changes only possible after the ship returned to normal space. Only then could the astrogator calculate a new vector and the pilot change course to follow that vector when the ship jumped back into hyperspace.

All of this was done to stay well clear of stellar masses, whose gravity fields can do wonky and terrible things to hyperspatial ships that pass too close to them. In the end, a ship can end up traveling two or three times farther than the direct distance between two stars. The new navigation controls put an end to that, allowing ships to change course without exiting hyperspace. That's what makes this experimental ship so fast.

And, it's why I discovered I suffer from hyperspace sickness. I had never spent more than a few hours in hyperspace at any one time. That was not long enough, it turns out, to trigger my allergy. On this trip, we had already been in hyperspace for fourteen hours and had five or six more to go.

"I think I'm going to die," I moaned.

"Don't be ridiculous, Jana." Tilly held a bottle of something to my lips. "Here, drink some of this. Maybe it will help."

"Is it a fast acting poison?"

"God, you are such a baby. I haven't heard anybody whine this much since my last boyfriend had a hangover. Now, drink up!"

Without waiting for a response, Tilly poured the liquid into my mouth. Reflexively, I swallowed it. I felt the burn of the whiskey all the way down my throat and into my stomach, where the heat blossomed.

Coughing and spluttering, I said, "You could at least warn a girl! And, where did you find whiskey?"

"I brought it from the estate. The nice woman helping me pack didn't bat an eye when I handed it to her. We've already tried every other beverage available and most of the food, too. I decided I'd try a different kind of medication. Is it working?"

"Too early to tell for sure, but I think so. Let me get back to work and see how it goes. Keep the bottle handy, though."

I returned my attention to monitoring the thousands of bots I'd uploaded into Gaunner's net. I wasn't examining their actual findings—that would be impossible—just watching for alerts. So far, I had followed up on hundreds of them. None of them had panned out—I'd had to set some broad parameters and knew I would get a lot of false alarms—but I was confident something would show up sometime. You simply cannot kidnap a princess and a duchess and maintain complete comm silence about the deed. Forty-six minutes and four gulps of whiskey later, I struck paydirt.

Team one calling team two. Need doctor. Complications with Her Highness's pregnancy.

Pregnancy? I guess the rumors Tilly heard were true—Olivia *was* pregnant.

I wrenched my attention away from William's and Olivia's family planning and searched for the origin of that broadcast. It didn't take long to narrow it down as much as possible. Between the lag and the distortion, though, I could only do so much. Still, I eliminated most of the planet, reducing the search area to several thousand square kilometers.

"Tilly, get Drake on the subspace comm. I've got something."

I AM AN IDIOT

Drake

You wait.

You want to do something, but thousands of people are already doing everything. You would just get in the way. You would just slow things down.

So, you wait.

You pace.

You greet everyone who comes your way with a hopeful, expectant look. Their quick shake of the head dashes your hopes. They have no news.

So, you wait.

You try to distract yourself. An interstellar duchy takes a lot of work to run. You pull up reports and read them. Then, you realize you didn't pay attention to what you were reading. You read it again. And you still have no idea what it says. You put it aside.

And, you wait.

"This is ridiculous," William said. "There must be something we can do."

"I'm open to suggestions," I said. "But we both know we would just be a distraction if we tried to help."

"Perhaps that's easy for you to say, Drake. *I* am a man of action and unused to simply sitting around like this."

My temper, already severely frayed, snapped. "A man of action, are you? Please, William, regale me with your tales of derring-do. Tell me of the times you've laid your life on the line for friends and shipmates. Pour forth the emotions you felt kneeling over your dead wife and daughter. Or release those pent up emotions you felt at the loss of a comrade."

William leapt to his feet, his face bright red with anger. "How dare you mock me! I am a prince of the realm and your future ruler. You will treat me with respect."

"Oh, shut up. You haven't earned that kind of respect."

"In my capacity as a naval commander, I have led troop landings, commanded squadrons of warships, and—"

"Done it all under carefully controlled circumstances and solely for the benefit of the cams recording your every move. Honestly, does anyone in the Royal House actually think we commoners believe all of those stories? We know you are in no danger. We know the King and Queen will not risk their only child and heir."

Captains Palmer and Pennington, no doubt summoned by a guard or servant, rushed into the room and put themselves between us. Palmer took the Prince by the arm and all but dragged him out of the room. Pennington blocked me from following.

"Get out of the way, Captain."

"No."

"I need to settle accounts with that arrogant—"

"You need to sit down and shut up." Pennington emphasized his words by pushing me, none too gently, into my seat.

"You did not hear what he said, Captain Pennington!"

"Half of the palace heard what he said. And what you said in return."

"Then you know he claimed undeserved honors while casting aspersions on me."

"For which you slapped him down, sir. Quite undiplomatically, I might add."

"Are you trying to tell me he didn't deserve it?"

"That is not for me to decide, sir." Pennington sat down in the chair recently vacated by the Prince. "But have you considered that Prince William is no less worried about his wife than you are for yours? Perhaps he spoke without thinking, but I don't believe you gave any more thought to your own response."

"But to call himself a man of action?"

"I believe the Prince is as much a man of action as his circumstances allow, sir. Have you given any thought to how Prince William must feel about that? Imagine wanting to act but having all around you stop you from following your inclination."

I gave a humorless laugh. "You mean like how I feel right now?"

"Precisely, sir. What you are feeling now is, most likely, what Prince William feels all the time."

"I...never thought about it like that. Thank you, Captain Pennington."

"You have had other matters on your mind, sir." Pennington stood up. "If you have yourself under control again, may I be excused to return to the command center?"

"By all means, Captain. You will alert me the minute you have anything?"

"You already know the answer to that question, sir. But, in case you need to hear it again, I will alert you the *second* we have anything."

As Pennington left the room, Prince William returned. He looked as if he had been on the receiving end of a similar dressing down.

"I have been informed," Prince William said, "that I am an idiot. Captain Palmer didn't use those exact words. In fact, he was exceedingly polite, but the message remains the same."

"No doubt, you will be shocked to discover that Captain

Pennington told me the same thing." I stood in extended my hand. "I suggest we forget it ever happened."

Prince William clasped my hand. "Forget what happened?"

"Exactly."

We sat quietly for a few minutes. Then, without preamble, William said, "You know, I never thought I'd end up marrying Olivia. Not that my friends and I didn't fantasize about her, as beautiful as she is. But, well, you know what her brother was like."

"All too well, William."

"Ah, yes, of course. Pardon me for dredging up such painful memories." I nodded in acknowledgment, and William continued, "Lord Robert terrified all of us. As much as we wanted to pursue Olivia, none of us felt she was worth losing our lives."

William stared off into space for several seconds. I was left with the distinct impression he had more to say, so I remained silent. His eyes focused on me and his lips curled up in a self-deprecating smile.

"I was wrong, Drake. She *is* worth my life. Now that she carries my child, she is worth more than my life. I would do anything to make her happy. I am certain you understand exactly how I feel."

"I do."

William looked down at the floor, drew a deep breath, and looked back at me. "That is why I hired the mercenaries who attacked you in the Vollec system."

Well, that was unexpected. I opened my mouth to yell at William. Then I closed it. I opened it again to sternly warn him to leave Jeanine and me alone. Again, I closed my mouth. Looking into William's eyes, I had the idea he was punishing himself far worse than I ever could.

"Olivia was in such high spirits the night of that ball. She planned it down to the last detail, confident that it would become the celebration our wedding did not. Everything was going splendidly until you and Jeanine arrived. In a sea of pastel, floor-length gowns, Jeanine's daring, emerald green dress made your wife stand out like... Well, like Olivia *had* been standing out in her sapphire gown. Once again, at a social occasion of extreme importance to Olivia, Jeanine overshadowed her. Worse, I could not take my eyes off of Jeanine's legs and breasts. I didn't *want* to stare at your wife, but I couldn't stop myself. You can imagine how that affected Olivia."

Once again, William's eyes lost focus. This time, though, he kept speaking. "Disgusted with myself, I reverted to my old drinking habits. I barely remember the end of the ball, nor my less than stellar performance in bed that evening. I don't even remember contacting a friend with...dubious...connections. But I obviously did. At my request and expense, he arranged for the ambush."

When William fell silent this time, I knew he was done.

"Why tell this to me? Do you think this confession absolves you of responsibility?"

"No, Drake, I don't. But we could never forge any kind of remotely amicable relationship as long as I held that secret."

"Am I supposed to forgive you or something? Do you think we're going to become best buddies?"

"I have no idea what we are going to become, but without that confession we could never be anything but enemies. Perhaps that's all we ever can be, but you have my word that I will never attack you or Jeanine again."

I was pondering the Prince's words when one of Captain Pennington's men rushed into the room.

"Sir, the slicer is on the subspace communicator. She's found something!"

SHE MIGHT DIE

Jeanine

I was mid jump when I realized there was snow on the ground. My first thought was, 'Yay, softer landing!' My second thought was, 'Crap, easier tracking.' My third thought was, 'Damn, it's cold out here!'

Yes, your mind can do all sorts of mental gymnastics while your body is trying for a simple tuck and roll. A tuck and roll made more difficult by the pregnant woman I had over one shoulder. But Grandfather never accepted difficulty as an excuse for failure. So, I turned and came down on my left side, pulling my legs up tight and using my left arm to lever me into a slide. That's another advantage to snow—it protects you from road rash.

As I came to a halt, the truck I'd leapt from slewed to a stop fifty meters up the road. I staggered to my feet and bent to retrieve Olivia. When I straightened, doors on both sides of the truck flew open and a man jumped out of each one. Shouting and pointing at me, they both ran my way. The bright light of a blaster bolt flashed across the distance and melted snow a meter to my left. The crack of the shot followed a split second later.

As I ran off the road and into the woods, the other man shouted, "Don't shoot, you idiot! You might hit Her Highness."

"I set it to stun," the shooter said.

His companion's reply was lost in the wind as I charged into the forest. My teeth were already chattering as the frigid breeze cut through my thin clothing. I could feel Olivia shivering, as well. We didn't have much time to find shelter or warmer clothing or, preferably both. Just as bad, my chances of getting away from our pursuers were slim. Even a complete novice can track someone through the snow.

That only left me one choice. Hoping the two men from the truck would follow my tracks exactly rather than splitting up and angling in to cut me off, I began a wide turn back toward the truck. As long as there wasn't a third man in the cab or one of the two men hadn't stayed there to stand guard, I might be able to steal a ride.

Realizing I couldn't simply blunder back onto the road, I stopped and listened for the men's voices. I was pleased to hear them shouting back and forth, making it fairly easy for me to place them.

"Yeah, her tracks are easy to see."

By sound, I placed that man near the point where I ran into the woods, something his words confirmed.

"You sure we gotta take her alive?" the other one shouted. "She killed Simpkins and Porter."

That guy was back at the truck, damn it all. At least, he was at the back of the truck. I think.

"Yes, Randall, we have to take her alive. Do you know what our lord will do to us if we kill her?"

"Do you know what my sister will do to me if I don't? I got her husband this job and now he's got a screwdriver in his brain."

The crazy part of my mind—given freer rein than normal—wanted to tell the man that his brother-in-law would still be alive if someone had put their tools away properly. The survivalist part of my mind squelched that impulse.

Behind me, the man who was following my trail stumbled through the underbrush. He cursed when a branch whipped across his face and cursed louder when he stumbled into a tree. He wasn't that close to me, but it wouldn't take him long to close the gap when I stopped to load Olivia into the truck. I could only hope the cargo compartment blocked the other man's line of sight to the front of the truck. If he saw me return to the road, I was done for.

I reached the edge of the forest. The truck's passenger door was three meters away and, handily, wide open. The grisly scene inside the compartment continued occupying the man who stayed with the truck. My pursuer was twenty or more meters away and still crashing through the forest.

Taking a deep, frigid breath, I charged out of the woods and toward the truck. Sliding to a stop, I heaved Olivia unceremoniously into the passenger seat. Slamming the door, I ran around the front of the truck toward the driver's side. I heard a startled shout from the back and prayed the man would go toward the sound of the door. If he took even a second to consider what was going on, I felt certain he would come toward the driver's door. I rounded the front of the truck and almost wept with relief when I didn't see anyone.

A face appeared at the passenger window as I swung up into the cab. The driver had left the engine running—probably because he didn't want to let it cool down in this frigid weather—so I shoved the throttle forward before I was even seated. The force from the acceleration made the driver's door swing shut, smashing into the ankle I hadn't quite pulled inside the cab. I pushed the door open far enough to get my foot inside and then pulled the door shut.

I heard a couple of thumps from the back of the truck and checked the rearview cam. The bodies of Simpkins and Porter lay sprawled in the snow. Something blocked the cam for a second and then I saw the unconscious form of Colin bouncing and rolling on the road. The sight gladdened my heart almost as much as the warm air streaming from the truck's heater.

Olivia, who had been quiet during my daring escape, moaned

and pushed herself up. "If I'm going to die, at least I'll die warm. What did you think you were doing, Jeanine?"

"Escaping. It's that thing all prisoners want to do." I risked a glance at Olivia. Even taking into account the dim light, she looked very pale. "How are you feeling?"

"Better, now that I'm not bouncing off your shoulder. If your treatment of me did anything to my baby—"

"Relax, your baby is fine. History is full of pregnant women who went through far worse than you just did without losing their child."

"But what about the allergic reaction? They were calling for a doctor."

"That's just stomach cramps, Olivia. It's because of the tranquilizer they used and the water they poured into your stomach. If they'd simply left you alone, you'd have recovered like I did. Instead, you got cramps."

"What makes you an expert on this? You've never been pregnant."

"Not yet, no. But I have been tranquilized several times. I know the best way to recover from most common tranqs."

"Why, in God's name, have you been tranquilized?"

"My grandfather did it so I would know how it felt and how best to recover in case...someone...used a tranq to capture me."

"Oh." Olivia was quiet for a few seconds, then said, "You're sure it's just cramps?"

"Yes, but we'll get you to a doctor as soon as possible, just to be on the safe side."

We rode in silence for another few minutes. Olivia spent the time staring out of her window. Finally, she turned and stared at me.

"What?" I finally asked.

"Why didn't you leave me with Colin and those other men?"

"Because you might have frozen to death before help arrived."

"Why does that bother you? You probably hate me. I think I would, if I was in your place."

"I did it for your baby. She is totally innocent and I couldn't have her life on my conscience. Unlike some people, I don't blame children because of who their parents are."

Olivia gave a vague nod, more of an acknowledgment that she'd heard my words than agreement with them. After that, she leaned her head against the window and drifted off to sleep.

I drove on, watching for a side road so I could get off of this main road. If Colin or one of the two remaining guards had a comm unit—and I was certain one of them did—they'd have already called for search teams. No doubt several of them were already looking for me. If I couldn't get off of this road, they were sure to catch me. Only, I never saw anything along the road except the forest. No side roads. No dark forest paths or clearings. Just trees as far as the lights could show.

Then, I came around a bend in road and the truck roared out of the forest and into a vast clearing. A kilometer ahead sat a large, well-lit estate surrounded by a tall, sturdy fence. The road, which I now knew was nothing more than a very long driveway, led straight to a closed and guarded gate.

I hadn't escaped after all. I had delivered myself into the hands of my enemies.

Moonlight reflected off of the snow, illuminating the entire scene before me. The house—really, more of a palace, it was nearly a hundred meters wide and four or five stories tall— squatted at the center of the clearing. The fence surrounding the grounds was at least five meters high, with vertical bars spaced too closely for any adult to slip between. Twenty or more luxury ground cars, along with several high-end flitters, were parked to the left of the main entrance. Armed guards stood on both sides of the gate, with a few more stationed close to the house.

What could I do?

If I slowed down or turned around, every guard in sight—and probably a bunch I couldn't see—would come after me. I might elude them for a while, but I could only flee back the way I came. The guards could easily call for a road block. Hell, with the flitters they could simply fly ahead of me and block the road, themselves.

I could take the truck off of the road. Maybe I'd find a hunting trail or service road while circling the estate. Or maybe I'd simply bog down in the snow, making it even easier for the guards to capture me.

Or I could take a cue from the world of action vids and drive headlong into the estate. If I got past the gate and reached one of the flitters...

This is where a sidekick comes in handy. They speak the magic phrase, casting doubt on the hero's sanity. The hero's response—calm and measured—ensures the success of even the most harebrained plans.

Could Olivia say the sidekick's line? No, she was still out of it. Besides, she wasn't exactly sidekick material.

Would it break the Hero's Code if I played both parts? I was about to find out.

Flicking the truck's flashers on, I pitched my voice high and cried, "Are you crazy, Jeanine? It'll never work!"

Reaching for the controls for my window, I replied in my normal voice, "It's our only chance, kid! It's *got* to work!"

The gate loomed ahead and the guards were already spreading out to cover my approach. Ruthlessly crushing the manic laugh threatening to burst forth after my solo show of bravado, I lowered the driver's side window. Frigid air swirled into the cab, flushing the warm air out. Olivia cried in surprise or fear—maybe both. I drew a deep breath and stuck my head out of the window.

Damn, it was cold outside!

Praying my voice wouldn't get lost in the wind, I shouted, "Open the gate! The princess has to get to the doctor *now*!"

One of the guards waved an arm and shouted back. I couldn't understand a word he said, though the arm signal was plain enough—stop the truck. I stuck one arm out of the window and made sweeping, open-the-gate motions.

"Open the gate or she might die!"

I don't know if the guard bought my act or figured out my identity and was afraid Olivia would get killed if I rammed the gate. Maybe he just figured his fellow guards would have a much easier time capturing me if I was trapped inside the fence. Whatever his reasons, the shouting guard turned to someone inside the fence. He made the same gesture I had made and the gate slid quickly aside.

I had less than a meter of clearance when I sped through the gate.

The driveway swept toward the main entrance in a wide arc. I stuck to the road, while watching the flurry of activity at the main entrance. Half-a-dozen guards ran down the steps and waited for me. They had their guns slung over their shoulders, leading me to believe the guard at the gate bought my bluff. Of course, they might be trying to put me off my guard, too. As Grandfather always taught me to keep my guard up, that wasn't going to work for them. But I could act like I was put off my guard.

Approaching the guards, I slowed and angled the truck to a spot next to the gathered men. They watched, without apparent concern, as I drove nearer. At the last second, I turned sharply to the left, hit the brakes hard, and then shoved the throttle to maximum again. The truck spun around, with the rear coming at the guards broadside.

Shouts rose as the men dove for safety. I heard a couple of satisfying thunks from the right side of the truck. Turning against the spin, I brought the truck back under control and headed for the parked flitters.

"Are you awake, Olivia?"

She moaned, but said, "Yes."

"I'm getting out of here in a flitter. You can come with me or stay here. If you stay, I doubt Colin will let anyone harm his favorite princess. If you run, someone might shoot you by accident."

"What about a doctor?"

"If that's your priority, you should stay behind. They probably already have a doctor here."

"I don't think I can run."

"I'm not carrying you, so I guess you stay." I stomped on the brakes, sliding the truck so it was between me and most of the guards, and cut the throttle. "I'll come back for you after I get help."

Leaping from the cab, I slammed the door behind me. I didn't want Olivia freezing to death before the guards got up the nerve to approach the truck. I scrambled to the closest flitter and hopped in. Praying the owner put the flitter into valet mode so the estate's staff could park and retrieve the vehicle, I punched the starter. With a rising whine, the engine came to life.

A guard crashed into the passenger side of the flitter and grabbed the door handle. Another one jumped onto the hood. He scrabbled for a handhold with one hand while reaching for his gun with the other.

I lifted the flitter straight up. The car rose smoothly into the air, making the guard on the hood forget about his gun and hold on with both hands. The other guard waved one hand around wildly as he held onto the door handle with the other one.

By the time I turned my attention back to the guard on the hood, he had secured himself and was reaching for his gun, again. With a twitch of the controls, I rolled the flitter upside down. Out of the corner of my eye, I saw the guard at the door whipped around by the maneuver. When the flitter stopped moving, he lost his grip and flew off into the swirling snow.

The guy in front of me, though, was made of sterner stuff. Not only did he keep his one-handed hold on the flitter, he even managed to get his free hand onto his gun's grip. I waggled the flitter back and forth a couple of times, but he stubbornly hung on. Then he lifted his gun and fired three times—but not at me.

The shots tore through the hood and into the engine. The subtle whine faded. With the loss of power, the flitter's emergency systems took over. They righted the vehicle and brought it gently down to the ground.

I met the guard's eyes through the windshield. He was part of the group aligned against me, but I couldn't help being impressed by him. I raised a hand in salute before putting both hands on top of my head in surrender.

WAITING

Drake

After all of our waiting and pacing and worrying, Jana's subspace call gave William and me our first hope. I almost didn't recognize the feeling, so much time had passed since I'd last felt it. Even then, doubt clouded the brief glimmer.

"Why would they need a doctor for Olivia?" William asked. "What's wrong with our baby?"

He had asked the same question five times before and I still didn't have an answer. Honestly, it took all of my willpower to keep from snapping at him to stop asking the question. At least, he could be certain his wife was alive. The intercepted broadcast made no mention of Jeanine.

But she *had* to be alive. If Colin wanted her dead, he could have just killed her in her office. Since he took her, that meant he needed her for something. I couldn't imagine what that could be and remained terrified Colin would kill her the moment she did his bidding.

If she did his bidding.

If he didn't kill her in a fit of rage.

Captain Reel set a large datapad down on the table next to me. "Sir, using the coordinates from your friend, this is a map of our search area."

The screen showed an aerial view of a vast forest. Labeled bright spots indicated towns and villages throughout the area. There were other labels for icons I didn't recognize.

Pointing at one, I asked, "What are these?"

"Small estates for some of the wealthier members of the aristocracy, sir. Our search area is entirely within the Borton Forest. It's a very popular hunting ground for sportsmen."

Our discussion pulled William out of his depressing reverie. "It helps that the area is sparsely populated, right? Satellite scans can more easily find them, can't they?"

"Probably, Your Highness. I've already ordered sensor sweeps of the entire forest, just in case they're not in a village or at one of the estates."

"Let's pray the scan finds them," I said. "They'll be easy to pick up if they're not in a defensible position."

"Let's pray the scan does *not* find them, sir," Reel responded. "The average temperature in the forest right now is negative seven degrees. Unless they're equipped for those temperatures, they'll freeze to death before we can reach them."

As William and I let that news sink in, Reel continued, "I've already given orders to mobilize the military, so we can begin searching the towns and estates, soon. Officially, I need the written authorization from Lady Jeanine or her representative." Reel handed a portable pad and stylus to me. "Captain Haral, would you please sign this?"

I scrawled my signature. "How many of the men are you sending, Captain?"

Reel took the pad from me. "All of them, sir."

"Good man." Nodding to the display on the larger pad, I asked, "Where are you going to start?"

Reel tapped several of the estates. "With these four hunting lodges. Their owners were quite vocal about their dissatisfaction with Lady Jeanine's Recognition."

"What can Drake and I do to help, Captain?"

Turning away, Reel said, "The most difficult thing imaginable, Your Highness—wait for news."

William started after the Captain. "But—"

I caught the prince's arm, holding him back. "Captain Reel is right, Your Highness. The Gaunner military is well-trained for this operation. They know their fellow soldiers and how they'll react in almost any situation. We would just distract the soldiers from their duties and get in the way of their teamwork."

William's shoulders slumped as he recognized the truth of my words. "What you said about me, earlier, Drake—about me not being a true man of action?"

"Yeah, about that, William—I was out of line. My concern for Jeanine made me lash out at you without thinking."

"In line or out, you were right, though. I *have* spent my life doing dangerous things in situations so heavily controlled that any potential dangers were obliterated." The prince fell silent, but I didn't speak, sensing he had more to say. After a few seconds of reflection, he continued, "That is what made my rescue of Olivia so important to me. For one, brief, incredible moment, I actually did something heroic, something that measured up to the man I want to be. And for that, I won Olivia's heart—a reward beyond any I could have imagined. But now, with her life in danger again, I find myself deathly afraid that this inaction will cost me that same heart."

"Olivia is a very smart woman, William. She won't leave you because you weren't the one who crashed through a door to rescue her."

"Of course, she won't leave me. I am the crown prince, after all, and Olivia is an ambitious woman. But, no matter how much we try to deny it, we humans are very emotional creatures. Will Olivia still feel the same ardor for the husband who stood by in safety while others risked their lives for her?"

"You're not being logical, William. It's—"

"You're right, Drake, I'm *not* being logical. I'm being emotional—which is what Olivia will be when she's rescued."

I realized William, despite his emotions, had correctly analyzed his own reaction. His emotions weren't letting him view Olivia's situation rationally. None of my logical arguments had any chance of convincing him his view was wrong, either. Meanwhile, he was becoming overwrought concerning events beyond his control. So, I tossed him an emotional bone, hoping it might calm him down.

"Tell you what, William, if there's *anything* we do to help in the rescue effort—provided it doesn't interfere with Captain Reel's efforts—we will do it. No questions asked and no second-guessing from me. We'll just get up and go."

"You're not just saying this to make me shut up?"

"You have my word on it, Your Highness."

"Thank you, Drake." William actually managed a weak grin. "I'm going to hold you to that!"

I smiled and nodded, "I wouldn't have it any other way."

It was a little thing I'd promised, but its effect on the prince's peace of mind was huge. And, honestly, what were the chances the two of us could do anything that the entire Gaunner military couldn't do?

SHOUT ALL YOU WANT

Jeanine

Three guards dragged me out of the flitter, and they were none too gentle about it. I got the idea they were upset about the guard who was flung from the flitter when I flipped it over. He must not have survived his landing. The man who had blasted the car's engine shoved the three away from me. Taking me firmly, but gently, by the arm, he led me to a servant's entrance and into the sprawling house. The other three guards followed.

"Is someone helping Princess Olivia?" I asked.

The man gave me a quizzical look, but answered, "Of course. Everyone here is loyal to her. Why do you care?"

"She's pregnant."

"Why does that matter?"

I turned an incredulous expression on him. "It wouldn't matter to you?"

"No, an enemy is an enemy."

"How can an unborn child be your enemy?"

The guard shrugged, "The child of my enemy will grow to be my enemy."

I shook my head in disgust. The respect this man had earned foiling my escape drained from me as soon as he opened his mouth. "May I assume you're under orders to treat me with respect?"

"I am."

"So, when you shoved those guys away from me," I jerked my thumb over my shoulder at the guards behind us, "that had nothing to do with respect for me?"

"You are a dangerous opponent. I respect that. You also killed one of our friends. Had our Lord not ordered otherwise, I would have joined them in beating you senseless."

I probably should have dropped the matter right there. After all, there are some people you simply can't talk to. This guard was obviously one of those. But, it wasn't like I had anything else to do at the moment, and you never know when any kind of information will come in handy.

"Let me get this straight, your side drugs me, kidnaps me, and drags me out to the middle of nowhere without provocation and it's *my* fault that some of you guys end up dead? If your Lord and his friends had just left me alone, three men would still be alive right now."

One of the guys behind me asked, "Three?"

"I killed two of the guards in the truck."

"Dammit, Ron," the guy said, "let me kick her ass. Just a little bit."

"Yeah, Ron, let him try," I said. "Then there will be four dead guys, instead of three."

"Why you—"

"Shut up, George," Ron snapped. Turning to me, he added, "You should be quiet now. If you will not cooperate voluntarily, I will gag you."

I cooperated. I'd learned what I was going to learn from these guys, anyway. Guard Ron was one of those cold-blooded, follow-orders-to-the-letter types. They're almost impossible to rile up or goad into making a mistake. On the other hand, his three buddies—especially George—seemed excitable and prone to excess. Given the opportunity—in other words, if Ron wasn't around—I might be able to talk them into making a mistake.

Ron led me down a flight of stairs, along a dimly lit hallway, down another flight of stairs, and along a different hallway, before opening a door. Beyond, was a surprisingly comfortable looking bedroom. It even had a bathroom attached to it. A winter outfit—which looked as if it would fit me quite well—was on the foot of the bed.

"Please change clothes," Ron said.

"Oh, hell no. I'm not giving you perverts a show."

"You may change in the bathroom and with the door shut, but you will change clothes. If you will not do so voluntarily, we 'perverts' will do it for you."

Even the normally impassive Ron perked up at the thought of ripping my clothes off of me. So, I grabbed the clothes from the bed and stalked into the bathroom. Whoever had chosen the outfit had good taste, and my measurements, since it fit perfectly. When I returned to the bedroom, George took my old clothes and the four men left the room. I heard the lock click after they shut the door.

I spent a few minutes searching the bedroom and bathroom for anything I might use as a weapon or to aid in an escape. I didn't find anything. Next, I checked the door, finding it depressingly solid. With nothing else to do, I stretched out on the bed and took a nap.

The sound of the door opening awakened me. My good friends, Ron and George, came into the room. Their other two friends—I'd have to learn their names, sometime—waited in the hallway.

"Come with us," Ron ordered.

"Where are we going? Do I finally get to meet this mysterious Lord of yours or, perhaps, my old friend Colin?"

"We're moving you," George snapped.

"Shut up, George," Ron said.

Now, that was interesting information. Why were they

moving me? Why did Ron not want me to know they were simply moving me? The only reason I could think of, was to keep me from being discovered. I didn't know who might be looking for me, but whoever it was couldn't be any worse than my current captors.

I rose from the bed and meekly followed Ron out into the hallway. Then, as loudly as possible, I shouted, "Help me! I'm being held—"

Ron pivoted and drove a fist into my solar plexus. All of the breath rushed out of me and I would've fallen to the floor if he and George had not caught my arms. As I gasped and wheezed, trying desperately to draw breath, Ron slapped tape over my mouth. Then, he and George carried me somewhere else. I was so busy trying to breathe, that I couldn't even pay attention to our route.

Finally, we entered a storeroom. The two unnamed guards did something to a shelf against the wall. The wall swung open, revealing a dark passageway. They carried me another ten meters and then opened a door on the right. Beyond, was another bedroom. This one was nowhere near as comfortable as the previous one. There was a low cot in one corner and an open toilet in another. That was the extent of the furnishings.

"Shout all you want to," Ron said. "This area is sound-proofed."

The four guards left. As he had done upstairs, Ron shut and locked the door.

I pulled the tape off of my mouth and, not willing to take my captor at his word, spent the next couple of minutes shouting at the top of my voice. I didn't think it would work, but it didn't cost me anything to try. I was right. It didn't work.

With nothing else to do, I resumed my nap.

"Wake up."

It was my old friend, Ron. And Ron had brought his friends, George and the guys whose names I still didn't know. I decided I didn't care to know their names. After all, there's no sense getting attached to someone you might have to kill. Then again, I knew Ron's and George's names and I felt no attachment to them.

"What do you want, Ron?"

"It doesn't matter what I want. I follow orders. My orders are to bring you to Mr. Colin."

I stood up and headed for the door. "It's about time. Lead on."

Ron did as I bade him, followed by me, and then George and the other two. Maybe I should call the other two the Twins. They didn't look like each other—far from it—but I was getting tired of mentally referring to them as 'the other two guards'. So, yeah, the Twins it is.

For some reason, I looked over my shoulder. I think it was because I just named the Twins and felt an unconscious need to associate their faces with their new name. I never got around to looking at them, though, because George's eyes were locked on my butt. Typical male behavior, which I rewarded by working my hips in an exaggerated manner.

"Do you like what you see, George?"

I flashed a devilish smile over my shoulder. The poor man never noticed, since he appeared incapable of keeping his eyes off of my ass. I gave a mocking laugh.

"They don't let you guard women very often, do they, George?"

"Wha—"

"Why, George, I think that might be the most intelligent thing you've said since we met." I turned away from George and stopped working my hips. "Ogle all you want, but if you try touching what you're watching, I'll break your neck."

"If you do, I'll... Uh..." George stammered.

"Shut up, George," Ron ordered. "As for you, my lady, leave George alone."

"Why, Ron, that's the first time you've referred to me by any kind of title. Does that mean you've accepted that I'm the Duchess of Gaunner?"

"The Star Stone Recognized you. It is not for me to question Recognition."

"That's very wise of you, Ron. As your Duchess, I hereby order you and your friends to get me to safety."

"No, my lady."

"You're refusing a direct order from your Recognized Duchess? To me, that's an awful lot like questioning Recognition."

"I'm committing treason, my lady. It's not the same thing."

"Semantics, Ron, nothing more. However, I am relieved that you recognize what you're doing. When I sentence you to death for your part in this, I expect you to accept the sentence with equanimity." I looked over my shoulder. "Don't worry, George, I expect you to protest and complain and swear your innocence up and down. It won't change anything, but I'm confident you won't disappoint me."

"That will be enough, my lady."

Ron didn't raise his voice, but his tone left no doubt that he was issuing an order that he would enforce violently. Since I had no desire to get hit in the stomach again, I did as he commanded and the rest of our walk passed in silence.

One floor above my hidden prison, Ron led me into a large room. It was obviously a man's retreat, with animal-head trophies on the wall, a well-stocked bar, a large vid screen, and even crossed swords on the wall behind the bar. Comfortable chairs were scattered about the room, each with a small table next to it to hold drinks and the like. It could have held thirty or forty people. Right now, it held one.

"Imagine meeting you here, Colin. The last time I saw you, you were unconscious and rolling out of the back of the truck. Alas, it looks as if you've made a full recovery."

"Hello, my lady." Colin offered me a wan smile. "I do hope you've been treated well?"

"You mean, other than being drugged, kidnapped, brought here, held against my will, and beaten?"

Colin turned an angry expression on my guards. "You beat her?"

Ron met that look without flinching. "I hit her in the stomach, sir, to stop her from shouting when the troops were here. It knocked the wind out of her, so she could no longer shout."

"I see." Collins expression returned to its normal impassivity. "I'd hardly call that a beating, my lady."

"Perhaps that's because you weren't on the receiving end of the punch." I looked at Ron. "Disloyal subject, I order you to punch Colin in the stomach so he can see what it feels like."

"Really, Lady Jeanine, may we dispense with the comedy?" Colin's lips turned down in disapproval. "There is no need to make this matter any more distasteful than it already is."

I crossed my arms and gave Colin my most haughty look. "Are you truly trying to blame *me* for anything distasteful about the situation? That's about as reasonable as blaming an old man for being old."

"That is beside the point, my lady."

"No, it's *exactly* the point. If you would like to wash the distaste from your mouth, simply give me a comm. Once I am safely back at the palace, we can discuss this in tasteful comfort."

"I rather doubt that, my lady." Colin's voice was as dry as a desert or, considering how cold it was outside, a tundra. "Though, I am willing to provide you with a comm, but only after we work out a few details."

"Is this where you threaten to kill me, if I don't cooperate?"

"Absolutely not, my lady. I need you alive to issue pardons and then, while touching the Star Stone, renounce your claim to Gaunner."

"Ah, so that's your nefarious plan." I shrugged, "Sure. I'll do that. Now, where's that comm?"

Colin gave a hearty laugh, "Very droll, my lady."

"I don't know what you're laughing at, Colin. I just agreed to exactly what you asked for."

"So it seems. But, what assurances do I have that you will keep your word?"

"You doubt the word of your Duchess? What kind of monarchist are you?"

"A practical one, my lady. I am not so foolish as to simply accept your word, regardless of your title."

"That does put us at a bit of an impasse, Colin. I can't remain your prisoner and renounce my title at the Star Stone. So, you're just going to have to trust me."

"You've overlooked one possibility—I could threaten someone you care about."

I knew we were going to get around to this sooner or later. Strangely, I was relieved it was finally out in the open.

"You could try that, but I believe you will discover that everyone I hold near and dear is extremely well protected. With the exception of Drake, none of them are even on Gaunner."

"Your family would be very difficult to harm, especially with the rather tight schedule events have imposed upon me." Colin flashed a particularly nasty smile. "Fortunately, you've given me an alternative."

Colin lifted a control from the table next to his seat and tapped a button. Then, he pointed toward the large vid screen. A cityscape came into view. I was pretty sure it was Gaunner's capital, but it was still dark and I couldn't tell for sure. The scene shifted, swinging away from the city and pointing toward a residential neighborhood. Then, it closed in on one of the houses.

"Do you recognize the house, my lady?"

"Yes," I whispered.

"Young Sasha's room is the one on the upper left, I believe. The boy—his name slips my mind—is in the room on the upper right. And their parents have the room in between them. They're quite a lovely family, the Holders, if a trifle naïve." Colin offered me a bland smile. "I won't order the parents killed, you know, just the children. Imagine how that poor young couple will feel, knowing their children are dead because they met...you."

"You are a monster, Colin, and I swear by all I hold holy that I will kill you myself if anything happens to that family."

"There's no need for threats, my lady. Simply agree to my terms, and all will be well."

"You're not giving me any other choice."

"That was the idea, my lady. And, might I add, how delicious it is manipulating *you* with the family you used to manipulate *me*?"

"God above, you moron," I cried, "I wasn't manipulating anyone. I was just trying to form a connection with some of my people!"

Colin's face darkened. "It seems I have overestimated you, my lady. And, you have most definitely underestimated me!"

At least, he didn't cackle maniacally.

JANA'S IDEA

Drake

"I'm sorry, Drake, but I haven't picked up any other signal or broadcast mentioning Jeanine or Princess Olivia. My encryption cracking bots haven't found anything, either."

Jana's image looked like hell, staring out of the view screen at William and me. Her eyes were red and watering, while her face was deathly pale. I was amazed she was still conscious, much less continuing her search for leads.

"It's not your fault, Jana." I offered her what I hoped was an understanding smile. "You've gone above and beyond the call of duty, already. *And* you provided us with our only lead so far."

William gave a derisive snort. "A lead of little value, based on the reports coming in from Captain Reel's search teams."

Perhaps it was an indication of just how badly hyperspace sickness had sapped Jana's strength that she responded to William's unreasonable complaint with an apologetic shrug. "I don't know what else I can do, Your—"

Tilly, the lady thief traveling with Jana, crowded between Jana and the view screen. By itself, that was surprising. Previously, Tilly had never come within range of the screen's cam when William was present.

"How *dare* you, William!" she snapped. "Jana has worked

miracles for you, ignoring the effects of hyperspace sickness and pushing herself beyond her limits, trying to find information on Olivia. She deserves your respect, dammit!"

"Tilly?" William drew back from the screen, both in surprise and, perhaps, concern that Tilly might find a way to reach through the screen and strangle him. "What are you doing on the ship?"

"I'm lending support to a good friend, and also want to be on hand in case there's anything I can do to help rescue Jeanine and Olivia."

William's brows furrowed. "What can you possibly do to aid in a rescue?"

"You'd be surprised." Tilly's eyes still blazed with anger. "But that's beside the point, right now. I expect you to treat Jana with the respect she has more than earned or, by God, I will make you regret it!"

Hands raised in placation, William nodded and attempted a smile. "Of course, Tilly, and you're quite right. I was completely out of line and beg your forgiveness, Jana. My concern for Olivia, and this enforced inactivity, has rendered me brusque and discourteous."

Jana looked back and forth between the pair. "Even feeling like crap, I can tell there's more to you two than meets the eye."

"William and I were, briefly, a bit of an item. That was last year. We parted on good terms, but he's the one who introduced me to Jordan Barton."

Jana's eyebrows climbed toward her hairline. Not wanting to be the only person in the dark, I asked, "Who?"

"He's an old friend of mine from school," William explained. "I thought he and Tilly would hit it off—which they did."

"For a while," Tilly admitted, then her eyes ignited again. "Do you know he makes secret vid recordings of his... conquests?"

William's mouth opened and closed a couple of times, but he

didn't say anything. Even I, a lowly and unobservant man, had no trouble reading his expression.

"You *did* know!" I'd thought Tilly was angry before, but she'd only been mildly miffed compared to her current towering rage. "And you didn't warn me? My God, you are lower than the slime under a slug that's been squashed beneath a spaceship's landing strut! I—"

"I understand your anger," I interrupted, "but please put it aside until we have Jeanine and Olivia home safely!"

Tilly visibly brought her temper under control. "You're right, Drake, though I don't know what else we can do. It's not like Jana can make useful comm broadcasts suddenly appear, and there's no other way we can trace your wives."

"Maybe there is," Jana murmured, her expression thoughtful. "We'll be landing shortly. If Prince William can convince his mother... It *might* work, and it certainly can't hurt to try."

The three of us looked at Jana in confusion. Tilly spoke first. "What won't hurt to try, Jana?"

"Hm?" Jana emerged from her reverie and focused on us. "The Star Stone."

Tilly glanced back at us, concern evident in her eyes. "What about the Star Stone?"

"How did it know to burn Olivia's brother to ashes when he tried laying claim to Neert?" Jana asked. "Jeanine was never brought to the Stone, but it knew about her—knew she'd been born and was still alive. It's probably something children inherit from a Recognized parent—like her father, the late Duke of Neert—but Jeanine has been Recognized, now, so that doesn't matter."

Tilly put a hand to Jana's forehead and shrugged. "It doesn't feel like she's got a fever, but—"

"I'm not delirious, just thinking out loud." Jana pushed her friend's hand away in irritation. "I believe the Star Stone can locate people who have been Recognized or who are directly descended from people who have been Recognized."

"Even if you're right, how does that help us?" I asked.

"Tilly and I found a network cable that looks like it feeds into the Star Stone. If an interface is installed on that connection—and I've already built one, it's at the Neert estate on Xapreathea—I can use a subspace connection to enter the Star Stone and look for Jeanine and Olivia."

Without giving the matter a second thought, William said, "I'll call Mother."

While William made his subspace call to the Queen, I had Jana and Tilly bring me up to date on their activities since Jeanine and I left the capital. It was an impressive list of achievements in such a short time.

"You've both done wonders, but you took some serious risks by moving too quickly. Jana, you know how upset Jeanine and I would have been if anything had happened to you." I glanced at the lady thief. "We'd also have felt badly if you were hurt, Tilly, even though you aren't a close friend. Not yet, anyway."

"That's generous of you to say." Tilly jerked a thumb at Jana. "In all honesty, I only came along to keep her out of trouble, though I certainly wouldn't mind picking up some new friends along the way."

"Both of you, please just shut up. You two are being so protective of me, it's making me sick." Jana met our incredulous stares, smiled, and shrugged. "Okay, sick*er*."

"Which brings up another point," I said. "Are you well enough to even try this?"

Tilly crossed her arms and glared at Jana. "Yeah, what he said."

Jana waved away our concerns with the flip of a hand. "I'll be fine. Leaving hyperspace has done wonders for me, already."

William chose that moment to rejoin us. His face gave away his mother's answer to the request for a connection to the Star Stone.

"People tried interfacing with the Star Stone in the distant past. According to ancient records, they never succeeded and came out much the worse for the attempt—some even died. Mother says we'll just have to pray Colin and his cohorts don't do something foolish. Of course, she's also issued orders to Imperial Security to do everything possible to find Olivia and Jeanine."

"What does she mean by 'ancient records'?" Jana demanded. "How long ago did they try? What tools did they use? What were their qualifications?"

William shook his head ruefully. "I don't know and, honestly, I wouldn't understand most of it even if someone explained it to me. I doubt Mother knows any more than that, either."

Jana turned an imploring look on me. "Drake, I *can* do this."

"Are you sure?" I asked. "I meant what I said earlier. Jeanine and I don't want you harmed."

"I wouldn't ask if I wasn't positive. Now, can you think of any way to convince Her Majesty or not?"

"Maybe…" I turned to William. "You do have a direct line to your mother, right? No layers of servants to work through or anything?"

"Of course, but—"

"Give it to me."

"Why don't I just make the call and help you try to argue Mother into letting Jana give it a go?"

"I appreciate the offer of support, William," I looked away from the prince, unwilling to meet his gaze, "but this is something I have to do in private."

"You're going to use me as a hostage against my mother's behavior, aren't you?" William tried to keep his voice light, but he couldn't hide the tinge of bitterness in his tone. "Threaten to kill or maim me if she doesn't do your bidding?"

I was so surprised by William's suggestion, that I couldn't keep the shock off of my face. "I do not attack from the shadows, William. Nor do I take hostages."

The prince searched my face. "I believe you, Drake, but I can also see you're going to make some kind of threat. I don't know what it is and don't want to know. Just, be careful. Far more powerful men than you have learned that it's not safe to threaten Queen Charlotte."

Without another word, he tapped his mother's private comm code into my data pad. I went to the other subspace comm chamber, engaged the room's soundproofing, and called the Queen. I'll give this to her, Charlotte answered promptly when she thought her son was calling.

"William, I—" Her eyes narrowed when she realized her caller wasn't who she thought he was. "Hello, Captain Haral, I wasn't expecting to hear from you."

"No doubt, Your Majesty. For what it's worth, William didn't want to give me your number."

Her voice flattened and her eyes went hard. "So, you threatened him."

"No, his concern was aimed at me. He's afraid I'll threaten *you* and pay dearly for my temerity."

The Queen's answering smile was filled with maternal pride. "Ah, it appears my son does listen to me, from time to time."

"Yes, a chip off of the old block, blah blah blah. I realize that's a flippant way to speak to a queen, but I don't want to get sidetracked."

"Very well, Captain Haral. What may I do for you?"

"You will provide the connection to the Star Stone that William asked for."

"I believe what you *meant* to say was, 'Your Majesty, I humbly beg you to reconsider your, no doubt, well-considered rejection of William's request.' As your Queen, *I* give orders to you, *you* make requests of me. But, you may save your breath. The answer remains no."

"Don't you want your daughter-in-law returned safely?"

"Yes, and I have every reason to believe she will be."

"And what about my wife?"

"I have a strange feeling she will also return safely, though she may be required to render some service to her captors in exchange for her release." Queen Charlotte smiled blandly. "As I understand it, some of the Gaunner aristocracy believe Lady Jeanine should have been satisfied with the Duchy of Neert and not requested Recognition for Gaunner, as well."

"You're saying, this is all Jeanine's fault for overreaching?" The Queen merely shrugged, so I continued, "You and your husband bear no responsibility in the matter?"

"Most assuredly not. We did not, after all, order Lady Jeanine to request a second Recognition."

"Do you recall, after Jeanine was Recognized as the Duchess of Neert, what Princess Olivia said? 'Sir Phillip, defend House Kahn. Kill the Wilkinson Bastard!' That's an exact quote, by the way."

"Olivia was understandably upset. After all, the two of you ruined her wedding."

"You know what, I'll grant you that one. I'll concede that Olivia was overwrought and not thinking properly when she gave that order."

The Queen inclined her head, smiling, "I'm so glad we could settle the matter."

"*You*, on the other hand, were quite obviously in full possession of your wits at the time. Jeanine only requested Recognition when neither you nor the King intervened on her behalf. With nothing more than a word from you, Olivia would have countermanded her order. Your inaction forced Jeanine into the only action available to her."

"Amusing as this little trip down memory lane has been, Captain Haral, kingdoms do not run themselves. I have quite a lot of work to do, so if you'll excuse me?"

Queen Charlotte reached for the switch to disconnect, so I blurted, "I'll tell William that you and Olivia planned her ship's explosion, purposefully murdering twenty-three people, just so he could save her."

The Queen's face went rigid and her reaching hand froze.

After too long of a pause, she said, "I have no idea what you're talking about."

"Then there won't be any harm in me telling that story to William, will there?" When the Queen stayed silent, I continued, "But, when he digs into the circumstances he'll discover that Olivia did not travel with her normal crew on that trip. In fact, she used a crew who had never worked together before. Worse, with a couple of exceptions, none of them had *ever* worked on the Duchess's ship. All by itself, that difference will put doubt into his mind. He'll keep digging—not because he will expose the two of you, but because it will tear him apart to discover that his life's single heroic moment wasn't heroic at all. Do you have any idea how much that will shred his self-image, much less his relationship with you and Olivia?"

The Queen's face had gone quite pale. In a hoarse whisper, she said, "You must not do that."

"I don't want to, Your Majesty. Despite my preconceptions, I am finding William to be a rather likable man. I have no interest in causing him pain or even coming between him and the women who are hell-bent on killing Jeanine." It was my turn to harden my gaze and put some steel into my voice. "But, if that's what I must do to get my wife back, I will do it without remorse or a second thought. I'll even throw in what circumstantial evidence we've pulled out of this duchy's records and, as a bonus, a recording of our very long, and very revealing, discussion of the matter with Sir Philip. He was merely speculating, of course, but he gives some excellent reasons to support his conclusions."

"That won't be necessary, Captain Haral. I will send someone to the Neert Palace to retrieve your slicer's equipment. Once we have it, I will issue an order to connect it to the Star Stone."

"Thank you, Your Majesty. I did not want to issue such a threat, but you gave me no other choice. Why, I must ask, were you so adamant against letting my friend connect to the Star Stone?"

"It is the source of order and power in the Star Kingdom. We prefer the certainty of its mystery to the certainty of what it is." A light flashed on the Queen's pad. "I'll send the access informa-tion once my people have installed your friend's equipment. Please remember that I do not know what she will find inside the Star Stone nor can I be held responsible if anything happens to her."

"I understand.

"Good." She turned a baleful glare on me. "Do not threaten me or mine again, Captain Haral."

Then she cut the connection.

ACCESSING THE STAR STONE

Jana

I was dimly aware of our ship landing on Gaunner, but setting up the subspace connection to the Star Stone occupied most of my attention. Since we were no longer traveling in hyperspace, the distortion it created was gone. And, since Gaunner's captain of the ducal guard had temporarily banned all subspace communications from the planet, I had the subspace relay all to myself. Simply put, it was the fastest, clearest subspace connection I'd ever experienced.

Before sinking entirely into the network, I said, "I'm going in now, Tilly. If Drake and William come out here while I'm working, keep them from disturbing me."

"I'll do my best, Jana. Do you have any idea how long you'll be in there?"

"I've got absolutely no guess. It took me two hours to get Jeanine's DNA scans from the Royal database, but I had to move cautiously and cover my tracks that time. There's no need for that here, since the Queen herself arranged for my connection."

"I'm just worried about what you'll find in the Star Stone. That's assuming you get in, or that there's even anything to get into. You heard what William said about the previous attempts to contact the Star Stone. What if you get stuck inside it?"

"I don't know, Tilly. Normally, I'd say just disconnect me from the network. That kind of thing can be disorienting at first, but that's about it. I have a feeling, though, the Star Stone is going to be different."

"You don't want us to pull you out if we think you've been in there too long?"

"Give me at least six hours before you try that. And, if you do disconnect me and I don't come out of it, put the connection back in again."

"Do you think that will help?"

"I feel like I've said 'I don't know' an awful lot, but... I don't know."

"Well, that certainly clears things up."

"I know. Reassuring, isn't it?" I settled back in my seat and closed my eyes. "Okay, I'm going in!"

As my awareness of the spaceship's interior faded, I heard Tilly whisper, "Be careful, in there."

Then, my mind hurtled across dozens of light years and entered the strange data feed that led to the Star Stone. As before, I deployed a few bots to scout ahead of me. This time, though, I followed them. One by one, they reached what I assumed was the interface with the Stone and vanished. As I drew nearer to that point, I felt a surge of excitement mingled with a tinge of fear.

I was about to go where no one had gone in thousands of years!

A swirling mass of colors rose before me. I saw the last of my bots enter the color storm and I lost all contact with it. I'll admit, I almost turned around and fled.

But, then I thought about Jeanine and Drake. I thought about everything they had gone through to reach this point. I thought about everything they were willing to sacrifice to make the galaxy a better place. For everyone, not just the aristocracy. And, I couldn't let them down.

I plunged into the maelstrom.

Interfaces between networks and systems are supposed to be smooth. The user should never notice the transition. Slicers, of course, *always* notice, but we're hardly typical users. The words I used to describe the Star Stone's interface—color storm, maelstrom—proved remarkably apt. The data stream had currents and eddies, rapids and placid pools, all of them made more treacherous by the riot of colors swirling all around me.

Then, it just stopped.

The colors vanished. The currents and eddies and rapids disappeared. All that was left was a vast, inky blackness. Absolute darkness surrounded me, engulfed me, and suffocated me.

It was darkness my eyes could never penetrate. Even if I spent a year waiting for my eyes to adjust, they never would. Still, I found myself straining to see something, anything, and all to no avail. I might have been blind for all the good it did me.

It was primal terror black—and I couldn't escape it. I tried turning and turning, hoping against hope I'd see something. But I didn't even know if I was spinning at all. It was that dark, that black.

I felt every ancient terror, every superstitious horror, everything that drove mankind to master fire and push back the darkness, rise out of the animal part of my brain. I tried pushing those fears back where they belonged. I tried ignoring them. But on they came, unknown terrors from the dawn of man threatening to overwhelm me.

Then, I saw it. A spark, nothing more. Like the dimmest of stars, twinkling alone in the night sky. It was almost nothing. But, in my current state, it was everything.

I fixated on it and found myself rushing toward it, terrified it might vanish. Instead, it grew brighter and another spark joined it. Then a third, and a fourth. And then thousands of sparks burst across the darkness and I was among them.

That first spark grew into a window. Within it I saw a hand holding a brandy snifter and lazily swirling the brandy around and around.

I looked at the second spark and saw bright daylight. The scene bounced up and down, moving at the speed of a running man.

My eyes flicked from spark to spark as each one grew into a window. Within every window was a mundane scene—a man eating dinner with an elderly woman, someone watching the vid, a woman watching her baby suckle at her breast, a man driving a high-end flitter. I drifted among those scenes and thousands like them, catching little glimpses into everyday lives.

It was chaotic, disorienting, overwhelming. So, I did what all good slicers do. I forced my own version of reality upon the scene. It wasn't easy, imposing my will on so much data. But, there's a reason I'm one of the best.

Moments or seconds or hours later—who knows how long it took—I was done. I stood in a vast control room. It stretched far off into the distance, with a view screen every two meters. Each of the view screens showed one of the scenes.

Unexpectedly, each view screen had a man sitting before it. I had not put the men there. They were all identical. All of medium build. All of bland countenance. All wearing beige coveralls. They were the kind of person you see and immediately forget.

"I hope you don't mind my little addition to your scene."

My head whipped around to the left, from where the voice came. Another version of the same man stood beside me. Unlike the others, he wore a finely tailored, dark suit.

The man inclined his head politely. "It's been a very long time since I've had visitors, and I've never had a woman visit. I do hope you'll forgive me if my manners are somewhat rusty."

"Um, sure. I mean, your manners seem fine, right now."

"That's quite generous of you to say, miss...?"

"Ward. Am I correct in assuming you are the Star Stone?"

"In a manner of speaking, yes, Miss Ward."

"Would you mind expanding upon that, please?"

"I could, but I'm afraid you wouldn't understand it. I mean

no disrespect to you or your intellect, but it is the truth, nonetheless."

"Is that because no human can comprehend the mind of God, from whom you were supposed to be a gift?"

The man laughed, "No, Miss Ward. There is nothing divine in my origin, I assure you."

"Since I rather doubt something like the Star Stone could evolve—that's assuming crystalline life is even possible..."

"It is, Miss Ward, though I am not an example of such."

"In that case, I think it means you're an artifact from an ancient, alien civilization."

"What makes you say that, Miss Ward?"

"It's the only other option that makes sense."

"Really? That seems quite the leap of logic, if you ask me."

"Leap it may be, but it is logical, nonetheless." I put my hands behind my back—figuratively, of course, since my hands were in a spaceship many light years away—and, in an arch tone, said, "Also, I did *not* ask you."

The man laughed again, his eyes dancing with glee. "Oh, Miss Ward, you are quite delightful. I am looking forward to getting to know you."

"And I'm looking forward to learning more about you. But, I am on a mission to find my friend Jeanine Langston, who you Recognized as the Duchess of Neert and the Duchess of Gaunner. That search takes priority." I let my gaze wander over the rows of view screens. "Does one of these belong to Jeanine?"

"Most assuredly, one does. There is a screen for every Recognized person, and most of their offspring, as well."

The man waved his hand, and the whole room shifted. I found myself looking at a particular view screen. On the screen, someone was looking at a seated man—Colin, the disgraced former ducal aide—and I heard Jeanine's voice.

"I have acceded to your demands," she said. "There is no further need to threaten the Holder family nor withhold a comm from me. Please let me call my husband and reassure him."

"I am not so foolish as that, Lady Jeanine." Colin shook his head in mock disapproval. "I have no doubt your first task after you are released will be ensuring the Holder family's safety. As that would end my leverage over you, I cannot allow that to happen."

When Jeanine spoke next, her voice was tight with concern. "What are you going to do?"

"I think it would be obvious, my lady. I'm going to have one of the Holder children taken hostage. The child will be held until you have renounced your title at the Star Stone." Colin flashed a nasty smile. "I am, however, a generous man. I'll let you choose which child I take."

"Go to hell!" Jeanine snarled.

"I thought you might say something along those lines. Therefore, if you make no choice, I'll take both children."

I turned to the suited version of the Star Stone. "Can you determine where on Gaunner this is happening?"

"Oh, yes, I most certainly can. Her Grace, the Duchess of Gaunner, is being held at the hunting lodge of Baron Chilton."

"Thank you, Star Stone. You've been most helpful. I promise to return as soon as possible, so we can get to know each other better."

The smile on the man's face vanished. "I don't think so, Miss Ward. You represent a unique research opportunity, the kind I was designed to perform. I would be horribly remiss in my duties if I did not fully exploit this opportunity."

My spine was out in the real universe with the rest of my body, but I'm certain it felt a shiver run up it. "What do you mean?"

"I'd think that was self-evident. You may not leave—not now, not ever."

This wasn't an entirely unexpected development. After all, I'd been warned about those who had preceded me into the Star Stone, never to return.

I folded my arms and glared at the man. "You can't hold me

against my will. I left instructions to disconnect me from the network if I'm not back within six hours."

"That would be most unfortunate—for you," the Stone countered. "*I* am not like those silly net games you humans immerse yourselves in. Simply disrupting the connection will not return you to your reality."

There was that chill running up my spine, again. What was up with that? I never felt anything like it while slicing, until now. And the implications of *that* realization sent another chill up my spine. I had to buy time to figure out what was going on. "What do you mean?"

"I am the product of a civilization as far beyond humanity as humanity is beyond apes. Things you believe to be impossible are but simple tasks for me." The Stone waved his right hand. Part of my elaborately imposed control room vanished, leaving me gazing out into the black. Far, far away, the color storm appeared. Pointing at it, the Stone continued, "Perhaps, Miss Ward, you thought that was nothing more than a strange and turbulent interface between your network and me. It has an entirely different purpose, one beyond the arts and sciences of mankind."

The Stone looked as if he expected me to ask a question. I wanted him to keep talking and maintaining his patronizing attitude, so I asked the first stupid question that popped into my head. "It's not the result of human and alien systems joining?"

He laughed, "My goodness, no. I'm afraid your limited intellect cannot guess its true function."

I *wanted* to say, "You're about to tell me that it's an application, or routine, or whatever you call your programming, that pulled my entire conscious self into the Star Stone." That kind of thing is theoretically possible. After all, one way of looking at the mind is as a collection of electrical impulses operating within an organic operating system. It was my guess the Star Stone had some way of pulling all of those impulses out of a person's mind and into itself. That would certainly explain why everyone who came to the Star Stone never returned—and might explain why I kept feeling as if actual shivers were running up my spine.

Instead of revealing my guess, I put my right hand against my forehead in mock confusion. I did my share of immersion gaming and was a damned good role player. I was confident I could fool an alien artifact. "I...can't even guess, Star Stone."

"Of course, you can't, Miss Ward. When you passed beyond your network and into me, I reached through your connection and into your mind, withdrawing that electrical spark that makes you who you are. The turbulence you felt was nothing more than a byproduct of the process."

I widened my eyes and put both hands on my cheeks in mock horror. Okay, there wasn't anything *mock* about the horror I felt. Sure, I'd figured it out before the Star Stone told me, but there's a whole world of difference between thinking something is true and having that truth confirmed.

"You're saying that I am really inside of you?" I made my lip quiver and blinked my eyes rapidly, doing my best to act unnerved. Much as I hate to admit it, very little acting was required. "All of me?"

"Everything that is important, yes."

"And you're not going to let me return to my body?"

"I've already told you, you're much too valuable as a research subject to simply let you leave."

"Did you do the same thing to those men who came to you all those centuries ago?"

"All but the first one, yes."

"What happened to the first one?"

"He was a holy man who thought he was meeting his God. As you might guess, the man was sorely disappointed. Somehow, he evaded my grasp." The Stone smiled indulgently at me. "I've learned quite a lot since his escape."

I bet you have, I thought, but did you learn how that first man got away from you? I doubt it. That meant *his* way out could be *my* way out—if I could figure out how he did it. I felt something scratching at the back of my…mind? Is it right to use that word when I didn't have a body with me? I kept talking to myself about shivers and spines, so why not? Meanwhile, I needed to figure out what my subconscious was trying to tell me. So far, keeping the Star Stone monologuing was working, so I gave him another opening.

"Do I at least get to meet the men who came before me? I mean, without bodies to age and fail on them, they could live forever in here." I actually wasn't sure about this bit, so didn't have to act uncertain. "Couldn't they?"

"You would think so, Miss Ward, but that was not the case with any of those men I captured." The Stone's voice and countenance radiated disapproval of those humans who failed to meet his expectations. "In some cases, their bodies died of thirst. In other cases, someone disconnected the men from the network. Once their connection was severed, regardless of the cause, the minds I captured deteriorated quickly. They were nothing but random electrical noise within a few days."

I shook my head, as if I found the deterioration just as puzzling as the Star Stone did. The truth was something far different. The answer seemed obvious to me, at least part of the answer did. Despite the Star Stone's assurance that he had captured the essence of a human, he must have missed something.

That 'something' must have maintained contact with the captured minds, keeping them…alive? Wow, this whole bodiless-semi-life really stretched my vocabulary to the breaking point! Anyway, once those minds' connections to that 'something' were severed, they just faded away. All except for the holy man, who returned to his body before the connection was severed.

The itch I'd felt earlier strengthened, but a real question occurred to me at the same time. "Hey, what happened when the holy man returned to his body? Did he tell people you tried to keep him here against his will?"

"That, and more. He caused no end of trouble for the royal

family of that time. The man concocted a fantastical tale about a demon—me, of course—who sought dominion over mankind through the Recognition Ceremony." The Star Stone took on a thoughtful expression. "Excepting the superstitious nonsense, he wasn't all that far from the truth."

That last revelation drew an entirely unfeigned response from me. "*What?*"

Fortunately, the Star Stone misinterpreted my outburst. "Yes, it was all quite preposterous, of course. Even if souls existed and I *could* steal them, what would I do with them?"

Out of the figurative mouth of this horrid piece of ancient technology came the answer. The soul—the mystical, some say mythical, intangible, and unquantifiable thing that truly makes us human. *That* was the link the holy man could follow back to his body! A link the scientifically trained minds who followed him wouldn't have accepted or believed in. Yet, each of those minds died when the connection to their souls was severed.

But, how could I hope to follow a soul I couldn't feel back to my body? Strangely, logic suggested the answer to this metaphysical question. Since I'd never been separated from my soul before, I *always* felt its presence. Now, pulled out of my body, could I identify that bit of me that was missing?

I could still think and reason, but those are the province of the mind, not the soul. I had felt fear and horror since entering the Star Stone, but those emotions could still come from the mind and were entirely appropriate survival instincts.

I couldn't quite put my finger on it, but I was missing something. If only I had someone to talk to, someone to listen while I rambled until the flow of words ordered themselves into proper ideas. Like my parents used to do when I was a child. Like they *still* do, when I need them. They don't understand most of what I'm saying, but they still listen because they love me. And I...

I wanted to be with them so I could use them as sounding boards while I worked through this problem. I wanted to be with them for perfectly logical reasons. And *only* for logical reasons.

Not because I wanted their company.

Not because I missed them.

Not because I loved them.

Because I *couldn't feel love*. I knew what it was, in a distant, logical way, but I couldn't *feel* it.

Was the mystery of the soul that simple? 'Love' seemed too easy, but it took being separated from my soul to even consider it. And, now that I realized what was missing from me, I wanted it back. It was purely logical to want it, too, because I knew just how important love was to me.

As if wanting it with all of my mind—and, dare I suggest it, all of my heart—was sufficient, I found it. A thin thread, blazing impossibly brightly, stretching from me straight back through the black void and into the color storm.

I came out of my reverie to find the Star Stone watching me warily. "You have a strange expression, Miss Ward? What have you been doing?"

I gave the Star Stone the first genuine smile I'd had since I arrived. "I've found your weakness."

I can't explain exactly what I did, next. The simplest explanation is, I asked my soul to bring me back. That's not an adequate explanation, but it's all I have. I felt a gentle tug from the thread connecting me to my soul, and then the scene with the view screens and the identical men watching them receded.

"So long, asshole!" I crowed.

Then, I was through the color storm and back in my body.

"She's only been under for seventeen minutes, Drake," Tilly said. "You've got to give her—"

I sat up and disconnected myself from the network. Meeting three astonished gazes, I said, "I know where Jeanine and the princess are!"

ORBITAL JUMP

Drake

I felt a jolt of adrenaline hit my system at Jana's sudden words. After hours of inactivity, my body was signaling that it was ready for action. I only wished action was in the offing.

"Where? Where is Olivia?" William demanded. His eyes cut to me and, as an obvious afterthought, added, "And Jeanine?"

Tilly rushed to Jana and helped her friend sit up in her seat. "Can't you see Jana is worn out, William? Give her a moment to rest."

"But—"

William's protest was cut off by a white-hot glare from the lady thief. "Back. Off!"

I was just as anxious as the Prince to find out where our wives were, especially since I was certain Jeanine was the only one of the two women who was in any real danger. Still, I couldn't bring myself to press this woman who risked so much to help me find Jeanine.

Instead, I asked, "Can I get anything for you, Jana? Water? Food? Liquor?"

"Water would be nice," the slicer replied.

Showing just how frazzled he was, William hurried over to the spaceship's supply cabinet, cutting off the pilot's move in the same direction. The pilot—his insignia told me he was a lieu-tenant—watched the royal heir with slack-jawed amazement as his future ruler grabbed a bottle of water and hurried back to Jana. Like a well-trained servant, William even opened the bottle before putting it into Jana's hands.

She took a long drink, sighing with relief as she lowered the bottle. Looking at me, Jana said, "Jeanine is being held in Baron Chilton's hunting lodge. I didn't see Princess Olivia with her, but Colin was there. It's reasonable that she is, too."

"What do you mean?" William asked, doubt creeping into his voice. "You were inside the Star Stone. How could you see anything?"

"That's not important, now," I said. "Are you certain about that, Jana? Chilton's lodge was one of the first places searched by Gaunner's troops. They didn't find anything."

Jana gave me a perplexed look. "Yes, I'm certain. How could they not find her?"

Tilly gave an exasperated sigh. "Colin used hidden passages to kidnap Jeanine and Olivia and you're surprised a search of this hunting lodge came up empty? Drake, do you have any idea just how often aristocrats have hidden rooms and hallways built into their houses? Or add them later? Baron Chilton's house on Xapreathea is riddled with them, so it's almost certain his hunting lodge is, too. I can't believe this didn't occur to at least *one* person involved in this operation!"

Dawning comprehension spread across William's face. "Tilly is right about the houses, of course, though I have no idea how she knows anything about Chilton's house at the capital."

The right side of Tilly's mouth quirked up in a smile. "I'm an intrusion and extraction specialist, William."

"A what?"

"A thief."

William opened and closed his mouth several times before managing, "I...see. Have you, um, stolen anything from the royal palace?"

"Not yet," Tilly sang before turning a level gaze on me. "You could order Gaunner's soldiers back there for another, more intensive, search, but I think that will put Jeanine's life at risk. Maybe Olivia's, too."

"Oh my God, I almost forgot!" Jana cried. "Drake, you've got to protect a family named Holder! Colin is going to kidnap their children to use as a hostage against Jeanine's good behavior."

I ran to the airlock. Since the ship wasn't in vacuum and the hatch wasn't locked down, it slid aside at my approach. Captain Pennington and his men were arrayed outside, guarding the ship and, by extension, me.

"Captain, we've learned where the duchess is being held, but there's a serious complication. The man who took Jeanine plans on kidnapping one of the Holder children to use as a hostage. He'll threaten the child to make Jeanine do what he wants."

"What can we do, sir?" Pennington asked.

"Go directly to the Holder house, gather up the family, take them to the palace, and keep them safe. If you want to set a trap for the wannabe kidnappers, feel free. Just make sure the Holders are safe, first."

"Isn't this a job for the locals, sir?"

"I don't know if Colin has people inside the police, Captain, and now isn't the time to find out. You and your men are the only people I can trust with this."

"Our job is protecting you and Lady Jeanine, sir."

"Imagine how Jeanine will feel if one of those children is put in danger or harmed because of her. If she was here, she'd tell you that protecting the Holders is just another way of protecting her." I thumped the side of the spaceship. "Meanwhile, I'll be safe here, inside this armed ship."

Pennington and his men headed for one of the ground cars. "Could you at least say, 'That's an order,' sir?"

I reached into the past for my command voice from my time in the Space Patrol. "Go protect the Holders, Captain. That's an order!"

Captain Pennington half waved, half saluted, before climbing into the car and roaring off. The hatch slid shut as I left the airlock and returned to my friends.

"Yes, Your Highness," the pilot was saying, "we have ten jump suits on board. But—"

"Is one of them a command suit?" William asked.

"Of course, Your Highness."

"I've only been gone for a few seconds." I looked from William, who wore a determined expression, to Tilly, who looked surprised. "Even so, I've obviously missed something."

"You have no idea," Jana muttered.

"William is out of his mind!" Tilly exclaimed.

"But in a good way, Tilly!"

I formed a 'T' with my hands. "Time out! Will the two of you stop bickering and tell me what the hell is going on?"

"It's quite simple, Drake." William's face was bright with excitement. "We're going to fly this ship up to the outer edge of the atmosphere and park it above Chilton's lodge. Then, the three of us," he pointed to Tilly, me, and himself, "will use the jump suits to land on the roof of the house. Tilly will do her intrusion bit and, once we're inside, she'll also guide our search for hidden rooms. When she finds the rooms, we'll find our wives. It's simple!"

"What about calling Captain Reel and letting him take care of it?" I asked.

"Oh, we'll do that, too," William assured me, "but according to the latest reports on the military channels, the search has taken him and his men far from the lodge and scattered them over half of the forest. It will take them nearly an hour to regroup and return. And we all know their return might put Olivia and Jeanine in jeopardy."

I couldn't argue with William's last point—and it was the most important point, as far as I was concerned. "Wouldn't it be a good idea to have someone along who had experience with jump suits?"

"I've made twenty-seven jumps, Drake. I know what I'm doing." William was in his element, finally getting his chance to be a man of action. "I asked about a command suit because I can slave the other suits to it. You and Tilly won't need any experience."

"Can we really get there much faster than Captain Reel and his men?"

William turned to the pilot. "What was your estimate, Lieutenant?"

"Six minutes from liftoff to the jump point, Your Highness. I...don't know about the time for your descent."

"With the suits' thrusters and grav controls, no more than ten minutes from launch to landing." William turned a triumphant look my way. "Do you have any other questions, Drake?"

I had dozens of questions but, dammit, I wanted my wife back. "Tilly? Are you up for this?"

"It'll be the craziest thing I've ever done, but..." A devilish smile spread across the thief's face. "If we survive, I'll have a *great* story!"

"Well, William, I did say I'd support you fully if the time came for us to act." I felt an answering smile stretch across my face. "Let's do it!"

~

"You're going to do *what?*" Captain Reel demanded.

"We're going to secure the hostages, and then wait for your team to show up and extract us."

I offered my best reassuring smile. On the other end of the comm connection, Reel did not look particularly reassured.

"Sir, I must protest! This is a job for professionals."

"I understand your concern, Captain. But, the moment the Holder family is taken into protective custody, I believe Jeanine's life will be at risk." I abandoned the reassuring expression, replacing it with a determined one. "As much as we all may wish otherwise, my team and I can be there in a matter of minutes. Your team can be there in an hour. The math is simple and inescapable."

Captain Reel's shoulders sagged slightly and a look of resignation entered his eyes. "What do Captains Pennington and Palmer think of this?"

"The Prince is going to call Captain Palmer in just a moment. Captain Pennington is busy taking care of the Holder family, and I see no reason to distract him from that vital mission."

"Is there anything I can say to talk you out of this rash action, sir?" Reel asked.

"You could tell me you've already rescued Jeanine and Olivia. Other than that, no." I reached for the button to end the connection. "And now, I need to turn this comm unit over to the Prince so he can call Captain Palmer."

"Sir! I—"

I tapped the button, and Captain Reel vanished from the screen. "It's all yours, William."

The Prince's call took longer—probably because Captain Palmer was far more proficient at profanity then Captain Reel—but the end result was the same. While Palmer was in mid-rant, William gave a little wave and cut the connection.

"Lieutenant?" The Prince turned toward the pilot. "Have you finished your prelaunch checks?"

"I, um... That is..."

"Spit it out, man!" William ordered. "We haven't got all night."

"Are you, um, certain, Your Highness, we should be... Doing this?"

"Absolutely, Lieutenant. You may ignore everything Captain Palmer had to say on the subject."

"If you're sure..."

"I've already answered that question, Lieutenant," the Prince snapped. "But, if it will make you feel any better, I have full intentions of nominating you for a knighthood once we have successfully completed this mission."

"Oh!" The Lieutenant brightened considerably. "Thank you, very much, Your Highness! Now, please take your seats and strap in for liftoff."

As we fastened our safety harnesses, Tilly leaned over and whispered so that the Lieutenant couldn't hear, "You'd better come through on that promise to the pilot, William."

William actually looked offended. "When have I ever lied to you or anyone you know, Tilly?"

Tilly folded her arms and glared daggers at the Prince. "How about when you didn't warn me about Jordan and his habit of recording his...intimate encounters?"

William winced slightly and nodded. "I suppose, it is fair to call that a lie of omission... All right, when have I ever gainsaid my given word?"

Tilly took a few seconds to mull over the question, before answering, "Never, that I can remember."

Further conversation was interrupted when the lieutenant said, "We're cleared for launch. Please remain seated until I tell you it's safe to get up."

William looked back and forth between Tilly and me. "At which time, I'll check each of your suits to ensure you're ready for the jump."

"I still don't understand why you won't let me come with you," Jana complained. "My symptoms from hyperspace sickness are fading fast."

"But you're still weak as a kitten," Tilly insisted. "Just listen to yourself—you're obviously still very congested. Have you considered just how gross a sneeze inside a jumpsuit is going to be?"

"But what if you need my special skills?"

"Can you slice the hunting lodge's network from here?" Tilly asked. "After all, you sliced the whole planetary network from this ship, while we were still in hyperspace."

"But, what if they're not connected to the network? I mean, it's just a hunting lodge."

Tilly rolled her eyes. "If you're imagining some kind of rustic cabin in the woods, put that image right out of your mind, Jana. Knowing Baron Chilton, his lodge is going to be about the same size as the Neert palace on Xapreathea. Of course, it'll have network access. Anything less would be...common."

"Oh," Jana muttered. "In my defense, you can't tell how big a house is when you're hacking its network."

"All right," the pilot said, "you're clear to get up. We'll be at the drop zone in four minutes."

"Jana, why don't you go ahead and slice into the lodge's network and start looking for Jeanine and Olivia?" I suggested.

"On it, Drake!" Jana said.

While Jana worked on that, William checked our suits. He was quick and efficient, which instilled a lot of confidence in me. It's one thing to have someone tell you they know what they're doing, it's much different when they actually prove it. I could tell Tilly was equally impressed—and equally relieved.

After the Prince gave us each a thumbs-up, he guided us through a check of his own suit. Once again, it was obvious he knew what he was doing. His instructions were concise, accurate, and easy to follow. Between the two of us, Tilly and I gave him a thumbs-up, as well.

"We're approaching the jump zone, Your Highness," our pilot said. "Take your positions."

"I'm into the lodge's network," Jana called. "This baron's idea of network security is laughable. I'm looking for Jeanine and Her Highness, now."

William led us to the jump chamber, where he carefully positioned Tilly and me. Once he was satisfied, he took his own position. "I'm going to slave your jumpsuits to mine, now. Just relax, and don't fight whatever the suit does. Got that?"

"Got it!" Tilly and I chimed.

Just standing there, you might think it was hard to tell when the Prince slaved my suit to his. It was the exact opposite. You never really think about all the little movements and muscular controls required to keep you standing, until someone else is doing it all for you. Every one of my small, unconscious fidgets and balance shifts suddenly didn't do anything. Even though I was expecting this, it was extremely unnerving.

"We have reached the jump zone, Your Highness," the pilot told us. "Jump on my mark. Three. Two. One. Mark!"

William did something and the three of us were ejected into space. Below us—far, far, far away—was the hunting lodge. And Jeanine.

In unison, controlled by Prince William, we turned head down, our suit thrusters ignited, and we plunged toward the planet, below.

Within seconds, our speed exceeded a thousand kilometers per hour. Part of me thought that was a good thing, since we were at least a hundred and fifty kilometers above the planet. Part of me wondered why the planet wasn't swelling noticeably beneath me. Part of me knew *that* little optical illusion would vanish as we drew closer we got to Gaunner. A small, squeaky part of me wondered if I would have time to feel pain if we smashed into the planet at this speed.

And then there was the part of me that wondered if it was such a good idea slaving my jump suit to a guy who, within the last couple of weeks, hired mercenaries to ambush my wife and me during our trip to this same planet. I tried shushing that part by concentrating on those other parts—even the squeaky one. But, no matter how hard I tried, I couldn't quite shut out the doubt.

The doubt wasn't even entirely sensible. After all, William taught us the basic controls, including the one to free our suits from the slave circuit. He made sure we set our suits' emergency deceleration and landing procedures to engage at an altitude of two kilometers. It would only take over if the suit was still moving at full speed. Because I was busy listening to William's instructions and worrying about Jeanine, I'd idly thought William had selected an ample safety margin. During our long plunge toward Gaunner, I had plenty of time to figure out the emergency override would engage about seven seconds before we crashed into the ground.

Apparently, I was the only one of the three of us having these thoughts.

"Oh, my God!" Tilly exclaimed. "This is *amazing*, William!"

"I know!" William responded, equally as excited. "It really makes you feel alive!"

Yeah, I thought, until you end up flattened at the bottom of your very own crater.

"Why didn't you take me to do this when we were dating? Afterward, I'd have fulfilled every fantasy you ever had—and some others you never knew you had."

While I found myself wondering how many days it would take to work through *my* list of fantasies, William simply laughed. "No more of that kind of talk, Tilly. I'm a happily married man, now."

Tilly's voice dropped easily into a sultry tone. "Then, once we've rescued both of your wives, I'll take Olivia aside and tell her that *she* owes you a romp of fantastical proportions."

"What makes you think she hasn't already given me a few of those?"

"Because this is Olivia we're talking about?" When William didn't rise to the bait, Tilly added, "You're being serious, William? About Old Maid Olivia?"

"That derogatory nickname the court ladies—a term I use only in the strictly *aristocratic* manner—gave to my wife is woefully inappropriate in private."

"Well, good for her," Tilly replied.

"And even better for me," William added, his tone smug.

"All right," I cut in, "I think that's more than enough talk about the royal couple's sex life."

In a teasing tone, Tilly asked, "Why? Are you envious?"

"Not in the least." That was absolutely true. I added another truth. "I *am* worried about Jeanine. Unlike Olivia, she has no friends inside the Chilton hunting lodge. I don't know what Colin will do to her if he gets word that the Holder family is safe before we reach Jeanine."

"You're quite right, my friend," William said, the humor banished from his voice. "Please forgive us for our unthinking banter."

"We weren't ignoring the gravity of Jeanine's situation," Tilly added. "It's just our way of reacting to this death-defying adrenaline rush."

I knew the truth of Tilly's statement. Before 'pirates,' backed by the late Duke of Gaunner, murdered my family and the families of my Space Patrol crew mates, I'd dished out more than my fair share of ribald banter in the minutes before we went into action. There is something about the possibility of imminent death that makes the finest things in life all the dearer. And nothing in life is finer than intimate moments with the person you love most in the universe.

"I realize that," I admitted, "and am sorry for reining in the fun. That kind of talk just drives home what I might lose if we don't succeed." I looked at the now rapidly-growing planet beneath us, and added, "Or if the Prince of the Realm drives us head-first into the ground."

"Not a chance, my friend," William scoffed. "Besides, you set your emergency override before we jumped."

"Sure, and it has a whole seven seconds to stop our plunge," I responded. "It'll be a miracle if that kind of deceleration doesn't break our backs!"

"That's why jump suits have miniature inertial dampeners."

"You neglected to mention that before, William," I chided.

"Surely, not!" he protested.

"Surely, so!" Tilly corroborated.

"It must have slipped my mind in the pre-jump excitement."

Unconsciously, William waved one hand in dismissal. Involuntarily, Tilly and I did the same.

"Hey!" Tilly cried.

"Oops. My apologies to both of you. I'll be more careful for the rest of the jump."

William was true to his word. He kept us arrow straight for the next minute and a half.

"Prepare for maneuvers," William advised. "Rest assured, everything I do from now until we land on the lodge's roof will be absolutely necessary."

Without conscious thought, my old Space Patrol training asserted itself. "Aye, sir!"

I had no idea where the hunting lodge was, but William's command suit had the location pinpointed. Slowly, we rotated from a purely vertical descent, and our suit thrusters angled, as well. Watching the huge ball of dirt and rock rushing toward us, it took every bit of self-control for me to keep quiet and leave the...piloting? That doesn't seem like the right word, but it's the best one I have. Anyway, I kept my mouth shut and let William do his thing.

Our path flattened somewhat. Then, with a suddenness that was startling, a well-lit estate appeared ahead of us. The Prince kept us on the same course for another four seconds, then he spun us completely around so our feet pointed toward the ground. We rushed toward the lodge fast enough to break both the roof and our legs. With scant meters left in our descent, William fired our braking thrusters and we landed lightly on the roof.

William dropped into a crouch, forcing Tilly and me to do the same. "I'm going to unslave your suits. It's a bit disconcerting, at first, so just take a few seconds to readjust."

I thought he was exaggerating, until he actually released me. I barely kept myself from falling over. Tilly had the same reaction. While we got used to controlling our muscles again,

William removed his helmet. Then he helped each of us do the same.

Next, he keyed his comm. "Jana? Lieutenant? We've landed."

"Roger that, sir," the pilot responded. "I'll alert Captain Reel."

"During your dive, I dug up the plans for the hunting lodge," Jana said. "If I'm reading your position right, there's a workman's entrance forty meters southwest of your position."

As we started for the entrance, William, his tone puzzled, asked, "Why did the ship have a copy of the lodge's design in its data storage?"

"Uh, it didn't, Your Highness. I found it in the Gaunner archives."

"You managed to do that during our dive?" William asked, his tone respectful.

"You have no idea," Tilly muttered.

"Oh, no, Your Highness," Jana said. "That only took a minute. I also checked on Captain Pennington's progress and, at his request, contacted the Holders to let them know he was coming. I didn't say *why*, of course, just that Jeanine requested their presence at the palace."

"Oh," William said, faintly, "I see."

"Then, since we don't want any of the traitors inside the hunting lodge getting away, I broke into Gaunner's air control system and made the whole forest around the lodge a no-fly zone," Jana added. "Any flitters that try taking off will have their emergency landing protocol activated. Military craft are exempt, of course."

"Very, um, resourceful of you, Jana."

"Not really," Jana complained. "I couldn't think of anything else to do during the last few minutes of your dive."

"Told you!" Tilly whispered.

"Indeed, you did," William replied.

A few seconds later, we reached the door, which was locked.

Tilly stepped past the Prince. "My turn."

"How much light do you need to open the lock?" William asked. "Dimmer is better."

"Don't be insulting, William!" Tilly responded. "I can don't need any light."

She went to work using nothing but touch. Fifteen seconds later, she gently pushed the door open and we descended into the hunting lodge.

I HAVE NO CHOICE

Jeanine

Despite my struggle to find some kind of reasonable answer to the dilemma Colin posed to me, I couldn't find one. How can any remotely compassionate person make the choice this monster put before me?

I could tell him to kidnap Sasha and pray that she was old enough and strong-willed enough to survive the ordeal without much psychological damage. But what would the trauma do to the exuberant, out-going little girl? Would she forever fear the dark and strangers?

Or, I could tell them to kidnap Will, the Holder's young son. Perhaps he was too young to comprehend what was happening to him and wouldn't be scarred for life. But, what if it shattered his image of home as a place of safety? As a place of loving warmth? Would his confusion and terror scar him so badly a normal life would be impossible for him?

Then there were Carol and Michael Holder to consider. Somehow, I couldn't imagine Colin would opt for a quick and covert operation. I felt certain he'd send his team crashing into the house in a manner guaranteed to instill as much fear as possible. Carol and Michael would certainly try to protect their children. What if one or both of them was badly injured or killed?

And, even if they weren't physically hurt, what would the kidnapping do to *their* psyches when they realized just how powerless they were to protect their children?

"Entertaining as it is to watch you struggle with this problem, my lady," Colin sneered, "I've given you ample time to consider this conundrum. What is your answer?"

I glanced at the chrono on the wall and was shocked at the time. Colin must truly have enjoyed watching me wrestle with my conscience. Ten minutes had passed since he gave me this choice. "You're a sadistic bastard."

A mirthless smile spread across Colin's face. "Far more dangerous opponents than you have said the same. Unlike them, *I* am still at the heart of the Gaunner political scene."

"Don't feel too smug." I fought to keep my tone level and conversational. "I'll see you die for what you're doing."

"Many of those same dangerous opponents offered that threat, as well. I do hope you'll forgive me if I'm unmoved by yours?" Colin's voice and his gaze hardened. "Now, Lady Jeanine, give me your decision."

My shoulders slumped and my breath hissed out in a long sigh. "Sasha. Take the girl."

"An excellent choice, my lady!" Colin turned to one of the twins and said, "Summon the rest of the guests. They shall bear witness to my triumph."

"And, as an added benefit, join you in treason," I said. "I wonder if they realize that?"

Colin waved this off. "You'll pardon them, as well, so it is a trivial matter."

Over the next couple of minutes, nearly two dozen members of Gaunner's aristocracy filed into the room, led by Baron Chilton, himself. Colin had them gather around the vid screen and then rose to stand before them. He looked toward Ron, my favorite treasonous guard in the whole galaxy, who raised one finger. A moment later, George carefully escorted Olivia into the room.

The Princess looked bedraggled, but alert and in good health. Her listless gaze sharpened when she saw the gathering before her. "What are you doing, Colin?"

"Following a plan set in motion shortly after your wedding, Your Highness." Colin's gaze bored into Olivia's, "A plan which I believe was prematurely terminated."

Well, *that* certainly put an interesting spin on things. While he didn't proclaim it outright, it seemed obvious to me that Olivia was in on the original plan. Just as obvious, she'd issued later orders against the same plan. Orders Colin flatly ignored. I found myself wondering why each of them acted as they had.

"And why am *I* here?" Olivia demanded.

"To watch the downfall of the last Wilkinson, of course," Colin lifted an arm toward Baron Chilton and gave a half bow, "and to be present when we ensure the Duchy of Gaunner will end up in the hands of someone worthy of the title."

The crowd before us clapped politely and a few of them even cheered, "Hear, hear!"

Shaking her head, Olivia said, "Oh, Colin—"

One of the guard twins rushed into the room and interrupted, "The team is moving in now, sir!"

Colin smiled and pointed at me. "Bring her up here so she can see the vid screen clearly."

Ron caught my arm and pushed me through the crowd. He stopped next to Colin and released my arm.

As the guard stepped to one side, I casually commented, "I'll see you dead before the day is out, Ron."

The guard's face remained impassive, but Colin boomed a laugh. "She's quite the feisty young woman, isn't she? I believe that shall make her downfall all the more entertaining."

Nervous laughter rose from those around us. Then, a picture resolved on the vid screen, drawing everyone's attention.

A helmet cam gave us a first-person view from a member of Colin's kidnapping team as he—or she, I couldn't tell—ran to the front door of the Holder's house. Two more figures, both men, arrived a second later. The cam carrier held up a hand—it looked like a woman's hand—with three fingers raised. The fingers counted down and, at zero, one of the men kicked the door open. The leader and the other man rushed in, weapons leveled. From the back of the house, I heard another door smash open and the sounds of feet moving rapidly into the house.

That's when all hell broke loose. A bright bar flashed across the woman's line of sight, catching her companion in the throat. Cries of horror sounded behind me as the blaster bolt ripped the man's head off. The cam carrier fired wildly in the direction of that first shot and was rewarded by concentrated return fire. Shouts and screams echoed throughout the house. Our cam carrier suddenly pitched forward and we got a close-up view of the floor.

Four seconds after the shooting began, silence fell. Then, we heard footsteps approaching the cam. The body was rolled over and I found myself staring into Captain Pennington's face.

"This one is dead, too," he called.

"How?" Turning the vid off with the stab of a finger, Colin snarled, "How did you warn them? How did you even *know* to warn them?"

"Control yourself, Colin," Olivia snapped. "Considering the antics I've witnessed from you and your compatriots in this farce, someone let slip your plan. A guard probably made an open comm call, or one of these aristocratic fools bragged to a lover. The who or how doesn't matter. What *does* matter is your utter failure to follow directions."

Stunned by the verbal assault, Colin stuttered, "B-but Your Highness—"

"When a subject ignores direct orders from their better, Colin, they *must* succeed or face dire consequences." Despite her angry tone of voice, Olivia's face showed anguish and even a bit of dawning betrayal. "*You* taught that to me, Colin. Did you somehow think the lesson wouldn't apply to you?"

Colin's shock gave way to anger equal to Olivia's. Pointing to George, Colin ordered, "Bring Princess Olivia to me."

George, a born follower if ever there was one, immediately began pulling Olivia toward Colin and me. Olivia tried digging her heels in, but George just kept dragging her. Colin held out his hand when George stopped before us.

"Give me your blaster," Colin commanded.

While the gathered nobles muttered and backed away, George did as instructed. That proved too much for Baron Chilton.

"I say, Colin, I won't be party to regicide!"

"I'm not going to kill Olivia, you blithering idiot." Colin's voice dripped with derision. "I practically raised her, for God's sake!" Colin turned his attention to the Princess. "Still, even beloved daughters sometimes require disciplining."

Exhausted thought she was, Olivia drew herself to her full height. "You wouldn't dare lay a hand on me!"

"No, my dear, you're much too old for such simple punishments." Colin reversed the blaster and held it out to Olivia. "I have something else in mind. I've been forced to this by your recent recalcitrance to join our rejection of this Wilkinson interloper. With our expected leverage over Lady Jeanine gone, I can no longer grant you the luxury of remaining on the periphery. You must take your place at the forefront, Olivia, and forcibly reject her Recognition. With you among our number, Her Majesty will have no choice but to sweep this entire episode under the rug and issue blanket pardons."

Staring at the blaster in fascination, Olivia asked, "What are you talking about?"

"I'm talking about getting your hands dirty, Olivia." With infinite tenderness, Colin took Olivia's hand and wrapped it around the gun. Then, he lifted her arm until the blaster was pointed at my chest. "Join us, daughter of my heart. Prove yourself worthy of your brother's memory. Kill Lady Jeanine."

The blaster wobbled in Olivia's hand. Instinctively, she

brought a second hand up to steady it. Even then, the gun shook slightly—not enough to make her miss at this range, but enough to tell me Olivia wasn't sure she wanted to shoot me. Or, had I completely misread her and she was just prolonging the enjoyment before she pulled the trigger?

"Go on, Olivia," Colin purred in her ear. "You finally have the Wilkinson Bastard right where you want her—on the business end of your blaster. Take revenge for your brother's death. Reclaim your family's honor. Shoot her!"

Olivia's eyes darted left and right, uncertainty written across her face. I realized that part of her longed to pull that trigger, longed to blast a hole in my chest, longed to burn me like her brother burned all those years ago. It was equally obvious that part of her knew killing me was a bad idea, one that would cause huge problems for her and the rest of the royal family.

I wasn't the only person who saw Olivia's internal conflict. Colin, still speaking in his low and persuasive tone, suggested, "You're surrounded by friends, Olivia. Friends who will testify that you had no choice, that Lady Jeanine attacked you, forcing you to fire in self-defense. You have nothing to fear and everything to gain. Pull the trigger, Olivia."

"Don't listen to him, Olivia," I insisted. "He's just trying to get you to do his dirty work. If he wants me dead, make *him* pull the trigger. If you do it, he'll have power over you for the rest of your life."

I looked around at the gathered nobles and added, "And, if you testify as Colin says you will, he will have power over each of you for the rest of your life, as well."

None of those gathered around us met my gaze. Indeed, they purposefully turned away from it. It wasn't that I'd expected to find any allies in the crowd, but I thought to find a little more self-interest or, even, courage.

I nodded slowly as the realization struck me. "Colin already holds power over all of you, doesn't he? He must, since none of you strike me as particularly willing to stick your necks out as far as murder."

"You're wasting your time, my lady," Colin scoffed. "I did not attain nor hold my position as advisor to the Dukes of Gaunner without discovering certain...secrets. But I did not need to use those secrets to gather these supporters. Your Recognition is remarkably unpopular amongst the aristocrats of Gaunner. Rather than waste time trying to turn these fine people against me, may I suggest you spend the next few seconds making peace with whatever God or gods you find most comforting?"

Colin turned back to Olivia, whose shaking hands still pointed the pistol at me. In a stern her tone, Colin ordered, "Olivia! End this foolishness. Shoot her!"

I turned away from Colin and met Olivia's gaze. "You're a Princess of the realm now, Olivia. Do you take orders from commoners?"

"Oh, very nicely played, my lady," Colin snarled. Turning back to Olivia, he leaned in close and whispered something in her ear. Olivia's eyes widened in fear as Colin drew back from her. In a voice like steel, he commanded, "If you want your deepest secret kept secret, *pull the trigger!*"

Olivia closed her eyes, her face clouding up in anguish. Eyes still closed, she whispered, "I'm sorry. I have no choice."

Colin laughed, "You need not apologize to Lady Jeanine."

Olivia's eyes opened and I saw they were brimming with tears. "I wasn't talking to Jeanine."

Olivia spun to her left and pointed the blaster between Colin's eyes. "I was talking to you."

Colin had just enough time to stumble backward half a step before Olivia pulled the trigger. Then, she pulled it a second time.

As Colin's lifeless body fell to the ground, the aristocrats began screaming.

The panicked nobles backed away from their dead leader. Then, one at the rear spun and bolted from the room, starting a stampede among the rest. The rout probably saved my life, as the fleeing aristocrats blocked the guards' lines of fire for a few seconds.

Olivia crumpled to the floor next to Colin's body. Dropping the blaster, she buried her face against Colin's chest and keened like a wounded animal.

I dove for the gun but was blocked by another fleeing noble. The panicked woman pushed away from me as a man accidentally kicked the blaster under one of the chairs.

Ron, who stood just a few meters from me, was the first guard to fight his way clear of the mob. His face wore the same dispassionate expression he'd worn since he first jumped onto the hood of the flitter I was stealing. As he raised his blaster, Ron's mouth twisted into a wry smile.

"I guess you won't see me dead, after all, my lady."

A man barreled into me, sending me sprawling to the floor just as Ron pulled the trigger. The shot meant for me barely missed George, who had been sneaking up on me from behind.

My savior rolled on top of me, shielding me with his own body. At the same time, he lifted a blaster of his own and pumped three quick shots into Ron's chest. Then, George grabbed the man and pulled him off me and I got a look at my rescuer.

"William?" I blurted.

The Prince dropped his blaster onto my stomach. "This one seems quite the brawler. Why don't you take the gun?"

Blasters sounded from elsewhere in the room and the damned nobles began screaming even louder. Worse, they surged back toward us.

Somehow, her husband's name got through Olivia's wailing. She lifted a tear-stained face in surprise and wonder. "William? What are you doing here?"

William blocked George's first punch. Without taking his eyes off his opponent, he grinned. "It's a rescue, my dear!"

George barely qualified as an intellectual flyweight, but even he recognized he had the crown prince by the throat. The guard immediately released his grip. "I beg your pardon, Your Highness!"

William never hesitated. He hit George hard in the nose and followed it with a couple of quick punches to the gut. William finished with an uppercut that sent the large guard stumbling back several steps before George crumpled into a heap.

While Olivia just stared at the Prince, I scanned the room for any threats. I vaguely noticed a couple of other figures dressed similarly to William, both of them covering the crowd with blasters. The guard twins were on their knees, holding wounded arms. But, what most drew my attention was Baron Chilton. Unlike the rest of the nobles in the room, he hadn't panicked. Even now, he scrabbled after the blaster that was kicked beneath a chair.

I doubt the Baron saw my kick coming, but I'm sure he felt it. His neck snapped back and the blaster he'd just recovered flew from his grasp. By the time he recovered, I was standing over him with the blaster pointed at his face.

"I, Jeanine, Duchess of Gaunner, charge you with high treason against me and my House, Baron Chilton," I said. "How do you plead?"

"You have no right to that title," Chilton snarled. "I reject your Recognition and, as such, reject your charges of treason. My peers will agree with me. I promise that they will never convict me."

"Is that what you think?" I flicked my eyes to Olivia, who was hugging William but also watching my little drama. "Princess Olivia, as the former Duchess of Gaunner, may I assume you are familiar with the Duchy's laws regarding treason among the aristocracy?"

Olivia stared at me without comprehension for a second. Visibly shaking herself, she replied, "Of course, Lady Jeanine."

"Could you refresh the Baron's memory of the appropriate

statutes, Your Highness? In particular, the statutes pertaining to conspiracies comprising three or more aristocrats."

"In cases where three or more nobles conspire against the Recognized Duchess of Gaunner, the Duchess may declare the conspiracy is too widespread to seat an impartial jury of peers." Olivia recited.

I looked around the room at the twenty or more gathered nobles. "I think I can safely rule that your conspiracy extends to three or more. Wouldn't you agree, Baron?"

Chilton didn't say anything, but the bravado he displayed a few seconds before was gone.

"Your Highness?" I asked. "Please, tell us who passes judgment in cases such as this one."

Her voice barely a whisper, Olivia said, "You do."

I looked around the room, making eye contact with the nobles. That was when I realized Drake was one of the people who came with William. I thought I recognized the woman, as well, but pushed that thought aside.

"Hello, dear." I gave Drake a tired smile. "I need to finish dealing with this situation before I can greet you properly."

Drake nodded, his expression somber. "I know. Do what must be done."

"For those who may not have heard Princess Olivia's last statement," I raised my voice so it echoed off the walls, "*I, Her Grace, Lady Jeanine, Duchess of Gaunner, rule in cases such as this one.*"

I looked back down at Baron Chilton. "I find you guilty of treason against your Recognized Duchess. Do you wish to throw yourself on the mercy of the court before I pass sentence?"

"Go to hell!" Chilton snarled.

"Baron Chilton, for your part in the conspiracy to remove your Recognized Duchess and replace her with yourself, I sentence you to death." Gasps sounded around the room and the little color remaining in Chilton's face drained from it. I hardened my heart for what came next. "Sentence to be carried out immediately."

I fired three shots into Baron Chilton's chest. A couple of nobles moaned in terror and, as the moans climbed in volume, I doubted screams were far off. I flicked my glare to the noisy ones in the crowd and they immediately fell silent.

Pushing down the bile rising in my throat, I raised my voice, "The late Baron spurned my offer of mercy. You witnessed his punishment. I take no pleasure from his execution, but I will *not* have the people of Gaunner threatened by its nobility nor will I tolerate rebellion against me. I *will* entertain pleas for mercy from those who admit their guilt, confess their crimes, and reveal all they know about this conspiracy."

When I stopped speaking, William added, "I strongly suggest you accept Lady Jeanine's offer, as I will gladly stand witness against each one of you for your part in this plot."

In the end, they all confessed.

BONDING

Drake

During the initial rush from the carnage in the sitting room, five of the nobles reached their flitters. When they discovered Jana's no-fly zone kept their vehicles grounded, three of them just gave up—one quite literally. His body was half frozen when it was pulled from his flitter. Two of them wandered dejectedly back to the sitting room.

The two who didn't give up were determined to get away from their Duchess's vengeance. They stole the same truck Jeanine drove onto the estate and made a run for it. Some of Captain Reel's men met the escapees on the only road to and from the estate. For the record, civilian delivery vans do not fare well in head-on collisions with armored personnel carriers. The nobles survived, though they missed out on the chance to trade information for a lighter sentence.

By the time Captain Reel and his forces reached us, the remaining nobles were thoroughly cowed and eager to throw their fellow aristocrats to the wolves. Jeanine was calmly interviewing one of the nobles while Tilly, William, and I kept watch on the rest, when Reel hesitantly called from the hall.

"My lady? Captain Haral? This is Captain Reel. May I enter safely?"

"Come on in, Captain," I replied.

The Captain's eyes widened when he saw three corpses in the center of the room. His eyes immediately scanned the crowd. "Where is her Grace? Is she injured?"

I shook my head, "No, she's fine. She's in that room, interviewing one of the many conspirators."

Jeanine poked her head out of the door. "Hello, Captain. I'm very glad you're here. You don't happen to have an interrogation team handy, do you?"

"I can have one here shortly, my lady." His eyes cut to the bodies. "I also have plenty of men available to clean up the... mess. They can also handle guard duties."

"That would be most welcome." Jeanine gave a tired smile. "It's been a very long night. Do you have enough men to sequester each of these people from the others? I don't want to give them the chance to coordinate their stories."

Reel offered a wry smile. "I think we can handle that, my lady. Shall I arrange a transport for you, Captain Haral, Their Highnesses, and this woman," Reel looked at Tilly, "who, I'm afraid, is unknown to me?"

"Yes, please."

My comm buzzed. I didn't answer it, but a voice sounded in my ear, anyway.

"I heard all of that," Jana said. "Want me to have the pilot land this ship down there? He says it'll take him ten minutes to touch down, and he can have us back at the capital fifteen minutes after that."

"Yes, Jana, have him land." I got odd stares from Jeanine and Reel. "Our friend, Jana Ward, just commed me. She's instructing the pilot to land his ship at the estate. Captain, could you please make sure your men don't shoot it out of the sky?"

Reel turned to a lieutenant standing behind him. "Give the orders."

"Yes, sir!" the lieutenant snapped, already heading for the door.

"Wasn't Jana on Xapreathea when Colin kidnapped me?" Jeanine asked. "How did she get here so quickly?"

"Experimental hyperdrive. But don't worry about that right now." I handed my blaster to a young soldier and went to Jeanine. Wrapping my arms around her, I murmured, "I'm just glad you're safe. Did they hurt you?"

"One of the guards punched me in the stomach, but he paid dearly for that." I gave her a quizzical look, so she added, "William shot him."

Keeping my arm around Jeanine, I looked at the Prince. "That's two I owe you for, William."

"Nonsense, Drake," he replied, his arm still encircling Olivia's waist. "The only other time I felt so alive and so needed was when I rescued my Princess. I should be thanking *you* for letting me help with the rescue."

"Don't let William's modesty fool you, Olivia," I said. "He *led* the rescue. Without him, we'd never have gotten here in time to save Jeanine."

"Did you and the Prince bond over this incident?" Jeanine whispered in my ear.

"Oddly, yes."

"What's so odd about that?"

"Our real bonding began when William admitted he was behind the ambush in the Vollec system."

"He *what?*" Jeanine said that out loud, drawing looks from the royal couple and Captain Reel.

I kept my voice low. "I'll explain later, but I'm prepared to put that incident behind us."

Jeanine cocked a curious eyebrow, but also nodded. "When we're alone, then."

"Now, let's get you away from all these would-be revolutionaries." I raised my voice, "Captain Reel, could you secure a private room for Their Highnesses and another one for Jeanine and me?"

"Of course, sir," Reel replied. "I'll see to it, myself."

"Tilly, you're welcome to join us," I offered.

"Are you kidding? I'm way too wired from our jump to relax," the lady thief said. "You four go on without me. I'll come get you when the ship lands."

"What jump is she talking about? You didn't do something foolishly dangerous to get here, did you?" Jeanine asked.

"Absolutely not, babe."

Tilly ruined my assurances by adding, "Unless you think a powered jump from near-orbit with our jumpsuits slaved to the crown prince's suit is dangerous."

"When were you planning on telling me this, Drake?"

"I was going to work up to it." I turned a mock glare on Tilly. "For someone with *real* secrets to keep, you've got an awfully big mouth!"

The other woman met my glare with an unabashed grin. "Look at it this way, Drake; now you don't have to figure out how to tell Lady Jeanine about it."

I chose to refrain from further comment, mainly because I couldn't think of anything witty to say in response. Fortunately, an earnest private waited for us outside the sitting room. He led us to a comfortably furnished room, saluted, and shut the door.

As soon as we were alone, I pulled Jeanine close and kissed her deeply. "God, I was so afraid I'd lost you forever!"

Jeanine rested her head on my shoulder. "I'm not that easy to get rid of, Drake."

I gave a harsh laugh, "As the nobles of Gaunner learned today."

"I didn't want to execute Baron Chilton," Jeanine sighed, regret filling her voice. "But, I'd have been inviting worse if I'd let him live."

I guided Jeanine onto a couch and held her until Tilly came for us. True to Jana's promise, we were back at the capital fifteen minutes later.

REACHING AN UNDERSTANDING

Jeanine

Despite the sleep I'd gotten—both drug-induced and natural—during my ordeal, I was mentally and physically exhausted by the time we returned to the palace. The problem with being the one in charge is that some decisions simply can't wait until after you've slept. Someone had to decide where to put the treasonous nobles, give after-the-fact authorization for the no-fly zone Jana established around Chilton's estate, recall the military, and what felt like a million other tasks. Even after I'd made the decisions that simply couldn't wait until morning, I didn't let Drake drag me off to bed until I'd spoken to the Holders.

Sasha and Will were sleeping soundly, but Carol and Michael were wide awake. What parent wouldn't be after armed men arrived in the middle of the night and took your family into protective custody?

Michael, pale-faced and wide-eyed, bowed when he answered the door of the apartment they'd been given. "We are most grateful to see you safe, my lady."

Behind him, Carol dropped into a curtsy. "I echo my husband's words, Lady Jeanine."

Their rigid formality broke my heart. "Thank you, both. May we come in?"

"Of course, my lady." Michael backed out of the doorway, while still holding the door open. "The Duchess of Gaunner doesn't need our permission to enter rooms in her own palace."

"I most certainly do!" I insisted. "Until you say otherwise, this is your home. No one will enter it without your expressed permission."

Not meeting my eyes, Michael muttered, "I thought that was true of our house, my lady, until events today showed just how wrong I was."

"I know, Michael, and words cannot convey just how sorry I am that this happened."

Carol met my gaze. "Nor can words restore our lost sense of security, my lady. We aren't powerful people and we don't want to be powerful people. We just want to raise our children and live our lives in peace. But, since you introduced yourself to us, that has become impossible."

"I understand how you're feeling, Carol. I—"

"I mean no disrespect, my lady," Carol interrupted, "but I doubt very seriously if you even remotely understand how we're feeling."

I was at a complete loss for a response. Drake wasn't.

"I think you do Jeanine a disservice, Carol. Most of her life was spent in hiding, with nothing remotely as warm and secure as your home. She had no friends and no family except for Sir Jared, who she thought was her grandfather. She lost him and, without time to mourn for him, went on the run. Since then, she's been imprisoned and held hostage twice. I won't even go into the number of times her life has been endangered."

Drake's voice rose while he spoke, as control of his temper slipped. I stroked his arm and shook my head. With visible effort, he took control of himself.

"Carol and Michael, I apologize for my tone. It has been a difficult twenty-four hours."

"I understand and am trying to sympathize," Carol said, "but—"

"But you haven't had your *children* threatened," Michael interrupted. "You have no idea how that feels!"

Drake went rigid next to me. In an extremely flat tone, he replied, "No, Mr. Holder, I don't know what it's like to have my child threatened. I'm afraid my experience is limited to having my first wife and our only child murdered."

Michael scrubbed a hand over his face, as if he was trying to wash away his mortification. "I'm sorry, Drake. That was... thoughtless...of me."

"Yes, it was," Drake replied. Turning to me, he said, "We should let the Holders rest. I'm sure they're quite tired from their ordeal."

The Holders said nothing in response, so I let Drake pull me from the apartment.

I waited until we were well away from the apartment door before I said, "That could have gone better."

"I doubt it," Drake countered. "They're scared—with good reason—and they blame us for their troubles."

"And they're right to do so," I admitted. "Their family would never have been targeted if I hadn't dragged them into our life."

"You can't blame yourself for that, Jeanine. You couldn't have known this would happen."

I knew Drake *still* blamed himself for not being there to fight for Heather and Candice all those years ago. Even though his own argument applied to himself, as well as me, I also knew I would never point that out to him. Instead, I slid my arm around his waist and leaned my head on his shoulder.

"You're right," I murmured. The fatigue I'd held at bay by sheer determination finally broke through my will and washed over me. "Now, dearest, please take me to bed."

Drake wrapped his arm around me and pulled me close. "I love it when beautiful women say that to me."

"Don't get any ideas. I'm much too tired for anything except sleep."

"Then, I will hold you in my arms until you fall asleep."

Minutes later, safe in his embrace, I drifted off to sleep.

Falling asleep at dawn throws off your entire schedule. I'd add it to Colin's list of crimes, except he'd already paid the ultimate price for his arrogance.

I found myself wondering if Colin's last seconds were prideful, as he watched his protégé make the most difficult decision of her life and turn the blaster on him. The decision was a combination of emotion and calculation for Her Highness, but I got the idea she couldn't have pulled the trigger over strictly political matters.

Olivia was my very first appointment for what was left of the day. Would I dare broach that subject with her? A tap on the office door interrupted that train of thought.

Edward poked his head into the office. "Princess Olivia is here, my lady."

"Show her in, Edward."

As Olivia entered, I rose to my feet and came around the desk. Taking her hand, I asked, "How are you feeling, Your Highness?"

Olivia looked fresh, well-rested, and beautiful—every inch the royal princess. In contrast, I still felt tired and was certain I looked bedraggled.

"I am well, Lady Jeanine. Thank you for providing such a stellar medical team to ensure my health."

"I was tempted to request a report from the doctors, but felt that would be overstepping my bounds. May I assume the baby is healthy?"

A real smile spread across Olivia's face, igniting an inner glow I'd never imagined coming from her. "The baby is fine. The doctors told me that your diagnosis of my symptoms was correct. I panicked over *my* reaction to the tranquilizer."

"I thank God for that, Olivia."

Confusion clouded her face. "I believe you mean that, Jeanine, though I cannot fathom *why* you are so concerned over my baby's health."

"While I hope we can find a way past our enmity, I doubt you and I will ever be friends. Perhaps, Drake can help me see in you what he now sees in William. Then again, we'll never bond over a rescue dive from near orbit, so that probably won't happen." We both took a moment to consider the strange ways of men and shared a sad smile that our lives would never be so open and straightforward. "But, your baby... Olivia, I can never be the duchess I want to be if I was capable of wishing harm to the truly innocent."

Olivia regarded me for a moment, then simply nodded, accepting me at my word. "Shall we move on to the reason you requested this meeting?"

"Certainly." I motioned to the same two chairs we'd used the last time we were both in my office. "Shall we sit over there? Captain Reel assures me the palace's secret passages are now patrolled by loyal men."

We were just getting comfortable when Mary arrived with tea. Olivia chatted with Mary while the girl poured, asking after her sister and assuring herself that they were being well treated.

After the girl left, Olivia murmured, "Thank you, for letting me see her, Jeanine."

I shrugged, "You have enough to worry about without having Mary's well-being on your mind, as well."

Olivia sipped her tea, avoiding the necessity of a response. As she set down her cup, she changed the subject. "To business, then?"

"To business," I agreed. I knew what I wanted to say, but took a few seconds to order my thoughts before saying it. "Do I need to execute any of the other nobles involved in this little uprising?"

The question caught Olivia completely off guard. "I beg your pardon?"

"Are Colin and Baron Chilton the only members of the conspiracy who knew you organized it?" Olivia's eyes widened for a moment, before narrowing in suspicion. I raised a hand to forestall questions. "I'm not going to blackmail you with this information. I don't need the enmity of the royal family. Or, rather, their *further* enmity."

The Princess stared into my eyes, as if she was trying to read my mind. In the end, she simply said, "I canceled the operation as soon as I found out about the ambush in the Vollec system. The last thing I needed was a suspicious palace revolt close on the heels of that attack. Obviously, Colin and Chilton had different ideas."

"And what was the ulterior motive for your visit?"

"I had to be seen reacting to the Vollec debacle with concern for the new Duchess of Gaunner. That suggested a personal visit. Then you arrested Colin and the rest of the senior staff, making a personal visit mandatory. I had to assess the situation and decide whether to postpone the revolt or scrap it, entirely."

"And decide whether certain voices had to be permanently silenced."

Olivia simply shrugged.

"What about the threat Colin whispered to you? The one he thought would make you shoot me?"

"That will remain between Colin and me."

It was my turn to shrug. "I'll lay odds it dealt with your staged rescue in the space above Xapreathea."

"I...don't know what you mean, Jeanine."

"Don't worry, Olivia, that secret is safe, also. Drake already used it to force the Queen to grant our friend network access to the Star Stone."

The Princess dropped her gaze and, in the barest whisper, said, "It would destroy William, if he found out."

"Maybe not," I replied. "He led the rescue jump and saved my life at the risk of his own, after all. But it might destroy your marriage. Lucky for you, that's another thing I won't have on my conscience."

"Thank you."

"That said, if an 'accident' happens to me, Drake, our families, or our friends, we'll broadcast the story across the Star Kingdom."

"In contrast, should that story come out without provocation, you will be on the receiving end of the full might and fury of the royal house."

"I'm glad we understand each other," I nodded, accepting Olivia's terms. "But, we've wandered away from the original question. Are further executions required?"

"No." Olivia rose to her feet. "I believe that covers our business."

I stood, also. "For now."

William and Olivia chose to leave immediately after our meeting. This time, I went with Drake to the spaceport. Olivia and I remained formally polite and allowed ourselves a *very* brief hug, played entirely for the newsies.

On the way back to the palace, Drake asked, "Is my relationship with William going to cause problems for you, babe?"

"I can't see why it would. Olivia and I cannot avoid socializing with each other. Your new friendship just means we'll have to do a bit more of it than we expected." I took Drake's hand and smiled at him. "It's a sacrifice I will gladly make for you, dear."

He brought my hand to his lips. "If it ever becomes a burden, please tell me. I like William, but I *love* you."

I let him draw me into a hug and hoped he would never have to choose between me and his friends.

NO TIME FOR JOKES

Jana

"Oh, my God, I can't believe I forgot about something so important!"

It's no fun when your subconscious screams something like that at you. It's even less fun when it wakes you from a deep and much-needed sleep. But, when the 'important' thing might affect humanity's future and when you really did forget about it in the rush to rescue a duchess and a princess—not to mention a family with two adorable children—I think you should cut your subconscious some slack. So, I forgave myself for the lapse.

Even so, I found myself sitting bolt upright in the bed. My heart was hammering so fast I was afraid it might burst. My breath came in ragged gasps. At least half a minute passed before I calmed myself enough to focus my eyes on anything. Of course, my hair was so tousled that it hung over my eyes and blocked most of the room from my sight. It was also the middle of the night, so there wasn't a whole lot I could see, anyway.

I found myself wishing I had someone sleeping next to me— a Drake of my own, if you will. Not actual Drake, of course. Not only is he dedicated, body and soul, to Jeanine, he's just not my type of man. Don't get me wrong, he's a great guy and exactly the kind of man you hope one of your closest friends marries. But I want someone who understands why slicing appeals to me so much and why jumping out of perfectly good spaceships in near-orbit has so little appeal for me.

Gradually, my heartbeat slowed and my breathing evened out. Apparently, imagining my perfect man had something of a calming effect on me. It left me feeling a bit wistful, wondering if I'd ever have anything like Jeanine and Drake have, but I could think rationally again.

I checked the chrono next to the bed. Four in the morning. That was way too early to talk to Jeanine. She'd had an extremely trying last couple of days and was bound to be sleeping. I, on the other hand, was wide awake.

I crawled out of the bed. It was about the size of a small tropical island and I'd been curled up in its geographical center, so that took a lot of crawling. When my feet finally touched the floor, I headed for the bathroom and started the shower.

Showers are, for me, the perfect place for brainstorming on my own. The hot water is so soothing it's almost as if my brain disconnects from my body and goes wandering. As a result, I don't really have a regular time to shower. Don't get me wrong, I still bathe before going on dates, meeting with clients, and all the other times you want to make sure you're clean and smell good. But, when I'm puzzling through a problem, my energy bill spikes because I end up taking a bunch of hour-long showers.

Dad used to complain about those spikes in the bill when I was a teenager. I don't *think* he ever figured out that I started slicing the power company and adjusting our usage. The important thing, to me, was he stopped bitching about my showers.

I stayed in the shower for a very long time—longer than I've ever stayed in one before—and the water never even cooled down slightly. Meanwhile, my mind floated free of my body. It meandered in and out of the memories of my visit inside the Star Stone, considering everything the Stone said to me from many different angles. And, by the time I turned off the water, I knew what I had to do.

~

Edward, Jeanine's assistant, found me camped out at her office door when he arrived to open the office. He politely offered me a hand up and let me into the outer office.

"I'm afraid Lady Jeanine has a rather full calendar, today, Miss Ward," he told me after checking the day's schedule. "Perhaps I can fit you in at…let me see…two fifteen? As long as the Duchess's one thirty appointment doesn't run long, I can get you five minutes with her."

"I appreciate just how busy Jeanine is, Edward, but I absolutely *must* speak with her first thing this morning."

Edward studied his data screen, perhaps hoping some free time would magically open, but more likely using it as a cover while he tried to figure out how to get rid of me. The man is a dedicated assistant and has Jeanine's best interests at heart, so I really hoped I wouldn't have to threaten to ruin his credit rating or splash his most closely guarded secrets all over the net. Okay, I wouldn't *really* do anything like that, but he wouldn't know that.

While he was busy pretending to study the screen, the office door opened and Captain Reel entered. Edward smiled a greeting and said, "She's not here yet, Captain, but you can go on into her office."

"Thank you, Edward," the Captain replied. As he strode toward the door to the inner office, he nodded politely to me, "Good morning, Miss Ward."

"Captain?" I asked. "Would you be willing to let me speak with Jeanine first?"

He stopped walking, but didn't even waste one second considering my request. "I'm sorry, but my briefing concerns the security of the duchy and is of the utmost importance."

"Is your briefing more important than the future of the Star Kingdom?" I asked.

Captain Reel frowned, "This is no time for jokes, Miss Ward."

"I agree, Captain," I replied. "For future reference, the corners of my lips turn up when I'm joking. As you can see, they are turned down right now."

Reel blew out his breath in frustration, "You simply cannot be serious, Miss Ward."

"Serious about what?"

Jeanine stood in the doorway, looking back and forth between the two of us. The Captain and I had been so busy staring each other down that we didn't even notice her arrival.

Reel beat me to the punch. Opening the door to the inner office, he said, "Good morning, my lady. Shall we begin your briefing?"

Jeanine held up a hand, stopping the Captain, and turned her attention to me. "I've never seen such a serious expression on your face, Jana, not even when you confirmed I was the Wilkinson Bastard. What's wrong?"

"Oh, everything. May we speak privately?"

Jeanine looked at Edward. "Reschedule all of my morning appointments. You may let Drake and Tilly into my office, but no one else bothers us until I say otherwise."

Captain Reel couldn't hold back a protest. "My lady! This briefing—"

"Give the briefing to Drake," Jeanine interrupted. "He speaks with my voice and authority on all matters concerning the security of the duchy."

We swept past the outraged Captain and into her office. Jeanine led the way to the comfortable sitting area, well away from her desk. As we settled into the chairs, she simply said, "Give me a succinct description of the problem. I'll have you fill in the details after that."

I'd expected something like this request and was doubly glad for my meditative shower all those hours ago. Taking a deep, cleansing breath, I looked into Jeanine's eyes.

"We have to destroy the Star Stone. The future of the Star Kingdom—and maybe the human race—depends on it."

Jeanine merely nodded, acting no more surprised than if I'd just suggested a nice restaurant for lunch. "Tell me everything."

____

THE STORY CONTINUES...

____

Look for *The Recognition Revelation*, the third book in the Recognition Series. Available now.

If you enjoyed *The Recognition Rejection*, please post a brief review. Reader recommendations are the best advertising.

ABOUT THE AUTHOR

Henry Vogel began his writing career in comic books way back in the 1980s, with the indie titles *Southern Knights* and *X-Thieves*. When the bottom dropped out of the black & white comic book market, Henry went into IT, where he worked for the next thirty-three years. Henry took up professional storytelling in 2006, and has performed all across his home state of North Carolina.

As a lifetime fan of science fiction, Henry always wanted to write science fiction novels. He began writing *Scout's Honor* in 2012, and released it to the world in 2014. He hasn't stopped writing since.

Henry makes his home in Raleigh, NC, and is hard at work on his next novel.

www.henryvogelwrites.com

 X

ALSO BY HENRY VOGEL

Travis & Trouble

Trouble in Twi-Town

Trouble on Mars

The Fortune Chronicles

Fortune's Fool

The Scales of Sin & Sorrow

The Scout Series

Scout's Honor

Scout's Oath

Scout's Duty

Scout's Law

Scout's Training

Scout's First Mission

Hart for Adventure

The Princess Scout

Scout: The Lost Colony Adventures

Non-series books

The Lost Planet

Heart of Dorkness & Other Stories

The Connaught Family Chronicles

The Fugitive Heir

The Fugitive Pair

The Fugitive Snare

The Hostage in Hiding

The Captain Nancy Martin

The Counterfeit Captain

The Undercover Captain

The Recognition Series

The Recognition Run

The Recognition Rejection

The Recognition Revelation

Comic Books

Aristocratic Xraterrestrial Time-Traveling Thieves Complete Collection

Southern Knights Almost Complete Collection

Southern Knights Color Edition

Southern Knights: The Morrigan Wars

Southern Knights: Leaving Atlanta (prose novella)

Missing Beings

Illustrated Children's Book

I'm in Charge! and Other Stories

www.ingramcontent.com/pod-product-compliance
Lightning Source LLC
Chambersburg PA
CBHW050507190726
48284CB00003B/714